BODIES IN PARADISE

PARADISE SERIES

BOOK 23

DEBORAH BROWN

BODIES IN PARADISE
All Rights Reserved
Copyright © 2021 Deborah Brown

Cover: Natasha Brown

PRINTED IN THE UNITED STATES OF AMERICA

BODIES IN PARADISE

Chapter One

Not even five minutes after my husband, Creole, blew out the door to work, it reopened and my best friend, Fabiana Merceau, snuck inside. Did she knock? Ring the bell? No. Instead, she'd whipped out her lockpick—which she pocketed with a smirk, swinging her long brown hair—and skinnied into the entry, confident that I wouldn't shoot.

I beckoned her into the kitchen, where I was making coffee. It was such a beautiful day—blue skies, a fluffy cloud or two—and I couldn't wait to sit outside on the deck. I put the seashell mugs that I'd scored from a local store on a wooden bamboo tray and carried it outside, through the open bank of sliders, to the deck that overlooked the blue-green water below. My favorite place to sit.

"Next time, maybe run by the bakery when you're planning on stopping by early," I said in a slightly admonishing tone, enjoying every minute. "Or… I know, bake something. Fresh from your oven would be fun."

"Madison." Fab feigned a big sigh. "You've had enough caffeine."

Creole and I had bought the house next door to Fab and Didier in "the compound," moving from our previous residence at the opposite end of the street. What was now our house and the other house on the cul-de-sac had originally been a wedding present from Fab's father after they'd bought the third house for themselves. They'd recently rented the remaining house to Casio, an ex-cop, and his kids.

It was nice to have our own house and furniture again. It was a long time coming, after my house suffered major fire damage and Creole's ended up full of bad memories.

Fab and I grabbed mugs of coffee and settled into a pair of chairs that looked out at the beach, where waves gently lapped the shore on the strip of sand that we shared.

"I'm still loving your surprise." Fab pointed at the dock and laughed. "Although it didn't go off quite as planned."

"I envisioned a dramatic unveiling once the dock was completed and was so wrapped up in it coming off as a surprise that I didn't think about not being able to hide a boat pulling up and offloading lumber and construction supplies." I'd had the dock constructed between our properties, extending from the beach out into the water. Included in the design was a large rectangular deck at the end that Fab and I had furnished with chaises for kicking back and enjoying the sunrise or sunset. At least the construction crew's arrival had caught everyone off guard, and that part was truly a surprise. It had been fun to watch it being built.

Fab wasn't easy to read unless you knew her, and I did. In truth, she still pulled one over on me more often than I wanted to admit. I'd upped my game and still wasn't close to evening the score, although I had a few tick marks in my column. If she knew that her face telegraphed when she wanted something, she'd be irked and would work to make sure it didn't happen again.

The approach of a boat going way too fast cut through the morning quiet. It caught our attention as it grew closer, skimming across the calm water. We watched as the sleek speedboat came into full view and slowed to a crawl. The man at the wheel waved his arm, and two men popped up, each holding one end of a body, which they hurled into the water without hesitation. The body hit the end of the dock with a thud that made me wince, then slid off into the water. Seconds later, the men popped back into sight, and another body followed, this one landing with a splash. The boat roared off.

Fab and I had jumped up after the first one landed and leaned over the railing.

"What just happened?" I stuttered. "Do you think they're still alive?"

"Neither resurfaced." Fab grabbed my hand and pulled me over to the stairs. "So probably not."

Once on the sand, I jerked out of her hold. "I'm thinking you can investigate on your own."

"I'm under strict orders to behave." Fab grabbed my wrist and urged me to keep up with her race walk.

"I'll bet you hung on every word of Didier's edict and promised ever so sweetly." Her grin told me I was correct. Didier knew from long experience that he needed to keep an eye on his wife or she'd go off half-wild. "We both know those two will most likely turn out to be dead, and that's your forte. Corpses make me barfy."

"My forte?" Fab's brows went up. "I'm here to investigate, not jump into the water and fish out a body. That's out of my skill set. If I see signs of life, I'll toss out one of the life rings."

I once again jerked out of her hold and skidded to a stop several feet back from the steps to the dock. "Once you've made a determination, I'm happy to call 911. Since I left my phone at the house, I'll run back." Meaning that I'd walk slowly and stop to pocket a shell or two.

"Nice try." Fab pulled both of our phones out of her pocket and handed me mine. "So much for my plan to prank you. I promise, though, that I'll make it up to you." She moved to the side of the dock and waded in up to the hemline of her sundress. She bent down and scanned the water, then retreated to the sand and circled around to the other side.

"Almost forgot that you rented your other

house to a retired detective." I turned and eyed the exterior of Casio Famosa's place, wishing he were out on his deck so I could wave wildly. "He needs to get his batoo over here and brush up on his detective skills. Probably a good idea for him to stay on his game."

"When you call him, be sure you mention his backside in that derogatory fashion," Fab said over her shoulder. She was now on the dock, moving toward open water and the point of impact for the first man.

"Please don't lean so far over; it's giving me the barfs." Fab ignored me. I called Casio. It rang twice and went to voicemail. How dare he? We needed to have a talk about re-routing my calls. He'd laugh until I did it to him. I called again. Same thing.

"Unfortunately, I don't have good news. There's no sign of either man." Fab straightened and circled the dock one more time.

I continued to call Casio, waiting a minute in between so it wouldn't go immediately to voicemail.

On about the sixth time, he answered. "This better be good; I'm in a meeting with the Chief," he grouched.

"Too loud." I jerked the phone back from my ear. "There's a dead body at your house. You might want to get it disposed of before the kids get home," I told him in a so-there tone, then hung up and turned off my phone. I'd turn it back on in a minute or two.

"Casio's going to find out you're full of it and then what?" Fab turned and headed back toward me.

"Too late. He'll be home by then." I fell in behind her as she came down the steps and sunk my toes in the sand. "He'll be bringing the cavalry, judging by the laughter in the background."

Fab's phone started ringing. She took one look at the screen and passed it off to me. "Didier. That tells us that the guys were all together when you called."

I thrust it back at her, and she stepped back, a "you're on your own" look on her face. It stopped ringing and started again. I ran after her, and she eluded me, laughing. I finally answered. "Are you on the way home?" I asked in a saccharine tone.

There was a pause before he said, "You're not my wife."

"You're right." I wanted to laugh but managed to stifle it. "Fab thinks that because I was a tad misleading to Casio, I should field any calls from you guys. So here I am. How fun is that?" In the silence, I heard a car honking and knew that the men were on the way home. "You better catch," I said to Fab and tossed her phone through the air without hesitation. She caught it. "That hottie French dude you're married to is being mean and not talking. You deal with him."

I fished my phone out of my pocket and turned it back on.

I only half-listened as Fab filled him in on the details. The call ended with kissy noises.

"The guys were having a meeting, and the Chief and Casio walked in, looking for snacks. Lark spoils everyone by stocking the pantry with a wide variety of junk food and inviting all to fill their pockets. Casio wasn't the least bit busy; he just didn't want to take his attention away from his cinnamon roll. Another Lark treat. On her way into the office this morning, she stopped by the bakery."

I'd hired Lark Pontana as the office manager of The Boardwalk, a joint family-and-friends real estate venture. Creole, Didier, and my brother, Brad had formed a real estate partnership, and the biggest project to date was The Boardwalk. It consisted of attractions, shops, restaurants, a collection of rides, and a hundred-slip marina, and continued to expand. They dealt with day-to-day operations; the rest of the family were silent investors and only got called on when a vote was needed for a new project.

"And so…" I threw out my hands.

"Get ready, because the guys are headed this way. Didier put me on speaker so he wouldn't have to repeat everything, and I heard Casio making the 911 call. He mentioned the sheriff's office sending out a boat or two, so don't be surprised when one motors up. It's been a while since we dealt with that agency, so I forget how they respond."

"I take it we're to hang around, like any other crime scene?" I asked.

"You know how the cops feel about eyewitnesses running off. You can bet there will be a hundred questions." Fab sighed. "It's the consensus of Creole and Casio that they're probably both dead or one or both would've crawled out of the water or at least be hanging on one of the ladders yelling for help."

"Let's go back and suck down the last of our coffee before everyone arrives."

Fab linked her arm in mine. "What we need is binoculars. I'm thinking we get cutesy storage boxes so they'll be handy."

"I hope you're not implying this will be a regular occurrence." I made a face at her. "I'm one-upping you and getting a telescope. When I'm not on dead-body watch, I can peek in your windows."

Fab ground to a stop, turned, and eyed the exterior of her house. "That would be boring."

Chapter Two

Halfway back to my house, Fab pulled me down on the sand next to her. "I'm thinking if we're easy to find, we won't have to listen to any lectures about being more cooperative."

"I can't believe that our properties are a crime scene."

"There's no chance that what we saw happen didn't. I'm hoping that the men tossed into the water are easily found and alive. Would be nice, but probably not."

After a while, we could hear vehicles roaring down our quiet cul-de-sac, and it didn't take long before Creole, Didier, and Casio trooped through Fab's house, across the patio, and down to the beach. Casio didn't break stride and continued down the dock. They'd picked up local law enforcement at the gate, and the officers were behind them. A boat labeled "Monroe County Sheriff" put in an appearance, cruising past the dock and looping around to come back and idle in the water. Two officers stood on the stern, binoculars in hand.

We waved and stayed seated as Creole and Didier conferred with the officers, standing in the sand at the end of the dock. Kevin Cory appeared to be the lead and, in the past, had been the usual one to respond to any calls that had to do with me and Fab or one of my businesses. Today, he had a new partner in tow. The officers broke away and trailed after Casio, moving up to stand next to him. The threesome waved the sheriff's department boat over, which then shut off the engine, and all eyes surveyed the water.

Kevin dropped down on the deck and leaned over the front for a look underneath. He stood and exchanged words with other two. Casio nodded and stepped onto the boat.

Creole and Didier, both over six feet and dark-haired, headed our way, their blue eyes boring into us. Fab jumped up and ran to meet Didier, and the two stood on the beach by their house. Creole walked over to me and pulled me to my feet, wrapping his arms around me and engulfing me in a hug. He pushed me back slightly, and his eyes scanned me from head to toe. "You okay?" I nodded. "One body got hung up on the underside of the dock. Face down. So… coroner is on the way."

"We were on the deck drinking coffee when it happened." I detailed what we'd seen and answered all his questions.

"Either we were singled out, or we somehow got lucky and it was random, with someone thinking it a convenient location for a body dump," Creole mused as he scanned every inch of the beach.

"Once we learn the identities of the bodies, we'll know if there's a connection. Even if Fab and I had irked someone off of late, which we haven't, what message does dumping bodies send?"

"It's generally a warning to keep your mouth shut. Could be wrong dock." Creole stared out at the water and watched as a diver went in. "Have Xander check for any similar incidents."

"You're not mad that I didn't call you first?"

Creole, who'd left his arm around me, tightened his hold. "If you could've seen Casio's face when you hung up on him..." He laughed. "I wish I had a picture; I'd blackmail him forever."

"I honestly thought he was home and not answering," I said.

"Since you turned off your phone..." His brows went up. "I read between the lines and figured you weren't standing over any bodies and what you wanted was a clean-up crew. Within minutes, Didier confirmed with Fab."

Kevin joined us. I'd bet that he was dripping sweat in that uniform of his, but you wouldn't know it. Whatever he put on his sandy brown hair, it stayed slicked back and in place. "What's your story?" he demanded.

I repeated everything I'd told Creole.

"You're sure both were bodies?" Kevin asked, his brown eyes boring into me.

"Not sure what else would be the same shape." I paused and added, "They didn't bother to disguise what they were doing."

"Once the body that's hung up under the dock is recovered, the sheriff's department will put more divers in the water," Kevin informed us. "If we're not able to locate the other one, keep an eye out. Depending on the currents, you never know where it will wash up."

I grimaced and snuggled closer to Creole.

"Anything you can tell me about the boat?" Kevin asked.

"Sleek. Cigarette style." I drew the shape with my hands. "Blue around the waterline, the top half white. Made for speed."

"If you spot anything out of the ordinary, don't investigate yourself—call 911," Kevin admonished.

"How's life at The Cottages?" I asked. He was a tenant of mine, snuck in by my brother. Did that make us friends? It meant we tolerated one another. Dead bodies didn't help.

"You need to get rid of a couple of your tenants; they're not normal," Kevin said with a grimace.

"Are you including yourself in that group?" I asked.

Creole chuckled.

"I happen to know that one or two of the ladies think you're hot, hot." I struggled not to grin. "They'd be appalled at what you're saying."

Kevin's cheeks reddened. "I know who you're talking about, and I don't date women old enough to be my grandmother. I'd also appreciate you not encouraging them."

"You could move." I ignored Creole's slight pinch to my side.

"One of these days, you'll stomp on my feelings one too many times... and I still won't move out." Kevin laughed and walked off.

"Really, Madison." Creole glared down at me, but that was short-lived and replaced by a laugh. "For all his complaining, I know he likes living there."

Didier and Fab joined us.

"Now what?" Didier asked Creole.

"There's nothing for us to do. The sheriff's department has it under control. I've worked with them in the past, and they'll do a thorough investigation."

"Didn't you have a friend that worked for Fish and Wildlife?" I squinted at Fab. "As I recall, he was an admirer who thought you were hotter than canned Spam."

"I really loathe you." She turned to Didier and rattled off something in French.

So rude, since she knew I didn't understand a word. Creole, who also spoke the language, chuckled. My guess: she was explaining Spam, since Didier's nose wrinkled, and then he laughed and winked at me.

My phone rang. I pulled it out of my pocket

and saw the face of Macklin Lane, the manager of The Cottages, on my screen. I groaned and turned it around for everyone to see. Gossip about the body couldn't have traveled that fast, and I was loath to find out what was up.

"Bonjour," I said, overly cheerful. The guys laughed. Fab arched her brows.

"If you could get your behind over here, sooner than not, that would be smoky," Mac said.

"Who's the boss?"

"Gotta go." She hung up before I could say anything, but not before an ear-curling sound vibrated through the phone.

I shook my head to stop my ears from ringing. "I need to put out a fire. I'd give you more details except Mac hung up, and knowing her, if I called back, she wouldn't answer since it sounds like she hustled off to put out a fire of her own. Not a real one, but you get the gist." I rolled my finger at Fab. "I need you to come along. If you're going to wiggle out, then Didier needs to back me up, and we'll reduce the number of favors he owes me by one."

Family and friends traded favors like hot currency. The rule was, when asked to perform, get off your high horse and just do it. No grumbling.

Didier's brows shot up, a smirk on his face.

"My husband doesn't owe you," Fab said in a high-and-mighty tone.

"Maybe not now," I said sweetly, which irked her more. "But one day he might, and I'll deduct it then."

"All the times Madison's backed you up and hasn't let you down, and you're saying no?" Didier looked down at her, thoroughly amused. Fab remained mute.

I swore he was about to laugh but held it in.

The two engaged in a staring match.

If it wouldn't have broken the mood, I'd have placed a bet with Creole. Who'd back down first? The answer…

"Fine," Fab seethed. "I'd love to come along. Unless you're driving, and then—let me be very clear—no way."

Both guys were looking at their feet, so I knew they were laughing.

"Have I told you lately how bestie you are?" I asked.

Creole pulled me into a hug. "If you need more backup, I'm on speed dial."

Didier was kissing Fab.

"Hurry up, you two." I motioned to Fab and Didier over my shoulder as Creole and I started up the sand.

Chapter Three

Speed demon Fab whipped around the corner and came to a squealing stop at the driveway of The Cottages, a u-shaped ten-unit property that I owned, along with the apartment building next door.

We both leaned forward and stared out the windshield at the pink Cadillac, which I hadn't owned for very long, that was now wrapped around the palm tree.

Fab backed into Mac's driveway, which was located just across the street. Mac liked being close to work, as it allowed her to keep her snoop on. Nothing frustrated the woman more than not knowing something that was unfolding in the neighborhood.

The neighbors had come out of their residences and were loitering on the sidewalk, some drifting into the street.

"My tree," I moaned.

"What about the love mobile?" Fab pointed.

"It was a hot gimmick for about a minute, then turned into a money-sucker. When folks found out they couldn't get their drunk on while getting it on in the back seat, interest waned." Mac had insisted time and again that people couldn't go on vacation and entertain *themselves*; we had to bring the fun and games to enhance their out-of-town experience.

We got out and crossed the street, standing with one foot on the curb.

"Maybe you should've pointed out to your guests that it's a convertible and the drawing card is that the top is always down unless the weather's bad," Fab said, like I didn't know all that.

"You're under the assumption that people care that their naked butts are on display, but you'd be wrong. Being the center of attention, traffic piling up, the wind blowing up their... are all selling points, but only one person had the nerve to say that to my face. We both know who that was, and despite my admonitions to stop, I'm certain I was ignored." I unleashed a huge sigh of frustration. "Crum called me out for ruining his business. I pointed out that encouraging criminal activities, such as sex in public, could also result in charges against him. One mention of the slammer, and he came to his senses." I circled the Caddie and inspected the front end. It took the bashing pretty well but would need repair—to get behind the wheel, you'd have to vault over the door. The palm which now tilted off to one side, was a concern. "Who was driving?" I shouted to those close by, hoping that one of them might answer. Three people had possession of a set of keys. I marked myself off the list, which left Crum and Mac. After sticking my head over the side and checking the interior, front and back, I twirled around and took stock of the several pairs of eyes focused on me, radiating eager anticipation of… I almost didn't want to know. "Driver?" I yelled again.

Several people jabbed their fingers toward the corner. I turned and scanned the street, including the bushes.

Fab sidled up next to me after also inspecting the Caddy and taking pictures. "The good news is I don't hear any sirens approaching."

A shrill whistle had us both turning. Mac barreled around the corner from the pool, in hot pursuit of a dog. Correction: goat… or donkey, or one of its kin.

"Catch him," Mac yelled.

A tall, white-haired, willowy woman, also in hot pursuit, slowed and veered off, entering a cottage on the opposite side of the driveway.

I stepped out of the animal's way. Cat rapport was my specialty — the rest of the animal kingdom, not so much.

Fab had a similar thought and also stepped out of the way, giving the animal a wide berth.

"If he jumps either of you, don't shoot him; use your animal-wrangling skills," Mac called.

Fab snorted.

Both of us fell short in the wrangling

department but didn't feel compelled to mention it, since it would soon be evident.

The squeals and shouts from the street ratcheted up and took on a new fervency. Fab and I pivoted as a tandem bike approached, weaving from side to side, the six riders yelling their heads off. In the front seat was Crum, who barked at the crowd that had gathered in the street. "Get the hell out of the way."

The bike barreled toward the driveway, and at the last second, the animal darted out and, startled, bleated, "Baah," at the top of its lungs. The bike swerved. The animal, unharmed, ratcheted up the ear-splitting noise.

Crum and another man kept everyone from hitting their heads as it lurched sideways, and the two men lowered it to the asphalt. Crum jumped to his feet and hauled the frame out from under the tangle of arms and legs. The profanity flowed. If you needed a refresher in dirty words, this would've been the time to listen up.

The white-haired woman barreled back out of the cottage she'd dashed into and marched over to Crum. She twisted her fingers in the back of his moth-eaten shirt and hauled him back. "You dumbass."

He twisted away, shouting, "Shut it," then stormed over to the Caddy. "What the hell happened to my baby?" He ran his hand along the side, heading to the front. He leaned down and inspected the impact point with the tree.

The woman—who I'd yet to identify as a neighbor, guest, or what the heck—was hot on his heels. The two put their foreheads together and engaged in a ferocious exchange of words, judging by body language, but managed to keep their voices down so no one could eavesdrop.

If this was one of his true loves, she would find out soon enough that he didn't do relationships; he had sex, and the women usually left in a snit, a few wanting to commit bodily harm.

Before Fab could move closer to listen in, I grabbed her by the back of her designer sundress. "You're the licensed PI; you step up and take the lead."

"No way," she hissed back.

"If you wander off…" I jerked on her arm, realizing at the same moment that I didn't have a good threat that she wouldn't laugh at. She dug her feet in but begrudgingly followed me over to check on the pile of people. I breathed a sigh of relief. They were laughing, not a sober one in the lot. One by one, they hauled themselves off the ground and straightened their clothing. One spit on a scrape on her arm. They headed down the driveway in a group. My guess was that they were all guests.

The animal, which I'd tentatively identified as a donkey, was back. He headed straight over to Fab and I, sticking his nose in between us and sniffing. We both jumped back at the same time.

Mac barreled up behind the animal, skidded to a stop, and slipped a leash over his head. "You two could've been more helpful," she snapped.

I looked over my shoulder, wanting to irk her some more, knowing full well who she was talking to. "Excuse me. I'm the owner. Another bone of contention—you hung up on me." I stared at the animal. "And so we're clear, I'm not a donkey-wrangler. Are you?" I asked Fab, who responded with an impressive eye-roll.

"This is a Nigerian dwarf goat," Mac informed me in a tone that suggested I should have known. The goat had turned his attention to Mac and was rubbing up against her. "You need to be careful because they'll do it with anything." At my incredulous stare, she added, "I looked it up on my phone, and they love attention and will mate with anything and everything."

I pictured that, much to my disgust, and burst out laughing. I caught Fab's grin and laughed again. Once I recovered, I faced down Mac's glare. "What in the heck? You better have a good explanation."

"I quit." Mac attempted to push the leash into my hands, but I threw them up and brushed her off. A militant look on her face, she crossed her arms over her massive chest.

Fab also put a foot of space between her and the goat.

"Fab, you got your gun on you?" I asked, knowing the answer. "If Mac makes a run for it, shoot her." I had mine holstered to the small of my back, but I couldn't be shooting employees.

Mac, who totally fan-girled Fab, grinned at her. "Car accident," she said evasively. "I'd hate to give you bad information, so we should wait until the facts come out."

Since when? Speculation over every little thing ran rampant in the neighborhood. "What can you tell us?"

"Saw a woman skedaddling that way." Mac pointed to the corner. "I'm fairly certain she's okay."

Translated, she knew the woman.

"I rushed out of the office when I heard the crash and headed over to check out the Cad. The goat was in the front seat. My first thought was we can't have him whizzing on the interior, so I let him out. Didn't occur to me he'd run off. The wretch."

I crooked my head and stared at the woman, hoping to intimidate more information out of her. Knowing her as well as I did, she was leaving several details out of her story. "Was there another vehicle involved in the crash and they skated off? Or possibly the goat was a distraction?"

Mac shuffled her faux bacon-soled flip-flops. "Since I'm the best employee ever, I called you, like you've requested ten dozen times." She continued to fidget. "Because of that, my attention was elsewhere. Goat boy reappeared, and I had to cut the call short."

"I'm assuming we're in agreement that there are three of us that have keys, but you're telling me that a fourth party comes out of nowhere, loads up a farm animal, and hops behind the wheel for a joyride and you know nothing?" I squinted at her and nodded at Fab, indicating, *Your turn.*

"Why haven't the cops shown up?" Fab asked. "Even though no one was hurt and an ambulance isn't needed, wouldn't they still come out? I'm assuming that the driver, climbed out and ran off? If this is an unknown party..." Fab's brows went up. "That person needs to be charged with theft and property damage. It would help if you could ID said person. While you're trying to come up with a waffley answer to my questions, how about a coherent story as to what the woman was doing behind the wheel? Grand theft auto gone awry?"

"That's a lot of questions." Mac turned her attention to the goat and clucked. "I think it's best to know the whole story before calling the cops." *Don't you think* in her tone. "You won't be needing a police report for insurance, since the policy only covers the other car. Saved bucks that way."

"Great idea," I said, thinking *clearly not.* "If the driver comes back and claims bodily injury and you haven't filed a report, are you paying out of your pocket?" I needed to calm down. Maybe later.

"As someone who always has her nose up everyone's... in their business, anyway. How is it you know nothing about what went down?" Fab leveled a glare that had Mac squirming again.

Mac's *I know nothing act* was just that — an act. But who was she covering for? Not Crum, since he'd been out pedaling around on that excuse for a bike. "I'll go find Crum. If he's as evasive as you, I'm calling the cops as a precaution and reporting it, so nothing comes back on me."

"Crum and the white-haired woman split out to the beach." Fab pointed in the direction of the gate that opened onto the sand.

"Let me guess." I glared at Mac. "Those two are doing it and she's a needy nutcase, since that's his type." I scanned the corners of the property in case they'd stuck around. I wouldn't put it past him to hide behind a tree until I left.

Mac shook her head, erasing her smirk after noticing that my glare hadn't lessened. "Nix is a guest who checked in a couple of days ago and booked the cottage for two months." She pointed to the one I'd seen the white-haired woman disappear inside.

"I'm not going far," Fab said as she walked over to the Caddy and stuck her head over the steering wheel. "No keys," she yelled. She got down and checked under the front end. Standing, she said, "Needs to be towed. But I wouldn't do that until it's determined whether the tree is stable, since it's leaning against the bumper."

I turned my attention back to Mac. "I didn't think I had to explicitly say, 'No goats allowed.' You need to find the owner and reunite them." I turned, walked over to the barbeque area, and took a seat on one of the cement benches. I knew that I hadn't gotten all the facts and wondered who Mac was covering for. I also didn't want to know. I scrolled through my phone. "Step-daddy dearest," I said when Spoon answered. My mother had waited years to remarry after the death of my father, and she'd made a great choice. They were both very happy.

Spoon groaned. "When you bring up the pervy daddy thing, I know something's up."

"You wouldn't believe how this day has gone, and it's not over yet," I groaned back, then told him about the Caddy.

"I'm sending a flatbed and a couple of my men." Spoon owned JS Auto Body, an appointment-only service. "They'll stabilize the tree and get the Caddy moved. I've got a friend who owns a tree service; he can give you his professional opinion about whether it can be saved." Between family and friends, we knew almost everyone in Tarpon Cove, which was located at the top of the Florida Keys.

"You're the best." I smiled, even though he couldn't see me. "There's more..." I almost laughed at his grumble. "You can be the first to share this tidbit with Mother, and she'll think you're more amazing than she already does." To put it bluntly, my family gossiped about one another, and everyone liked to be the first to share any bit of info. I told him about the body dump.

"What in the heck? Any clue what happened?"

"None. I'm waiting for the second body to be found and both to be IDed. Then I'll have a check run and find out who they are and if there's a connection." It'd be a start. "More husband points for you—let Mother tell Brad." Though my brother probably already knew, since the guys would be back to the office by this time.

Spoon laughed. "What'll happen is that Madeline and I will have the same hot news to share."

"If Brad finds out first, I'll tell him to act surprised when he hears it from Mother."

"You want the Caddy repaired?"

"Junk it. I'm more upset about my palm tree."

"It won't be hard for me to find a buyer to take it as-is," Spoon said.

"Huge thank you," I said, and we hung up. "Just so we're in agreement," I said to Mac, who'd sat down on a bench opposite me and boldly listened in on the conversation, "Spoon is sending over a tree dude; my first choice is that he saves the tree. If not..." I sighed. "Then I want it removed, roots and all, and replaced. Once I find out who you're covering for, if they have two nickels, it will be their responsibility to pay up."

Fab had come over and sat down. "My advice, when you find out who was driving, is to use not calling the cops as a bargaining chip."

Chapter Four

It didn't surprise me when I glanced up and saw Crum come barreling around the corner from the pool area. He edged over to the Caddy and once again ran his hands over the sides and across the front, inspecting the damage. He gave it a gentle pat and changed course, heading straight over with me in his sights. "You two mind hitting the road so I can have a private talk with Madison?" He nodded to Fab and Mac.

"I'm not going anywhere." Fab returned his fierce stare.

"You might need a friend, and that would be me." Mac pointed to herself. "So you know, I kept my promise."

Crum threw himself down on one of the benches and manspread as wide as possible. Thankfully, he had on shorts.

I reminded myself of the mental note I'd made long ago not to look below his chin. "Not to be rude, but I'm expecting a work crew or two to show up. I'll be running off as soon as they arrive."

"I... uh... I'm not here to lay blame but to

assure you that my sister will take responsibility for the minor accident." Crum motioned over his shoulder. "Nix somehow got the impression that I owned the luxury auto."

I'd bet she got the idea because he told her that and struggled not to roll my eyes, since no one in their right mind would describe it as "luxury" anything. Maybe back in the day.

"It's possible that I bragged a time or two about the love rides, and so she jumped to the conclusion that I was the owner. Thinking the car was mine, Nix helped herself to the keys and took it for a spin. She only meant to take it around the block. Coming back, she got distracted, and the crash happened."

This day was giving me a headache. "Why not march your sister over here, hang her out to dry, and let her explain for herself? Then she can write a check for the damages, if she's got the nickels... and in this case, a lot of them."

"I told her I would broker a deal that didn't include getting hauled off to jail, since it was a misunderstanding and she didn't mean any harm. I convinced her she wouldn't like being arrested and said, if she didn't want to take my word for it, I could hook her up with a couple of folks that have been and they can relate how a day behind bars goes down." Crum shuddered.

"If Nix doesn't have the dough, then we could kick her to the curb, re-rent her cottage, and recoup some money that way," Mac suggested.

At my raised eyebrows, she added, "She's prepaid."

"If the story is that it was all a misunderstanding, why run off?" I asked. "Unless she was drunk? Or has a warrant out from her previous place of residence?"

"We're Crums, not hoodlums." He straightened his ramrod posture even more, if that was possible, and ran his fingers through his white hair, which stuck up on end, and today was no exception. He caught my glare and knew I wasn't letting it go. "Nix's baby jumped out of the car, and she had to chase it down. That's not what I would call it, but then, it's not mine."

"Are we talking about the goat?" I eyed the animal still in Mac's custody, who'd laid his head on her knee and was chewing on the end of her leopard print tunic. He kept eyeing my legs, which unnerved me.

Crum nodded reluctantly, unwilling to make eye contact.

"In case you were unaware, we have a 'no pets' policy," I reminded him. "No matter how exotic his heritage, he's got to go. We'll let your sister out of her reservation and refund her money, no problem."

"Hold your horses, girlie." Crum chuckled to himself. "Give me a few to check around the neighborhood and see if anyone wants to pet-sit."

"That's a great idea, except that it might be

illegal. You should check with the county and see what the rules are regarding goats. Doing otherwise would invite the cops to show up and pound down your door. The most likely scenario is they'd arrive with animal control; then your sister would have to prove she had a code-approved place to house it to get it back." Red flags were popping up, and what seemed like an easy solution could go south in a hot second and become my problem. Not happening.

"What about those friends of yours that run the goat resort?" Fab asked, the picture of innocence.

I wasted a glare on Fab, who had her head down—laughing, judging by the garbled noise she'd just made. "That could be an option. It's a farm on the outskirts of town. Your sister could negotiate visits, so the two could spend time outside while the goat eats grass or whatever they do."

"We're talking about a goat." Crum snorted. At my *So?* expression, he added, "Just that it sounds fancy and spendy."

"What it is is an animal rescue, and for a generous donation, they can be very accommodating. Something to think about if you want to continue to hang out with your sister here at The Cottages. Goat-free." Sanctuary Woods was an animal rescue that my friends and family supported. They'd also become family friends.

31

"I've got their number." Mac held up her phone.

"The good thing is that they already have a goat, or something close," Fab reminded me.

"This one can have a playmate." I pasted on a stiff smile. "Does Mr. Friendly here have a name?" Bored with Mac's clothing, he'd turned his attention to her legs.

"Goat." Crum's tone suggested that I was dumber than a stump.

I glared until he looked away. "Great. Goat will have new friends to hang out with, lick on…" Whatever. "Another good reason for his not staying here: there are too many opportunities for trouble."

A flatbed rolled up and double parked, JS Auto Body painted on the side. The pickup behind it maneuvered into a tight parking space.

I was tempted to make a run for it. I took a breath and turned to Crum. "So we're in agreement. Nix is reimbursing me for all the damages, and if not her, then you. She's also dealing with her goat issues. This deal has a twenty-four-hour expiration on it. Except for the goat, which needs to be gone in the next hour. If I have to follow up after that, I won't involve the cops, but I will send a thug to beat the moly out of you and force your sister to watch."

Crum's eyebrows shot up. "You need to calm down. I gave you my word." He turned to Mac. "Get me the amount owed, and I'll get you a check." He stuck his hand out to me.

"You know how I feel about hand-shaking. Ick. How about a knuckle bump in front of witnesses?" I extended my fist.

Billy Keith rounded the front of the trucks, tucking his windblown, sun-bleached hair behind his ear, and I stood, hoping my sigh of relief at having the perfect excuse to run off wasn't noticeable. I waved and hurried to meet the go-to guy that Spoon often sent when Fab or I had a problem. He skipped the excuses and always came through. Two good-sized men appeared next to him. The three trooped over to the Caddy and inspected the damage, then turned their attention to the tree.

I walked over to them, Fab at my side. Mac stayed to deal with Crum and the goat. "You guys will be the center of attention in your tight jeans and t-shirts. Beware: you'll have the women here drooling on you." They laughed.

"What happened?" Billy asked, a frown on his face.

"Oh, let me." Fab took center stage and sauced up the details as she told the events as we knew them. She had the men hanging on her every word and laughing. All three spotted the goat and shook their heads.

"Do you know anyone beefy or scary who might want a part-time gig?" I asked Billy.

"What are you up to now?" He stared at me suspiciously.

"I object." I laughed. "We used to have a guard, of sorts, but he met the love of his life and moved in with her up in the Panhandle. I'm thinking of maybe hiring another one to keep the guests in line."

"I'm not certain a guard could've prevented this from happening, since it wasn't a stranger lurking around." Billy's smile was deceptive. He came off as a regular guy, but if you came looking for trouble, he'd finish it.

"You're right." There would've been no preventing this from happening unless Mac or I had been standing by the car.

"You don't have to worry," Billy reassured me. "The guys will get this cleaned up, and the Caddy hauled away. Before we get ready to leave, I'll check with you and update you."

"I'll be around. I'm going to check on a couple of tenants."

Billy nodded, and he and the other two turned their attention back to the car.

"What happened to the neighbors hanging in the street?" I asked Fab.

"Got bored with no cop action and went back inside where they have air conditioning." Fab pointed me toward Miss January's. The woman was tipped over the arm of her chair, passed out. "I'll knock and tell that boyfriend of hers to get her out of the sun."

We walked over to Miss January's porch and were greeted by the sounds of her snoring.

Neither of us wanted to wake her from her stupor. Fab jumped up the steps and beat on the door, which flew open. Whatever complaint sat on Captain's lips as his enormous frame filled the doorway, he bit it back, staring at Fab and then over her head at me. Fab said something, keeping her voice low. He nodded and scooped Miss January into his arms, carrying her inside.

"Does a grunt count as conversation?" Fab asked when she joined me and we cut diagonally across the driveway.

"In Captain's case, that would be a full sentence." Based on past conversations, he'd shown himself to be a man of as few words as possible. "I need to make sure that Joseph is still breathing, and then I'll be ready to get out of here." Both he and Miss January were original tenants. According to their doctors, they were living on borrowed time, but they just chugged along, not caring what anyone said or thought about anything. "Come with me. You think he's... tolerable. Although his girlfriend is our favorite."

"Woah." Mac ran up, the goat leading the way. "You two can't skate out of here and leave me to deal with everything."

She meant the goat, and yes, I could. If I had to, I'd say it was in the manager's handbook and hope she didn't remember that we didn't have one. "There's the problem. You've shown yourself more than able to handle almost every situation. I don't expect that to change. Quit again and see how that works out for you." I turned to Fab. "If you don't back me up here, you'll be doing her job."

That made Mac laugh. Her attention turned to her ringing phone, which she whipped out of her pocket and hung back to answer.

"This'll be quick," I promised Fab. "Don't let me dally. It's past noon, and I need a drink to improve my flagging personality."

"Being the great friend I am, let's go to lunch. Tomorrow."

I groaned. "I don't even want to know. I had a feeling you were holding back, and here it comes. Save it for later. I don't think I can deal right now." We reached Joseph's door, and I unleashed my best cop knock to get the old veteran's attention. No answer. "Joseph," I yelled. Still nothing. "Guess he's not home. I'm surprised Mac didn't tell me." I peeked in the window to make sure he wasn't asleep in his chair. Nope.

"Mac's irritated with you." Fab's smirk told me there was more coming. "She had it all planned that if she couldn't find alternate accommodations for the goat, you'd take it home. Mac doesn't want to be bothered and expects you to step up." Fab gloated at being able to impart that tidbit. "So you know what a great friend I am, I told her there was zero chance he was getting in the Hummer. If you were to take him home, she'd have to use her truck and deliver him to you."

Most people thought it was Fab's car rather than mine. That's because I hardly ever got to drive. It'd stopped bothering me when more than once she maneuvered us out of what could've been a terrible accident and we walked in one piece. On the goat issue, we were in agreement.

"You'll be happy that I didn't share what I was thinking with Mac... that she was a complete hot mess, just like the rest of the people here."

I stepped off Joseph's porch and scanned the driveway. As I was about to leave, a window across the driveway shot up. A woman stuck her head out and yelled, "Joey's passed out by the pool. Says he hasn't been drinking, but who believes that?" She slammed the window shut.

I waited for the glass to crack and hit the ground and breathed a sigh when it didn't. "Joey? With her snotty attitude, she sounds like a woman who didn't get any. I hope he's not hooking up with the guests and I'm the last to know."

"I'm fairly certain that he can't... uh... and on the off-chance that I'm wrong, you should give him the talk."

I pretended I hadn't heard a word of her suggestion. "That would mean he was cheating on Svetlana." I grabbed her arm before she could get away and tugged her toward the pool.

Joseph's snoring greeted us as we rounded the corner. He was sacked out on a chaise tucked under the tiki bar, his rubber girlfriend asleep on his chest. The blond-haired, blue-eyed Svetlana, Svet to her friends, was one of my favorite tenants. She never got into any trouble.

I crept through the gate, grabbed a beach towel, and covered him, warding off a scorching burn. I squashed his cigarette butts with my shoe, just in case, then scooped them up and tossed them in the trash. Just as quickly, I was back out the gate, which Fab held open.

"What if he sleeps out here all night?" Fab asked.

"Wouldn't be the first time." I eyed Mac coming our way. "I'm thinking if we go to the right, we can outrun her and get back to the car before her and her leashed friend."

Fab laughed, her amusement increasing at Mac's militant scowl.

Before Mac could grouch me out, I asked, "Would you keep an eye on Joseph and make sure he gets back to his cottage okay?"

"Just one more problem on my endless list," Mac snapped. "Nix called and informed me she has a migraine and needs to lie down. She graciously gave me permission to board the goat for a few days. But not before I had to listen to mumbling I could barely decipher—something along the lines of, 'It's all Crum's fault.'"

"I guess I won't be meeting her today." Yay! I

didn't have the energy for round two with a Crum. If she was anything like her brother, you had to be on your game or get mowed down. "Did you get in touch with Sanctuary Woods?"

"Her words: 'We have plenty of room, dearie, but you'll have to deliver him.' If you need me for anything, I'll be escorting the goat to the resort. Unless you've got someone else that will do it."

I turned to Fab, gearing up to enjoy her explosion. "How about if we—"

"No. Way," Fab spit out.

I struggled not to laugh, my face feeling the pinch.

"Delegate," Fab barked at Mac.

Mac crossed her arms and glared.

"Here's some incentive. You take care of it so that none of us has to hear another baah—" Fab made the sound effect. "—and I'll take you shoe shopping.'

I winked at Mac and stared down at her multi-colored crocheted slip-ons with knitted balls for eyes. It surprised me that she'd swapped the bacon flops for them, but I didn't question her choice.

Mac eyed Fab's designer leather slides. "Hmm... you know... our shoe fashion sense isn't copasetic. It might take several trips before I found anything. I'll take a favor instead."

"Done," Fab snapped.

On the way back to the car, I stopped to talk to

Billy. The Caddy had been hooked up, and the other two men were ready to pull out.

"I understand that you're not interested in keeping the Caddy." Billy waved as the tow truck started down the street. "I've got just the buyer, and he won't drag his feet sealing the deal."

"You're the best. Freebies galore at Jake's—" The popular dive bar I owned in the middle of town. "—so take advantage."

"As for the tree, we were able to stabilize it so it won't fall over. Spoon's arborist friend is on the way. I'll be surprised if the verdict isn't replace."

I sighed. "Not what I wanted to hear, but the last thing I want is for it to fall on anything or anyone."

Chapter Five

"I'm certain we could squeeze in lunch," I said the second the car door shut. "I need a margarita to get through the rest of the day."

"No time today." Fab's attempt at a sympathetic look failed.

She hit the gas as though today was the day I'd make good on my threat to jump from the car. I might have given it serious thought if we were on the main road and close to a restaurant. Since we were on one of the back streets, it would be a hike to the highway. She wound through the neighborhood and took a couple of shortcuts, passing a dog that barked furiously as we cruised past. She pressed a button on the visor, and the security gate opened as we arrived at one of the warehouses that Creole and I owned. We'd decided not to make any upgrades to the street side of the building, leaving it with an unassuming "nothing happening here" air. We'd bought three side-by-side properties, the other two now leased to a boat dealer. My first warehouse purchase, a little farther down the street, and the three floors of this building were also rented.

Fab also owned two buildings of her own at the other end of the street. At my and Didier's suggestion, she'd moved her office and mine to the top floor of this warehouse, which put us close to The Boardwalk offices and our husbands on the first floor. The second floor was leased to the ex-chief of police out of Miami, who'd opened his own security company upon retiring.

Fab pulled around the back and parked. We couldn't miss the black Escalade with tinted windows, signaling that Fab's longstanding client, Gunz, was around somewhere. He hadn't opted for the patio area, with its large table and numerous chairs, so one less place to look.

"If your client picked the lock, I'm shooting him," I said, getting out of the car. I knew full well he didn't have a key, and if I had my way, he wouldn't be getting one.

Lark waved from where she stood under one of the glass roll-up garage doors that had replaced the old shuttered windows and opened up the interior of the previously drab space. She looked like a tropical flower, dressed in a flowing multi-colored sundress, her brown hair in a ponytail and sunlight bouncing off the stack of bracelets that lined her arm. She unleashed an ear-splitting whistle meant to get the attention of Arlo, her Golden Retriever. He barely slowed, on the hunt for something in the grass that ran along a strip of water at the back of the property. She followed it up with a longer, shriller version of the first whistle, and Arlo came running.

"The guys wanted me to flag you down before you went upstairs," Lark told us as she beckoned us inside, at the same time scratching Arlo's head.

We couldn't miss Gunz's massive bulk behind Lark's desk, his feet up on the corner. The man had made himself at home. You'd almost think he worked here. The truth was, he was somewhat tolerated by the guys, after promising he wouldn't knowingly send us on any jobs that would get us hurt or worse. From his smirk, I knew the guys, who were sitting at the conference table nearby, had already questioned him about whatever job he had for Fab, so there went that excuse for backing out.

"Isn't he the cutest?" Lark whispered.

I turned to Arlo, wondering what dog trick I'd missed.

"Nooo..." Lark giggled and pointed in Gunz's direction behind her cupped hand.

After doing a double take, I said, "You and I need to have a talk."

"If it's about..." Lark tapped the tips of her fingers together. "I already know." She laughed and skirted past me to her desk.

Creole finished his call and crossed to me, dropping a quick kiss on my lips.

"Sorry I didn't—"

DEBORAH BROWN

"No worries. Fab called."

It was a rule that when a job went awry, we were to call and report in. At first, it'd meant for trouble but had been expanded to anything out of the ordinary, and that certainly described the morning.

"That reminds me... we can't stay long," I said, loud enough for all to hear. "Our newest family member—a goat, and I'm open to suggestions on a name—anyway... he's out in the Hummer, and Fab is helping me get him home. I don't want him to get heatstroke. I thought he would make a good playmate for the cats." Creole started out with a grin, which disappeared. The others had lapsed into an uncharacteristic silence. "He's very affectionate, so don't be surprised when he comes sniffing."

"A goat!" Creole whipped over to the doorway and craned his neck to see the Hummer. "It better not be true."

I exchanged a grin with Fab, who'd sat down next to Didier. Witnessing the exchange, he shook his head.

"For anyone who believed that story—and that's what it was—you've been pranked," Brad announced with a laugh.

I sat next to my brother and leaned in and kissed his cheek. "You staying out of trouble?"

"You know me." Brad chuckled.

"I do, and that's why I asked."

Creole came over and sat next to me. "You're

not very funny."

I fake frowned.

"I have a goat-free announcement," Didier said. "The divers recovered the first body, which is at the morgue." He'd been reading off his phone and shoved it back in his pocket. "They've stopped the recovery process for the other body."

Swell.

"Let's hope it doesn't wash up on our strip of sand," Fab said.

I seconded that. "Did body number one drown?"

"The bullet in the middle of his forehead did the job," Didier said.

Fab and I both grimaced.

"I have friends on the force, and as soon as I heard, I put out a request to be kept in the loop." Gunz wiggled back in his chair, getting more comfortable, if that was possible.

"How long before they release a name?" I planned to order a background check the second I got it. We all wanted to know if any of us knew one of the victims.

"Good question," Creole said. "Kevin told us that the man didn't have any identification on him, so hopefully they can match his prints."

"Be nice to know why our dock was chosen," Didier mused.

I seconded that.

"I've asked the boat dealer next door to ask around," Creole said. "He said it won't be easy to locate the boat based only on type and paint color."

"I'll also pass the description along to a couple of friends that work the docks," Brad said. "If they don't know, they probably know someone who does." Brad had been a commercial fisherman for years before he sold off half the business to a friend and joined the family in real estate.

Gunz caught Fab's attention and tapped his wrist.

Fab stood. "We've got a meeting."

"I'll wait here for you," I told her.

She scooted closer, leaned in, and whispered, "The heck you will."

Creole, who'd heard her, laughed.

Gunz stood, grabbed his briefcase, and headed to the elevator, Fab behind him. I didn't bother to keep up, sure to earn another glare from Fab. I preferred to walk the two flights. I hadn't stepped foot in the elevator since the time it shook on me. The repair guy claimed to have fixed the issue. Whatever.

"You have a surprise upstairs," Lark said to me as I passed her desk. "I wouldn't have opened the door, but the guys insisted and also admonished me not to warn you." She shot the three men, who were staring her down, the stink eye.

I paused and asked, "Is it going to be bad?"

She furtively shook her head.

"Next time we're late, don't feel obligated to entertain Fab's client. I know Gunz can be 'tudey."

"He was a perfect gentleman." Lark giggled. "He's so funny; all we did was laugh."

I swallowed my groan. Gunz's track record with women stunk, as evidenced by the scar on the side of his nose where some chick had removed a hunk with her teeth. "We're going to have a talk." Later. When I had more time.

I waved and bounced up the stairs. The door stood open. As I walked in, I couldn't miss Xander Huntington sitting at one end of the ten-foot oblong desk that Fab had had custom-made for me out of shiplap. He was our Information Specialist, meaning he could dig up info on just about anyone, and if something was out of his skill set, he had contacts. He waved with a grin.

"Are you the surprise?" I asked as I walked over and dropped my briefcase and purse on the other end of the mammoth desk.

Xander nodded. "I have a business deal to pitch you."

"I hope this means we'll be sharing office space again, but what about Toady?"

Toady was a friend that Fab and I met out in Alligator Alley, and he lived in one of Fab's warehouses. Part of the agreement they'd made was that he was to keep intruders off the property. Needing more room for his business ventures, Xander had worked a deal for office space, and in exchange, he dug up information that Toady needed on his jobs, most of which were referred by Fab. They were the ones that Didier had banned Fab from taking. Dangerous wasn't a word in Toady's vocabulary—he met it head-on.

"The good news is that Toady's found his soul mate. Now that she's moved in, they need their privacy." Xander glanced around furtively, then whispered, "She's loud."

"Loud?"

"Hah... ah... ahh..." he said, then gasped.

I covered my face and laughed; I could feel my cheeks burning.

"For my sanity, I decided that Fuchsia and Toady needed space and it was time to get my own," Xander said. "I thought I'd stop by and pitch sharing space again. I ran it by the guys downstairs, and they all thought it was a good idea. Creole had Lark let me in, saying it would be a great surprise. Hope he was right."

Fuchsia? Couldn't wait to meet her. "You're a perfect fit for this office." I smiled. "There's plenty of room for another desk. We'll pick out something ugly and show it to Fab: 'Don't you love this?' I guarantee something amazing will get delivered the next day."

"Before we do that," Xander cautioned, "it would probably be best if you asked her... and not in front of me, since she might want to say no. Then it would be awkward."

"Can't have any awkwardness." I flashed him a shifty smile that had him doing a double take. "Fab," I yelled across the room, "Xander's moving in. He needs a desk and whatever else, and I'm certain you can take care of it."

Fab didn't skip a beat and yelled back, "In the meantime, he can use your desk."

I winked at Xander, whose cheeks were on fire. "No worries about Fab dragging her fashionable heels; we won't have to share for long. Happy you're back and that we'll be sharing space again. It'll be good to know someone's here, since we're not most of the time. You can keep an eye on the place."

I crossed to Fab's desk and sat in her second chair, which I'd pushed up against the wall with the admonition not to move it. Not the perfect position, but at least I could watch Fab and her client in action.

"As you both know…" Gunz stopped to suck down water from his designer bottle. "I'm heavily invested in real estate. One of your jobs is now to check out any property I'm interested in and get back to me with a report on the condition, neighborhood, that sort of thing. I forwarded a sample of the report I'll need for each address."

"Don't you think a licensed appraiser would be better for this job?" I knew Fab hated it when I asked Gunz questions, but too bad.

Gunz's expression bubbled with anger as he

bit out, "I had one."

"He die?"

"I wish. Turns out, the b— was checking out my properties all right. Billing me through the nose and selling the information to other investors."

"I'd have thought your killer reputation would've preceded you and no one would dare screw you," I said.

"Word's spread that I've cleaned up my rep and don't kick ass like I did before." Gunz oozed frustration. "So game on. Once I found out, I fired his ass, and what did he do? Spread word that I'd gone soft." He growled out the last word. "Now if he were discovered face down in a ravine, you can bet I'd be the first suspect."

"Then figure out a way to hit the guy in the wallet and make his humiliation public." Fab checked her phone and handed it over to me.

"You and I..." Gunz winked at Fab and tapped his temple. "I put the word out that he's blackballed and if anyone uses him, that's the end of any business relationship with me."

I gave the report a fast perusal. "We'll do our best to duplicate this and make sure you get the info you need."

He nodded, liking that we were on board.

I didn't need to be part of this and excused myself, going back to my desk and sitting opposite Xander. I updated him on the morning and the information I'd be needing. "Can you also check for other bodies dumped in the same way?" Then I told him about The Cottages, which had him laughing.

"You should hit up your funeral friends, since they have a connection in the coroner's office and that guy's always willing to share."

Fab and I had made friends with the owners of Tropical Slumber Funeral Home. They'd hid us from trouble a couple of times, and in return, we "bodyguarded" at their shindig funerals. What better place for a fight to break out?

"Good idea. Fab can do it." I texted her, so I wouldn't forget. "They find her more entertaining than me."

Xander didn't appear to believe me.

Hearing Gunz's size twenties hit the concrete on the way to the door, I deduced that he and Fab had concluded their meeting. "Like I told your husbands, I don't expect you to stick your neck out. You ever sniff trouble, just hit the highway," I heard him tell her before the door closed.

That was one thing I appreciated about Gunz—he always stressed our safety first, unlike Fab's other clients.

She came over and sat down, slapping her hand on the desk. "I'm not doing the reports."

"Figured as much and came up with a solution—hire Lark. Then boost Gunz-o's bill. Problem solved." I smiled at her. "According to the guys, she never says no to any request and

DEBORAH BROWN

doesn't drag her flats on turnaround time. They had to step in a few times when Boardwalk tenants wanted to take advantage and turn her into an errand girl."

"Gunz never complains about what I charge as long as I give him a heads up. I also don't take advantage, and he knows that. It seems like he and Lark get along, so that's a plus."

Xander's brows went up.

"I'd like you to stress the no-dating policy." There wasn't one, but that was easily rectified. "You know he leaves his women in a frustrated mess and they inevitably end up trying to kill him. Remember the one that shot at us?" Maybe that was another client, but the reminder got the message across to Fab. "The guys are happy with Lark, and I don't want her leaving."

Fab nodded and turned her attention to Xander. "Can you set up a notification for any news stories related to this morning?" She passed her phone to him. "This needs to be a secret because Didier wants me to stay out of it. Once he started on the safety speech, I just readily agreed."

"I'm uncertain why you haven't figured out that your sneak-around ploys don't work for very long." I glanced over at Xander in time to see his smirk disappear. "You could have Xander send it to all our phones, and then you're in the clear."

"No thanks. That would mean I wouldn't be

52

the one to spread the news."

I tried not to, but laughed anyway, and she joined in.

"Please tell me you'll put Gunz's job off until tomorrow?" I asked. "One good reason is that we need to organize what information we'll need so we're not making multiple trips. Another reason, if you need it, is I've had enough of this day."

Chapter Six

The next morning, Creole was in the middle of making coffee when my phone rang. Fab's face popped up on the screen. "You're canceling our road trip?" I asked when I answered. One less Gunz job was fine with me.

"Can you be here in five? I'm offering waffles to sweeten the pot."

I looked down at my ankle-length t-shirt dress. I didn't usually go trotting down the block in it, but what the heck. "Can I bring Creole or should I ditch him?"

Fab laughed. "Just know that if you do the latter, he'll track you down."

I shoved my phone in my pocket. "Put on a shirt, babe, so we can hop to the neighbors' for tasty chow."

He gave me a scrutinizing once-over.

"Waffles."

He unplugged the coffee and moved past me, grumbling, "Whatever Fab is up to better be good." He was back in a minute, hooked his arm around my shoulders, and we went out the back and cut down the beach.

We walked across Fab and Didier's patio and

through the open glass doors. The kitchen island had been set for the four of us.

"Bonjour." I waved frantically, which amused Didier. I slid onto a stool and licked my lips at the glass of fresh-squeezed orange juice he set in front of me.

"Smells good." Creole sat next to me after Didier declined his help.

"My wife has news, which she's excited to share but which will wait until we've finished eating," Didier arched his brow at Fab.

The conversation was often funny as we devoured our food at a fast rate. It was good to be back together for breakfast. The guys stacked the dishwasher, even though I'd offered for Fab and I to do it, which meant that I'd do it and Fab would direct me.

Didier refilled our coffee mugs.

"Warning, this picture is a bit gruesome," Fab said, mostly for my benefit. "To speed things along, I got with my source, who called on theirs, and they identified the body fished out of the water as Richard Paul. Here's a picture taken right after he arrived at the coroner's office." She retrieved her phone off the countertop, clicked on the screen, and handed it to Creole. So much for her promise to stay uninvolved.

Translating for Fab, she called our digger friends, who called their coroner friend, who always came through. If he ever cashed in all the favors we owed, it would be a doozy.

"He's not as bloated as his friend will be when he washes up," Creole said. "Never seen this man before."

I waved off the phone, not wanting the image of the corpse seared into my brain.

"I didn't recognize him either," Fab informed us. "I texted the info to Xander, and he sent back a preliminary background check that showed the man to be a small potatoes hoodlum with a lengthy rap sheet of petty crimes. No missing persons report has been filed."

"Don't forget about your latest phone alert." Didier's brows went up.

It surprised me when Fab blushed.

"Local news is reporting that there's an eyewitness to the disposal of the body. A woman. Yet to be identified." Fab screwed up her nose in distaste.

"You can bet they're digging," Creole grouched.

"That means that one of us is the witness in question?" I mused. "Unless someone else is bragging." One could hope that local media was being led on a chase.

"It's probably you or me, and if they're able to track one or both of us down, you can bet we'll be hounded." Fab continued to scroll through her phone.

"I'd think it would take help from someone within the sheriff's department to find us," Didier said.

"What this means is that we'll need to keep our eyes peeled for anyone snooping around." Creole picked up Fab's phone and looked at the picture again. "Forward all this to me, please."

"I'll copy all of you," Fab said.

"Not me." I screwed up my nose. "You can share the less gruesome highlights." Fab's grin let me know that I'd be hearing more details than I wanted to. "Are we still on for the Gunz job?"

"The window for coming up with an excuse as to why you can't go has closed. So yes."

"Give me a half-hour." I slid off the stool. "Lay on the horn, and I'll come running."

The guys smirked.

Creole walked me out the same way we came. "Yesterday, Didier and I questioned Gunz about the job. Seems tame enough, and he assured us that he's not expecting any trouble, but…"

I stood on my tiptoes and brushed his lips with mine. "Once I shoot my way out, I'll get hot on the phone."

Creole swung me around, tickling me. I screamed. He hoisted me over his shoulder and ran up the steps.

Chapter Seven

Fab flew down the Overseas like the highway would disappear if she wasn't in the lead, ignoring that it had been built eighty years ago and wasn't going anywhere anytime soon. There was the chance of a hurricane nipping off hunks, but even rain rarely wiped out the whole road.

"Do you think you could get us to wherever we're going without making me puke?" I grouched.

"I'm not a fan of the windows down, but if you're going to be sick, then by all means."

Her superior tone was so annoying that I didn't bother with a comeback.

"The turn is coming up." Fab pointed in an off-hand way. "As you know, Gunz is partial to his real estate holdings being local. Claims he doesn't have time to drive all over creation."

"Which he wouldn't do anyway. He has you."

Fab turned off the highway, and there wasn't a house on the street that didn't need a little TLC. She cruised slowly through the neighborhood, scanning for addresses, which weren't always in plain view. She found the property easily enough and slowed before turning into the driveway of what appeared to be a run-down single family home.

"I thought Gunz preferred properties that only required a spit shine to get them rented?" I squinted out the window, shaking my head. I could hear the cha-ching in my head as I mentally tallied reno costs.

"It's been designated a historical structure," Fab said in a snooty tone as she pulled onto the gravel patch at the front.

"Whatever." I laughed at her and caught sight of her smirk. "Gunz-ola is being conned. I don't believe any structures have that designation here in the Cove. He needs to check with the appraiser's office before forking out for a title that no one gives a squat about. At least not around here."

"Would you stop with the names? One of these times, it'll slip out, and what kind of excuse will I come up with?"

"Easy. Since I'll be the offender, you roll your eyes. If it's you, then you better come up with something and quick." I turned my attention back to the dump in front of us. "Rehab or bulldoze?" I tapped my chin. "I know what I'd do."

"You're not being helpful."

I saluted, much to her disgust, I was certain, because it made her laugh.

"You know more about real estate than I do,

so what's your opinion?" Fab asked.

"We haven't seen the inside, but based on the crumbling exterior, my guess is that it will be in the same shape. If that's the case, then a complete gut job. The renovation budget can skyrocket, depending on the work he wants done and whether he wants top-of-the-line finishes. Probably best to go for somewhere in between. Cheapest isn't always best." I looked out the window and down the street in both directions. "I'd run the numbers of the neighborhood before investing a dime. Capture the best and worst aspects of the property in pictures, and the rest of the block as well. If he's still interested, then he can send out his contractor for an estimate." I glanced at the neighboring house. It was in the same neglected shape, but there were cars in the driveway.

"First on the list is checking for squatters."

"I'll be waiting right here while you're having all the fun."

"You better get out of the car," Fab grumbled as she slid out and rounded the front.

I waved through the windshield.

She crossed her arms and glared.

She almost had it down. Almost. All she needed was a few more lessons from Mother. I shook my head in response.

She marched around and opened the passenger door. I'd forgotten to lock it. No matter, she had the keys. "You can't allow your best friend in the entire world to go in by herself."

I got out. "I concede that you have a point, and you can expect to hear that line of reasoning tossed back at you. Here's the best I can do for you — I'll go as far as the front door... close enough, in my opinion. I'm inviting my friend along." I drew my Glock from my waist holster. "The first sign of trouble, and I'm out of there. In fact, if anything goes south, pick me up at the corner."

"You'd leave me to fend for myself in a shoot-out?"

"Maybe not. It's been a while since I've nicked anyone, and I wouldn't want to get out of practice."

Fab smirked. "I don't really want to crawl through the overgrowth to get to the front door. Let's check around back."

"If anyone is lurking inside, they can't see out the windows, so you'll have the element of surprise."

Fab led the way, phone out and clicking away.

The overgrowth was ridiculous. So happy I'd changed to crop sweats and tennis shoes. We tramped around the side of the house. We tramped through the knee-high weeds along the side of the house and curved around to the backyard, a weed-filled open space, the fence leaning in places, where it came close to kissing the ground. There was a large screened-in patio, the door missing. The rotted structure was hanging on by a nail or two, and built long before treated wood, which wouldn't be my first choice for Florida. The siding on the house had taken a beating and hung off in places, matching the rest of the house.

Finally, we reached the back door of the house. Fab reached out and opened the screen door, which fell to one side and hung precariously, one side tied to the doorframe at the top with a rope.

"Forget knocking. If someone were here, they'd be poking their head out about now to check out the source of the racket."

"I'm going for the element of surprise. You better not ditch me."

"It's quiet at least. That's a good sign. Hopefully." I had my Glock positioned at my side, not willing to reholster it until I got back in the car. "I'll stand guard at the door. Once you've cleared every room, holler, and I'll come in. Maybe."

Fab had her lockpick in hand, but noticed that the door wasn't closed and shoved it back in her pocket. She toed the door; then, with a kick, it opened into the kitchen. The interior was covered in a thick layer of grime, and a smell emanated from it that had both of us covering our noses. Based on the filth and the variety of dead bugs, no one had used the place in a long time.

I grabbed the back of her shirt. "Dead body? Maybe," I whispered. As promised, I stayed by the door and tried not to look too closely at the surroundings. Instead, I mentally took a roach count — toes up verified they'd taken their last breath. Twelve. I shuddered.

Fab moved cautiously forward and poked her head into the living room, waving me back with her gun-free hand. "Anybody home?" she yelled and continued out of sight.

I swear if anyone answers, I'm on the run.

Fab was back in seconds and gave me a nudge. "Hustle it up and don't touch anything."

She didn't have to tell me twice. I beat it out into the backyard, and the first thing I did was fill my lungs with fresh air.

"Dead bodies," Fab whispered.

"How many?" What was it with these empty properties and dead bodies? It wasn't our first find.

"One in the living room, who hasn't been dead as long as the two in the bedroom, and uh... they've been deceased a while, based on... well, you know."

We rounded the side of the house and came face to face with two cops, their guns drawn. Thankfully, we'd both reholstered ours.

"Hands up," one yelled. Past his shoulder, I could see their cars blocking the Hummer in the driveway. "Have a seat." He pointed to a dirt patch.

We did as instructed.

"I guess we don't have to flip to see who calls 911," I whispered.

A third car pulled up, and Kevin Cory got out.

"It's not often that I can say I'm happy to see him," Fab whispered.

"I wouldn't say our relationship with him has worked to our benefit in the past, so hang onto your lukewarm enthusiasm."

Kevin closed the distance and spoke to the two officers, then walked over to us. "We got a call about a couple of armed robbers, and look, it's you two." He motioned for us to stand.

"I'll check out the inside." One cop started toward the house.

"You might want to hold off for a second," Fab called out. "I should give you a heads up on what you're going to find."

"What?" Kevin demanded as the other cop back-stepped to where he could hear what was said.

Fab told the officers why we were there and about her discovery, her nose wrinkling, letting them know to be prepared for the smell.

"I'll call it in," Cop One said and walked back to his car.

"Did you mention to the other officers that you're both carrying?" Kevin asked. We shook our heads. "Set them on the ground."

Fab and I once again did as we were told.

Cop Two came over and bagged them.

"When did you two start doing property inspections?" Kevin asked, clearly suspicious of our story.

"When you've got a good client and they ask, you do it," Fab said. "In the five minutes that we've been here, we got to the back door, which was open, and I yelled inside and didn't get an answer. Besides checking out the general condition of the property, I needed to find out if someone was living here, legally or otherwise."

"Were you able to make an ID on any of the bodies? Friends, perhaps?" Kevin asked.

"They're all decomposed." Fab grimaced. "One not as bad as the other two, but still."

"You two are sure racking up the bodies," Kevin said.

"Speaking of... you fish the second body out of the water yet? ID the first one, perhaps?" I asked, even though I already knew.

"No, to both." He made it sound more like *none of your business.*

"Do the divers with the sheriff's department have a clue when number two might show up?" I asked, even though I knew it was a long shot that I'd get any info out of the man.

Kevin shook his head. "You two will have to go to the station and give a statement."

"Can we drive ourselves so we don't have to leave the Hummer here?" Fab asked.

"That's not the way it works. You'll need to leave the car and go with us to the station."

"How about letting us call our lawyer?" I asked.

"Make it snappy. And remember this bonding moment when I want something." Kevin smirked.

I raised my eyebrows at Fab. Tank was more her friend, although he would take my calls.

She slid her phone out of her pocket and made the call. When he answered, she got to the point. "Need you to come to the police station." Then she told him what had happened. To whatever he said, she answered, "Got it." After hanging up, she said to me, "He's going to put his pants on and meet us."

"T. M. I."

"He probably wasn't—"

"Stop," I cut her off. I was about to call out to Kevin when I saw that he'd walked over to meet the coroner, who'd just arrived. The fifty-something got out of his van and waved to Kevin. The two talked and then made their way around to the backyard.

Cop Two roped off the front of the property with crime scene tape. No clue where Number One disappeared to.

"What a gruesome job." I shivered. Since it appeared we would have a little time before being carted off, I called Creole, and it went to voicemail. "Did you call Didier?" I asked Fab.

"I flipped a coin, and both sides said, 'Madison can take care of it.' I guess I forgot to tell you. Oops."

Next call, the office, where I found out the guys were in a meeting. "I'll let you be the bearer of the news," I told Lark, and then detailed the events.

"They're not going to be happy." Lark's pout could be heard through the phone.

"Tell the guys that once we're released, we'll bum a ride off Tank, our lawyer—" I couldn't remember if she'd met him yet. "—and come straight to the office."

"If your plans go south, give me a jingle, and I'll pick you up," Lark offered.

"Gotta go. Kevin's stomping in our direction," I said and hung up.

"Ready, ladies?" Kevin opened his car door. "You two haven't been guests in a while, but the place looks the same." He grinned.

Fab and I looked at one another and shared the same thought: *Cop humor and not funny.* Neither of us said a word as Kevin drove to the station.

Once we arrived, we were taken into a private room one at a time and asked questions, then signed a copy of our statement, all under the watchful eye of Tank, professionally known as Patrick Cannon.

A few hours later, Fab and I walked out of the building to freedom. Our husbands were waiting in the parking lot and jumped out of the truck when we appeared. Fab walked straight into

Didier's arms and buried her face in his chest, and he helped her into the back seat of Creole's monster pickup truck. Creole wrapped his arms around me and lifted me into the front seat.

"I'm betting Fab has pictures," I said, knowing everyone could hear.

Fab made a muffled noise, which Creole decided was affirmative. She pulled out her phone and made a call. It wasn't hard to figure out she was talking to Gunz, updating him on his investment opportunity. She ended with, "If you learn anything, please call."

"I'm betting the price on that property just went down," I said. "The bank that owns it isn't going to want to deal with dead-body cleanup."

Creole had just turned onto the main highway when a loud explosion rocked the ground, and our heads all turned in the same direction. Flames leapt into the air off in the near distance. "What the..." He slowed and hung his head over the steering wheel, then pointed to the west. "What's over there?"

"Residential, some commercial, could be anything," I said.

Fab knocked him on the shoulder. "Check it out."

That didn't surprise me, since she'd have already been chasing the plumes of black smoke. What surprised me was that Creole made a sharp turn off the highway. Fab called out a couple of questionable turns, shortcuts that at first glance appeared to be dead ends, and Creole didn't balk, maneuvering the streets to where we needed to be.

He rolled past the blaze seconds ahead of the fire truck and parked far enough away that we wouldn't block arriving law enforcement.

Fab stuck her head out the window. "No more mini tacos for us," she lamented.

"No..." I leaned forward and looked over Creole's shoulder at the burning roach coach. The converted Airstream had been burned to a crisp. "I hope no one got hurt."

Fab and I liked eating here. Besides the good food, there was a small water view on the miniscule strip of land. Only drawback—no bar.

Creole had his head out the window, surveying the damage. The firefighters went to work and doused the last of the flames in short order.

Two cop cars pulled up.

"Good thing there were no cars in the parking lot." Fab cocked her head from side to side. "They must have been closed, or there might have been casualties."

Everyone we knew ate at the family-run truck, which had been around forever. Mini tacos were a favorite of Fab's and mine, and we always enjoyed them at one of the picnic tables overlooking the slice of water.

"Time to get out of here." Creole pulled away from the curb. "Before a cop walks up and starts asking questions. Our luck, it'll be Kevin, and I think you've seen enough of him today. Besides, it would be hard to explain how you ended up at two crime scenes in the same day."

I cast a glance at Fab. "Would that be a record for us?"

Fab shook her head in disgust. "Maybe."

Chapter Eight

The next morning, Creole and I were sitting out on the deck, drinking coffee and watching the sideshow of Fab and Didier prowling their patio from one end to the other. Fab stopped every few feet to stomp her foot, which brought smiles to Didier's face, along with a couple of laughs.

"What are they doing?" I asked.

"Fab's planning another update to the already tricked-out security system. She's having cameras installed on the beachside exterior of all the houses and the dock, in case someone gets the idea to dump another body." Creole made a face. "But... mean old Didier vetoed the 'no trespassing or you'll be shot' sign that she planned to hang on one of the dock posts to warn anyone cruising by in a boat."

"I'm for a 'no trespassing' sign. That way, if anyone's willing to take the chance of a bullet hole or two to test it out, we can feel justified in giving them what they want."

"Didier agreed with you, but wifey didn't care for the shortened version."

We continued to watch the entertaining twosome. Fab snuck up behind Didier, who probably thought he was safe with his back turned, and with a running start, pushed him into the water. His dark head surfaced to her laughing face. He splashed her, soaking her pants with water, and whatever he said, she laughed again, then turned and bolted back toward the house.

Didier swam to shore and stalked up the sand.

"Something tells me that Fab is in big trouble, and she'll love every minute of retribution." I laughed. Just then, my phone rang. I picked it up off the table, showing Creole the screen, then answered and hit the speaker button. "It's early for you to be calling. Another goat?"

Mac snorted. "Thankfully, no. I lucked out the other day. Cootie came home, the two old goats sized each other up, and it was instant simpatico."

Fab and I had met Cootie Shine out in the mangroves. Thankfully, he gave us a lift back to civilization, or it's possible we'd still be out there. When he was evicted for poaching, I hired him and his almost-wife, Gertrude Banner, to manage the apartment building I owned next to The Cottages. Since Cootie could fix anything, the guys availed themselves of his handyman services at the Boardwalk, and they kept him busy.

"All I know is that Goat got away from me, and catching him was near impossible since he was busy running the neighborhood. Then

Cootie whistles and Goat comes running. Couldn't hear what the old goat said to the young one, but Cootie got his leg humped, and after that bonding moment, Goat followed the man to his truck. As soon as he had the door open, the damn thing hopped in. So relieved to wave the two off to greener pastures. Happy ending." Mac unleashed a melodramatic sigh.

Creole covered his mouth and laughed.

"Have I told you lately how much I appreciate that you badgered me for a job and I had the foresight to hire you?"

"That's because when I showed up, you'd had enough and were entirely over herding drunks, not to mention the criminals that were living here at the time." Mac chuckled. "The good old days. If you were truthful, you'd admit that I was the first normal one to come in off the street and you scooped me right up."

"I haven't regretted a day. Maybe one or two, but we can look past those."

Mac laughed. "One incident is all I'm copping to, and what I have to tell you will clean the slate. Da, da, da…" she yelled, and I pulled the phone farther away. "Got a check for the damages to the Caddy and replacement for the palm tree, which I'll be hustling to Nix's bank to cash. In exchange, we won't be prosecuting. Slim chance of that, but she didn't need to know."

"So you took life in prison off the table?" I asked in a faux 'tudey tone.

"No one got hurt."

"Did Crum pay? Or did Nix cough up the moola?" I asked.

"Nix didn't haggle; she whipped out her checkbook, wrote the check, and assured me it wasn't rubber. It was a little too easy—wanted to threaten her with the SWAT Team—and since that didn't happen, it squeezed some of the fun out of the shakedown."

"Who is Nix?" Creole barked.

"Nice move, putting me on speaker and no warning. Your hair tips would frizz if I did that to you."

"Saves me from repeating everything. So much news, I'd forget something, and then his hair would frizz." I turned to Creole. "Crum's sister. The parents spit out two of them. She's in town for a visit." I couldn't remember if I'd specifically mentioned the sister or only referred to her as goat woman.

Creole tugged on the ends of my hair and grinned.

"They weren't able to save the tree?" I asked.

"Tree dude will truck one over as soon as I schedule it. He promised you won't be able to tell the difference," Mac assured me.

"I can't wait for my introduction to Ms. Nix. I don't have a speech prepared, but the gist will be not to take anything else that doesn't belong to her." There were a couple of other trees she could've taken out, which I'd prefer not to risk. "Thank you for squeezing the money out of her."

"I'm hoping for a quiet day."

"Good luck."

We hung up.

"I'm going to pay a surprise visit."

"I know you well enough that I knew that's what you were planning." Creole took my face in his hands and squeezed my cheeks, his eyes dancing with humor. "In case you planned to ask—and it pains me to disappoint you—but..." His lips quirked. "I'm not available to go to The Cottages with you today."

"You need to practice your facial expressions." I shot him a couple of my better ones, which made him smirk. "If I were placing a wager—and you know me, any old excuse—what worries that pretty head of yours is that one of the older ladies will jump your hot frame and ride you. No worries." I flexed my biceps. "I'll gun up and be your personal bodyguard."

"Now there's a good excuse for me to stay away, since I didn't have one ready." The sides of Creole's lips turned up. "You shoot one or two and your business will nosedive."

"Pleaz... Once the news of a shootout gets out—" I shot up the sky with my fingers. "—even the locals will burn up the phone lines for reservations."

"You need to behave, and so do your guests." He gave me a stern look.

All I wanted to do is lean in and kiss him. "If that's the way you're looking at the oldsters, behaving will be the last thing on their minds." I laughed at his scowl. "I will try to behave myself." *I smiled a how am I doing?* grin. "Should I not succeed, I expect a free pass."

He stood and pulled me to my feet and into a long kiss. "I'll walk you out."

Chapter Nine

I'd sent Fab a text and got no response. Before leaving the compound, I called, and it went to voicemail. I doubted I'd see her until tomorrow. I cruised through the entry gate that, along with the security fencing installed around the perimeter of the property, had been another gift from Fab's father.

Out of curiosity, and since I'd perused the local news site online and was disappointed—they only had two lines about the Taco Bar explosion and no good pictures—I decided a drive-by was in order. It surprised me that there weren't any lookie-loos milling about. One would think the news hadn't spread, but that was difficult to believe. The once-pristine, albeit older, Airstream had been reduced to a burned pile of rubble. Clearly a total loss. I felt bad for the family-run operation and hoped they would recover.

I rolled down the window and snapped a few photos of my own before heading back to the main highway. A few streets later, I turned off and cut around the corner to The Cottages. Approaching the driveway, I slowed and mourned the loss of the palm tree, eyeing the massive hole where the roots of the old one had been. Tree Dude had been careful not to wipe out the rest of the plants, and only a few would need to be replaced. Turning in, I scanned the driveway—not a porch-sitter in sight. All was quiet, or so it seemed, and I parked in one of the guest spaces in front of the office.

The office door opened, and Mac skated out in a short tartan skirt and a t-shirt knotted at the waist. She was wearing a pair of shoe skates that had seen better days fifty years ago.

I waved and walked over to her. "Heard any news about the Taco Bar?" If she'd gone bar-hopping last night, she was sure to know the latest.

"Arson. Although I can't tell you my source." Mac glanced toward Kevin's cottage, so I knew it was reliable information.

"When do I get to meet the illustrious Nix?" I eyed the front of the cottage I'd seen her going into yesterday. I should welcome her with my best cop knock.

"Be nice. She paid," Mac said in an admonishing tone. "Honest mistake."

In some convoluted way maybe, but I didn't say it out loud.

"I wouldn't be surprised if Crum had bragged about town that he owns The Cottages." Mac spit on her finger and wiped the bug pin on her shirt.

Except that most people in town knew me and

would laugh at him.

"Nix only lost control because the goat came up behind her and licked her face."

I grimaced. "Let me get something straight — the woman checked in with a goat, and mentioning the 'no farm animals' policy slipped your mind?"

Mac threw her hands out. She stumbled and twirled and came back steady on her skates. "It's not Cottages policy to toss the cars of every guest, so I missed the horny devil. It happens." She sniffed indignantly. "Be satisfied with your happy ending, because I'm telling you, Nix's got the gumption to take the case to court and enjoy every minute, even though she'd lose."

"You need to stop dancing on those skate things." I stared down at her feet for the umpteenth time. "You're going to fall, and I'm really not in the mood to go to the emergency room today."

"It's good for my muscle tone." She lifted her leg and twirled it around.

I grabbed her arm to keep her upright, and we both almost ended up in a heap on the pavement. "If I get scratched up, I'm shooting you."

"That can't be your solution to everything." Mac huffed. "You've got to change it up once in a while to be taken seriously."

"It usually works. Maybe not with you. Besides, it's not easy to keep coming up with new tricks." I flashed a deranged smile that I'd been working on. I couldn't determine from her double take if I'd mastered it or not.

"There's another slight hiccup," Mac stammered.

I hated it when Mac waffled. It meant trouble. I was about to demand, *What the heck now? Tell me already*, when I heard a door slamming. Something told me I better enjoy the last few seconds of calm. I glanced over my shoulder, and the white-haired woman from yesterday, wearing a camo-patterned tennis skirt and top, strode toward me, her knee-high sneakers with red laces slapping the ground and a militant, take-charge look on her face. I blinked and refrained from rubbing my eyes, certain they were playing a trick on me. The woman had a pig at her side with a pink ribbon around its neck, the other end wrapped around her wrist.

"Before you go off your spool, I was about to tell you," Mac whispered. "I honestly had no clue she had one until I caught her on the security camera in the middle of the night, taking it for a walk. I'd already tipped a few and wasn't in the right frame of mind to be running down the street, chasing her ass, yelling, 'What the hey hell?' and 'Have you lost your mind?'"

"So saucing it up stopped you from creating a scene in the driveway or somewhere close by?" I found that hard to believe.

"Ladies' night at Custer's—lift your top and get a free beer. Now how do you pass up that kind of offer?"

How indeed? I couldn't think of a better way to spend the evening than baring my chest to hooting and hollering locals at that rathole bar. Custer's sat on the outskirts of town and catered to locals, more aptly described as hardcore drunks, who wanted to drink on the cheap. After several go-rounds with the health department, they'd managed to stay open, serving screw-top wine and beer. I'd heard that they recently got a full liquor license again.

"Madison Westin?" The woman strode up. "I've heard that you're the owner of this fine establishment." Not a note of sincerity in her tone. "Nixon Crum, but you can call me Ms. Crum." Her lips curled up, clearly amused with herself.

"I think I'll call you Nix, like everyone else around here, including your brother." We traded snooty stare-downs. I'd honed my skills on her brother and wasn't coming in second in this game.

"One thing we have in common… I find hand-shaking abhorrent," Nix said, ignoring my comment. "It only makes sense, if you think a second about all the places one has to stick them—and most do and don't wash up…" Her eyes swept over me from head to toe in the same imperious manner as her brother.

Crum came barreling around the corner and skidded to a stop. At least he had on ill-fitting shorts, which were bunched at the waist, a bag clip barely keeping them up, the grey waistband of his tighty-whities sticking out the top. "No hard feelings, since we lived up to our end of the agreement," he said with a fake smile.

"Except that stinkin' overpriced tree," Nix grumbled and glared at where it had once stood. "No one liked my suggestion of a nice cactus. Way, way cheaper, by the way."

Cactus! My nose in the air was the only answer she was getting. I was tempted to moan and groan some more about my loss but decided there were more important issues. The pig! "That—" I pointed to the animal. "—needs to be relocated. Today. We're happy to refund any unused deposit so you can stay close by."

Nix straightened to her full height, towering over me by what seemed like a foot and looking down her nose. "Your demand may work on other, more uneducated people, but I know my rights."

I didn't even bother to hide my eye-roll. "Let's skip the IQ comparison, shall we? Been down that road with your bro, and it's already been agreed that his is higher and yours can be too," I said in a cheery tone, ignoring the nudge in my back. "The pig will be gone within the hour. If not, I'll bring in my eviction team to move you and your bro-ski to the curb, and you can keep each other company elsewhere."

"How dare you?" Nix jumped forward, spit

flying from her mouth.

It was her lucky day that it didn't hit me. I wouldn't shoot her, but I'd be damn tempted. I took the high road and ignored her, but kept an eye on her as I turned to Crum. "What's it going to be?"

"Don't you worry," Crum assured me and leapt at his sister, hooking his arm around her shoulders and holding on despite her struggles. He untied the ribbon from her wrist. "Come along, Porky." He clucked and somehow got the two back to her cottage.

Guess he didn't want pig cooties at his place. "One hour," I yelled after them. Nix stiffened and put up a struggle on the porch. Crum pushed her through the door, whispering furiously. I turned to Mac. "Is now the time to yell after their snooty asses that I'd like a thank you for not calling the cops? What are the chances of her brother getting her packed up and moved out? I know full well he's not going anywhere." Not expecting an answer, I asked, "Porky?"

Mac shrugged. "Turns out it was one of their favorite characters from when they were kids."

"Cartoons in the dark ages, who knew?"

Mac laughed. "Be nice."

"I've been way nicer than Fab would have been if Nix had been talking down her nose at her, showing her impatience at having to deal with an inferior human."

"When you're a retired scientist, you can lord it over folks. How many of them are running around?" Mac smirked. "Speaking of... where's your shadow?"

The only reason I believed Mac's tidbit is that she wasn't a liar. "Fab would prefer that you phrase it the other way around." I thought back to the morning escapade on the dock and smiled, wiggling my brows. "She and the husband have their phones turned off for some alone time."

"Oh man, I'd go for that in a hot second." Mac grinned, which disappeared as Crum bore down on the two of us, Mac in his sights. "If Porky's about to be my problemo, I want a raise."

"Sorry about all the miscommunication," Crum said as he sauntered up.

I refrained from snorting. Just barely. I pasted on what I hoped was a sincere smile, but I would bet it came across as smarmy.

"Since Harold and Porky are siblings... in a way..." Crum seemed momentarily flustered but quickly recovered. "I'm hoping that the farm can take one more. That way, in addition to being able to visit, Nix can easily pick them up when she's ready to go home."

"Harold?" *Who the heck...*

"The goat," Crum sputtered like I was a simpleton. "There's no need to worry; we'll get this worked out, and there won't be a need to kick anyone anywhere." He focused his attention on Mac as he walked backward toward the cottage. "So you'll take care of Porky?" He nodded as though it was a done deal.

Breathe, Madison. I thought his name was Goat. "For a fee," I yelled.

He waved as he turned, his long legs closing the distance to his sister's cottage in a few strides.

"He'll haul finds over from the trash, useful or not, and since I have zero chance of getting cash out of him, I'll have to sell everything at a yard sale." Mac sighed.

I laughed. At her look of disgust, I mumbled, "Sorry."

"Nix isn't as tight-fisted, and they're her children."

Children? I squirmed.

Several female guests walked out of their cottages at the same time. They were of varying ages, sizes, and shapes, but what they all had in common was they were clad in the scantiest bathing suits they could paste on. As though their meet-up had been planned, they congregated in the driveway, arms loaded down with beach bags, and after an exchange of greetings, headed to the pool, their laughter drifting back to us.

Mac glanced at her watch. "Crum's exercise class starts in a few minutes. It's a favorite with the ladies, so we're not going to say anything negative, are we?" She eyed me suspiciously.

"I'll try. Maybe." I nodded to Porky, who was being led in our direction by Crum. "Are you calling Cootie for help again?"

"Cootie and Rude are at a funeral for a snake-wrangler friend. Rude was excited because they're going out on a boat and each person gets to pitch a fistful of the man overboard."

I assumed that meant they'd cremated the dude. I squeezed my eyes closed, blocking any images. Porky stopped to pee. "Any plants that die, make sure they get replanted before I find out. And don't dig them out of the neighbor's yard," I said to Crum as he got closer.

Crum attempted to hand off Porky.

I waved him off and his *what the heck?* glare spoke for itself. "So we're clear — the animal sanctuary is not a free service, and you can expect a boarding fee to cover expenses, feeding, care, etc. Agreed?"

"Nix won't balk at any of the charges, as long as they're reasonable. Me, I'd have eaten them already."

"How could you? Your niece and nephew?" Or whatever.

Mac poked me again.

Crum was short on humor. It pained the man to deal with stupid people, and this was one of those moments for him. "I'll guarantee the bill." He sighed.

I knew that was painful, since he pinched nickels until they screamed.

"Do not tell Nix," he admonished. "Because when it comes time to dole out the cash, she'll take the animals and skip out if she knows I guaranteed payment. Porky's going to the same place as Harold? I want to reassure Nix so she won't worry."

"Let's hope," Mac grunted. "I've yet to call. One of these days, my number will pop up and they won't answer."

"If Blanche can't take Porky, then she'll refer you to someone else." I doubted that would be the case because the woman always went out of her way to help.

"I've got to run; my ladies are waiting." Crum handed Mac the ribbon and sprinted toward the pool.

"He's aware that the *no sex with the guests* rule is still in place?" I asked.

Mac nodded. "Now if he could just keep it in his pants when it comes to the ladies in the neighborhood." She took her phone out of her pocket. "Don't go anywhere. I'll need help loading Porky into my truck." In anticipation of my 'no way' response, she'd already called Blanche and started to explain the situation. The two women laughed a few times. Porky and I stared at one another. "I really appreciate this." Mac shoved her phone back in her pocket. "Blanche's sending over someone to pick up Porky. Thank goodness. She didn't skip a beat when I explained the situation. One would think she gets calls for pig boarding all the time."

We both looked up, hearing a door slam. Nix

strode down the driveway and straight to Porky. "I wanted to say goodbye." She bent down, hooked her arms around his neck, and made kissy noises. He appeared annoyed and obviously wanted to get back to sniffing the grass.

"Porky's ride will be here soon," Mac told her.

"I'll take him for a walk while we're waiting, so he won't get bored." Nix took the ribbon and headed to the street.

"It was nice meeting you," I called out and waved to Nix's back. She didn't acknowledge me or slow a step.

"Now that she's far enough away that she can't hear me..." Mac lowered her voice. "The pig is why she took off right after the accident. Upon impact, it escaped, and I'm not clear on the exact details. Once its hooves hit the pavement, it went on the run with Nix after it. When she couldn't catch up, she headed back here. One look at you, she figured you were the owner and ducked into her cottage."

"And what? Porky found his way back on his own?"

"Nix grabbed a bike and found him just down the street, with a neighbor feeding him dog food."

Anyone other than Mac, and I wouldn't have believed her. "Is that her... pickup?" I stared down the driveway at the nose of a truck with multiple layers of green paint in various shades, which poked out from the side of the cottage. It looked older than her, but I kept that to myself.

"It's a 1950 Ford flatbed. I suggested that since it still runs, why not spiff it up? Nix's nose hiked in the air was the only answer I got."

"Good for hauling her livestock. I'm going to sneak out of here before something else happens. Can you save any more emergencies for next week?" I waved and had to restrain myself from running. I jumped into my SUV and drove sedately out of the neighborhood, taking one of Fab's shortcuts to the office.

Chapter Ten

As I got to the warehouse and parked, my phone dinged with a message from Xander saying he had names for me. I texted back, "See you in a few." Before going upstairs, I decided to steal a quick kiss from my husband. I walked through the raised doors and waved to Lark, who watched me approach. Arlo lifted his head, barked hello, and lay back down.

It surprised me to see a tall, statuesque brunette waiting for her coffee to brew while she rooted through the cupboard. She turned and caught me staring at her. "We ran out of coffee upstairs."

Upstairs? An employee of the Chief's? I was certain I'd met her before, but where?

I poked my head into the office space that the three men shared, which took up over half the square footage of the entire floor, and winked at Creole, who was on the phone, as was my brother, who was laughing it up with someone. With slinky in my sights, I crossed to the conference table where the woman was sitting. "We've met, and I'm sorry to say I've forgotten your name." I barely got the words out before I remembered. "The artist from the beach. And you work upstairs?"

"Allegra Kent. Nice to see you again, Brad's sister." Her smile was phony, and it was clear that she didn't mean a word of it.

Overprotective little sister. In my defense, my brother had a type, and it wasn't stability. "I thought you moved."

Brad, who'd hung up, raced out of his office and planted himself next to me, shooting me a side glare that I easily translated as *be nice*.

"Brad and I had a good laugh about that little lie." Allegra patted her lips. Brad groaned. "It was my idea to get you to stop asking questions." She scooted her chair back, walked over to the counter, and filled her thermos. "So we're square, neither of us —" She pointed between Brad and herself. "— have ever been into each other. Nice guy, though." She winked at him and slunk out, coffee in hand.

"Talk about being kicked in front of a moving vehicle," Brad grouched. "Stay out of my personal life."

I got in his face. "There's no way that's going to happen." I struggled not to smirk.

"You really are a pain in the a —" he ground out.

"Dare you to say it. I'll tell Mother." I swallowed a laugh.

"We're not five, and that threat doesn't work

anymore. It sounds like you need a reminder that squealing on me violates our super-secret pact of not telling on each other unless faced with certain death."

I leaned forward and kissed his cheek. "You listen to me—I'm here for you no matter what, and don't you forget it. I apologize for being a tad overbearing when I met Allegra. Just being protective, and that's not going to change anytime soon. Know that, even though I'm annoying at times, I am here for you."

"Same here."

Brad's phone beeped, and I turned my attention to Lark, who hadn't missed a single word and had a grin on her face the whole time. "Tell the tenant on the second floor to buy his own coffee." That widened Lark's grin.

Woe to the Chief for giving her a hard time when she was first hired. He hadn't completely wiggled back into her good graces. Lark came off as an easygoing hippy chick, but she had a bite to her.

"Dude upstairs can hire who he wants, but we should know who they are so we don't shoot an innocent person, thinking we've got a trespasser," I said.

"You don't need to worry about intruders. I got my rifle loaded with rock salt," Lark assured me. "That will have them yowling and on the run, as opposed to dead. Makes the cleanup less messy."

Brad, who'd come up behind me in time to hear everything, groaned. "We're going to have to have a meeting and make up a host of new rules."

"Yeah, okay." I waved him off and turned my attention back to Lark. "What's the artist doing working for the Chief?" Pottery or something had been her gig when we first met.

"No gossiping," Brad said over his shoulder as he went back to his desk, his phone ringing.

"Ignore him," I said.

"She prefers Allie." Lark lowered her voice and pointed to the ceiling. "An ex-DEA agent and friendly with the Chief, although she made it clear that she wasn't doing him either. She was hired for her kick-ass skills, but didn't elaborate. A little tip: she doesn't care for questions; one or two, she's fine, but after that, she gets annoyed."

Brad was back in a flash and leveled a stare at the two of us when we stopped talking. "What happens in this office doesn't get shared with my sister," he grouched.

"Don't listen to him." I made a face at Lark, who laughed. "I'm going to order lunch and have it delivered. Call me when it gets here." I waved to the two of them and bounded up the stairs to the third floor.

I wasn't used to the new location yet, but happy that we'd made the move. The interior was almost a duplicate of the previous office. Once again, Fab had put her decorating stamp on it. I was happy to have my desk facing the floor-to-ceiling windows that I'd had installed, replacing the old ones and bringing them up to hurricane code. The sun streaming in made it less of a grubby hole.

I waved to Xander, who was on the phone and sitting at the far end of my desk. I spread my paperwork out and scooted my chair over, then pulled out my phone, called Jake's, and placed an order for a little of everything.

"How many people?" Cook grumped.

"Five? No, seven. Better plan for ten. And an assortment of beer." I ignored his clucking noises. "Hopefully you can con someone into delivering."

"Got it taken care of." He hung up.

"You feeding an army?" Xander asked when I hung up.

"With any luck, there will be leftovers, and they make the best breakfasts."

"I just emailed you the names you're wanting."

I opened my laptop and easily found the message. "You're the best."

"Shouldn't we wait for Fab?" Xander looked over at the door.

"I'm banking on her being a no-show. She's suffering retribution for pushing her husband off the dock." I told him about the morning. "It looked fun from my vantage point, and I'm thinking I should christen Creole with a little salt water. Except he wouldn't have to chase me; I'd dive in after him."

Xander laughed. "Thanks to you, and promises of rounds of drinks, I got an in at the coroner's office and can call directly now, so this news is hot off the press."

"I'm happy that the digger dudes came through for you."

"The three bodies in the house were easy to identify, even though they had no IDs on them; their fingerprints pulled up rap sheets a mile long. Most of the charges stemmed from drugs." Xander read off their names. "I ran background checks on the men, all in their thirties, and they've been in and out of jail since they were teens."

I made a note of the information and would return to it later. "Sounds like they crossed the wrong person and paid big. How is it that they were basically left to rot and hadn't been discovered earlier?"

"The previous owner of the house died, and apparently there were no heirs. It sat empty until the taxes went unpaid long enough that the county took it over and put it up for auction. Pretty sure it was illegal for Fab to be poking around inside." Xander laughed. "I know it wasn't you. If not for the two of you, the lucky buyer would've been in for a smelly surprise. The sale is on hold for now. I was told that when it comes back up for auction, it won't come with any kind of cleanup."

I wrinkled my nose.

"I've got a report ready to send Big Boy before he comes tromping up here, demanding answers."

"Good idea." I nodded. "Besides getting screwed out of other deals, Gunz got burned once, buying sight unseen, and he knows that Fab won't give trespassing a second thought and will thoroughly check out the properties."

"You'd think the county would find it hard to get a buyer, but I did some checking, and they changed the law—that someone died there no longer has to be disclosed."

"If it's cheap enough, buyers will line up, do a basic rehab, and flip." I grimaced. "Even though you don't have to disclose crimes that happened on the property, you know the second the new owner moves in, the neighbors will be banging down the door—'Oh, did you know…?'—the picture of innocence as they relate the ghoulish details, which will get embellished in the retelling."

"The first noise I heard in the night, I'd be, 'Oh no, the ghosts are partying.'"

I laughed.

"More news," Xander said with a smirk. "The second body, which floated off with the currents, surfaced just south of you. Mark Bowe is the unfortunate man's name. He got hung up on the boat of a man who made the discovery as he was about to fire it up for a ride."

Yikes. "That means we don't have to be on dead-body lookout."

"The two men, Bowe and Paul, owned a warehouse north of town. What kind of business they were engaged in is unclear. The cops checked it out and found it empty. The sign advertised a lumber yard, but according to a neighboring business, the billboard had been up for years, long before the new owners took possession."

"What did the records say about who owned the place?" I asked.

"It was purchased a couple of years ago by BP Inc., and the paperwork doesn't yield a clue about what they were into. They didn't file for a business license, and since the building didn't attract attention, no one went around to ask questions. So far, I haven't found any other records under their names."

"Smells illegal, and if it was, then they must have been conducting business at night so as not to attract attention."

"The neighboring businesses all kept regular hours, and they either didn't have any information or didn't want to get involved." Xander pulled a file from his briefcase. "Another interesting tidbit is that no missing persons reports had been filed on any of these men. Five men missing for who knows how long, and not missed by anyone."

"Someone had to know. Another case of not wanting to get involved because they knew they were up to their eyeballs in illegal and were afraid, not wanting it to come back on them."

"My source said to call anytime, so I'll keep checking back. Only costs me a beer or two."

"Take him to Jake's. Everyone there knows you and knows it's on the house. Just don't drive."

"Not doing that." Xander nodded.

"Another job. Would you research the street that we all live on? Who lived there before? Anything newsworthy? I've got my fingers crossed that you come up with zero."

"On it." Xander scribbled a note on a pad in front of him. "I've got a case that I'd like help on."

"You're switching roles and becoming a client?" I hoped he wasn't in any trouble.

"This is for a friend of a friend." He chuckled at my raised eyebrows. "Thanks to Crum, our mutual friend Tessa was able to make up her back schoolwork and ace the tests to start high school."

Fab and I had helped Tessa and her brother, who were both homeless, find her grandmother and get off the street. Their grandmother, Blanche Bijou, was the one who ran the animal sanctuary.

"Tessa made friends with a senior chick that she met in the library. The girl turns eighteen in two months, and her mother told her she had to move out on her birthday. Here's the kicker—the mother's forbidden her to take any of her personal belongings. Claims ownership because she paid for the stuff, which isn't true for everything, as some were gifts. The daughter's only allowed to keep the clothes she wears out the door."

"I can't believe... why would her mother do that? Even if she's been a big pain in the backside. To say that the relationship sucks is an understatement."

"Jealousy. The final straw for the mother was that Lena got an acceptance letter to an out-of-state college. Her mother had picked up the mail that day and ripped open the envelope, and by the time Lena got home from school, she was raging mad—how dare Lena apply anywhere without her permission, and she wasn't paying. Lena told her she'd applied for a scholarship, which made her mother angrier, and she snorted out that it was a pipe dream, since she was too damn stupid."

I could see where Xander wouldn't turn his back on this girl. It was too close to his own circumstances. His father had died while he was in college—a straight-A student with a bright future ahead of him—and the first thing his stepmother did, without a word to him, was stop his tuition and dorm payments. He was getting the last laugh, having sold a social media app that netted him six figures.

"What is it you want me to do?" I asked.

"Lena wants her stuff. All of it, and especially her childhood memories. I don't see how Mrs. Craig has the right to keep everything." Xander hissed out his annoyance. "The day after her mother issued the threat, she began collecting items, hiding them in the garage and telling Lena she threw them out."

"How do you know that?"

"Once I met her and heard her story, I offered to stop by her house when her mother wouldn't be there. The two of us had a look around and found the boxes she'd stuffed in the corner of the garage."

"I'm happy you didn't get caught," I said.

"It was my idea to go to a thrift store and replace the items in the boxes, which we did, and store her personal items in Billy's garage."

Billy, who worked for Spoon, had offered Xander a place to live when he first came to the Cove. They'd been roommates ever since.

"Does Billy know what you two did?" I asked.

"Billy said if Mrs. Craig weren't a woman, he'd have offered to rearrange her face. He then offered to talk to her, and I told him thanks, but a bad idea, since she was apt to call the cops. The last thing I want is for any of us to end up in jail."

"Good advice." I settled back in the chair and stared up at the ceiling. I already knew what Fab would do—confront the woman, like Billy wanted to do.

"The mother smashed her computer," Xander continued. "Figures if Lena can't turn in her homework, she won't graduate and no college."

"Most parents want the best for their kids. And the father?" I asked.

"He died when Lena was a kid, and her mother changed after that—once loving and kind, she withdrew and turned cold."

"Can Lena explain her dilemma to her teachers?"

"Too embarrassed. She's able to use the computer in the library. That way, her mother doesn't know what she's up to. She goes to school early and stays late and never takes her books home, for fear her mother will throw those out."

"What Lena needs is a lawyer, and I can make that happen," I assured him. "Her mother can legally kick Lena out at eighteen. Keep her belongings? Probably not. But she probably knows it would take the services of a lawyer to fight that, which Lena can't afford, so there's no one to tell her daughter that she can't railroad the girl." I frowned at him. "If you two get caught sneaking her stuff out of the house, you will definitely get in trouble. Lena is a question mark. Once the cops hear the whole story, they won't think much of the mother, but it wouldn't stop them from arresting you."

"What do I tell her?"

"Tell Lena that I know a lawyer that takes pro bono cases and hopefully this one won't be too involved. If it becomes necessary, does she want to take her mother to court? Once she's served, she could immediately kick her out. If that happens, does she have a place to go?"

"Don't know." Xander shook his head. "I'll talk it over with her."

"Also tell her that there will be no cost for the attorney." I'd call in a favor or six if I had to. "Once she meets with him, he can tell her what her rights are and advise her on a course of action. I hope the law isn't on the mother's side or that she gets a judge who rules against her. There's also the chance that once words like 'lawyer' and 'court' get bandied about, her mother will back off. Talk to Lena and get back to me with what she's decided to do, and I'll contact Tank. I suggest that she at least find out what her rights are."

"I'm thinking if Lena threatens her mother with legal action, she'll clean out her stuff in one fell swoop."

"Doesn't sound like there's a winning solution in this case."

"Don't forget to send me your bill." Xander smiled.

"Don't you worry your pretty head." I stared at the brown mop that framed his face and dancing eyes and bet that it had the girls doing a double take. "It's a freebie all the way around."

My phone rang, and Lark's face popped up. "Chow arrive?" I asked upon answering.

"There's enough here to feed the whole block."

"We'll be right down."

Chapter Eleven

Creole downed the last of his morning coffee and put the mug in the dishwasher. He did a double take and leaned over the sink to stare out the window, where everything was still dripping from last night's downpour and dark clouds had rolled in, threatening another drencher. Then he backed up and reached into the back of the junk drawer (every house should have one), pulled out a Glock 9, and turned to me. "Not sure what's going on, but stay down."

He was out the door before I could snap back, "Yeah sure." I reached into the same drawer and withdrew a Beretta, slowed to slip into a pair of flip-flops, and beat it out the door.

I approached Creole as he stood at the end of the driveway, his head turning one way and then the other. He shoved his gun into his waistband and hightailed it across the street.

Didier raced by in hot pursuit of a scruffy thirty-something man, the two headed toward the entry gate. The man caught sight of Creole about to intercept him and attempted to change course. His hesitation gave Didier time to come up on him and kick his feet out from under him.

The man landed face down on the grass, and Creole stuck his tennis-shoe-clad foot on his butt and barked. The man nodded and didn't move.

I waved at Fab, who was headed my way, and met her halfway. We stood on the side of the road. "Intruder? Man make a wrong turn?" I turned my head one way and then the other. Not a single car parked anywhere on the street.

"Didier was about to leave for work when he caught sight of this guy roaming around. Before he flew out of the house, he told me to stay put." Fab shook her head, conveying how stupid she thought the idea was.

"Mine had similar instructions, and here we are—a testament to how well we listen."

We both laughed.

Creole and Didier appeared to be weighing their options as the man continued to shake his head. Creole fisted the back of the man's t-shirt, hauled him to his feet, and searched him.

"We can't eavesdrop from over here." Fab grabbed my arm, and we hustled across the street.

We got the stink eye from our respective husbands as we joined them.

"I'm assuming this man isn't a friend of either of yours?" I directed the question to Creole and Didier.

"He's trespassing," Didier snapped.

The man eyed the guns that Fab and I were holding at our sides.

"He was just about to tell us what he's doing here," said Creole, who still had ahold of the man's arm.

"Honest mistake." His body shook with fear as he lifted his eyes to the four of us. "Had a little car trouble and wanted to use your phone." He sounded unsure, waiting to see if we were going to believe him.

"Where's your car parked?" I raised my brows at the man and got rewarded with a *who's the cop here?* look from Creole. Ex-cop anyway. I made a motion that I'd zip my lips.

"It's... it's out at the street." He waved as though unsure of the location. "No idea that this was private property when I walked up."

"How did you get in the gate?" Creole demanded.

"It was open?"

"You two are being way too nice." Fab moved up between Didier and Creole, and Didier stepped closer to her. "At this rate, we'll be here all day and still won't know anything, except that this man's a pitiful liar. I say we shoot him... one little body part at a time." She unleashed a 'crazy girl' smile on the man, and he stepped back but didn't get far, brought short by Creole.

"You've got my vote." I raised my hand. "I suggest that we do it on the grass so blood doesn't leak everywhere. It's messy to clean up."

Didier rolled his eyes with a slight shake of his head.

"Come on," the man whined. "Let me go, and I promise not to come back here ever again. No need for cops or anything."

"No one mentioned the cops, but that's a good idea." Creole took his phone out of his pocket.

"No," he screeched. "Seriously, you can't do that. Just tell me what you want, and I'll do it. I don't want to go to jail. The cops show, and it's possible they may find that I have an outstanding warrant."

My guess was it wasn't for jaywalking. Most likely a felony.

"Here's the deal." Creole tightened his hold on the man's arm. "Tell us the truth, starting with your name and why the heck you're wandering around here, or I'm going to assume you're here casing the houses, and then I'll break your neck."

"Name's Rick Pierce," he spit out. "I should've known the job was too good."

"You got ID?" I whipped my phone out of my pocket.

He shook his head. "In the car."

"Your birthdate?" I typed in the info and sent it off to Xander with a message: *Holding this guy. How much trouble is he in?*

"Start talking," Didier snapped.

Fab shot him a moony smile.

"A guy approached me at Custer's." Rick shuffled from one foot to the other. "I'd been pointed out as a man who does odd jobs, and he paid me a C-note to get the names of the people that lived on this street. It seemed like easy money but took me a few days, since I had to tuck myself behind that tree out front and wait for a chance to get in the gate. It took a few cars, as they all sat their asses right there and waited for it to close." He shook his head, not believing someone would do that.

I caught Fab's smirk. It was a good rule, as it turned out. Now, how to stop the next person willing to wait days for an opportunity to sneak inside?

"Okay, so now we know how you got in. What was your plan to get the names of the residents?" Creole asked.

"Easy—the mailboxes. Didn't realize it would be so fancy-ass that you wouldn't have any." Rick looked around. "Mail Dude deliver to the door?"

No one answered him.

"Do you have a backup plan?" Fab asked.

"Didn't figure I'd need one. I barely got to looking around when that one jumped out of nowhere and gave chase." He nodded to Didier.

The driveway wasn't actually nowhere, but okay.

Rick danced against Creole's hold on him.

Creole dropped his hand. "Move and I promise you won't get far."

"I've got a new plan." Rick pasted on a hesitant smile. "I'll get back to my contact with made-up names. I was supposed to take pictures, but I imagine you're not going to go for that. My excuse for not having them: broke my phone, which I dropped somewhere around here." His eyes swept back to where the chase started.

Fab took off in that direction and checked over every inch of the grass; it didn't take her eagle eyes long to find it. She retrieved it and took several minutes to scan the screen. Walking back over, she dropped it on the ground and stepped on it.

"What the...? Was that necessary?" Rick demanded.

"Watch your tone," Didier growled.

"If you hadn't already snapped a few pictures, maybe not." Fab shrugged. "I've run over a couple with my car, but that's the first one I've crushed underfoot. It was fun."

"How am I going to call and report that I got the job done?" Rick whined.

"Tell us about this contact of yours," Creole demanded.

"Introduced himself as John, no last name. Pretty sure he's a regular at Custer's, since a couple of the men I drink with acknowledged him. He pitched the job, seemed easy enough, and I was out of there with the money in my pocket. Now what am I going to do?"

"You were willing to put your backside on the line with no clue as to the kind of person you were dealing with?" Creole said with disbelief. "My guess is that he's not going to take it well if you lie to him and pass along phony information."

"John happen to say why he wanted the information?" Didier asked.

"No, and I didn't ask."

"How about a description?" Fab asked.

"Guessing at six foot, dark hair, Florida vibe, like everyone else in there." Rick's antsiness ramped up at having to answer questions.

Creole and Didier stepped away, and after a brief conversation, turned back. "Let's go." Didier nodded toward the gate.

"If there's a next time…" Creole glared at Rick. "You won't be walking out of here."

Rick nodded, relieved that he was being allowed to leave.

As the three men walked toward the gate, Fab whipped out her phone and sent a text, then made a call. "The number I just sent, can you get the information off of it? I got a bit carried away and crushed the phone under my shoe. It's about that Rick character that I already texted you about. I'm thinking he's not the smartest and will probably get another phone with the same number. Maybe you can monitor any activity." She told Xander what she was looking for and that if he could delete pictures of the compound, do it. Then hung up.

"The only way that man was getting arrested is the outstanding warrant. I doubt the cops would've done anything, especially if he stuck to his story that he wandered up by accident," I said.

"We need a sign."

"Yes, we do."

It didn't take long before the guys were back. Creole had his phone out and sent a text. "I just forwarded a copy of the license plate to Xander. I'd have sent a copy of his ID, except he didn't have one."

"We're keeping Xander busy today," I said.

Creole held up the screen, which showed a run-down white sedan. "Couldn't identify the make and model and asked Rick, who didn't know."

"Creole and I figured it was stolen," Didier said in disgust.

"Let this be a lesson." Creole clapped Didier on the back with a look of amusement. "Cheap help is not a good business strategy." He turned to Fab and me. "Our friend here hasn't been to Custer's, so I'm going to take him, show him the fine establishment. Tentative plan is to buy some info off the owner."

"I've met him a time or two," I said. "He's a wily character who's been around forever and knows the intricacies of the lowlife element. He wouldn't think twice about back dealing you if the price was right."

"You're better off bribing one of the servers," Fab said.

"Better yet, leave it to Fab and I. We know

how to get in and out. Our favorite is the alley entrance, as I recall."

Creole leaned down and fixed me with that dark-blue stare of his. "No."

"That's a maybe." I winked at Fab, who laughed.

"It's about ready to pour again. Talk later." Creole hooked his arm around me.

We headed back up the shell driveway that Creole had trucked in as a surprise for me, and Didier and Fab headed back to their house.

Chapter Twelve

We'd barely got the door closed when it started to rain. At the same time, my phone rang. I headed to the island, taking it out of my pocket and glancing at the screen—the manager of my bar: Doodad, aka Charles Wingate III, which he would never answer to. I glanced at the time. "It's early for him," I mumbled and shoved the phone across the countertop to Creole, who grabbed waters for the two of us and sat across from me.

Creole made an X with his fingers in front of his chest. "No way. Not answering. He's only going to ask for you, and I'll end up handing the phone over."

I reluctantly picked up the phone. "Yesss," I answered and hit the speaker button.

"Not sure how to order this..." Doodad laughed hesitantly. "The intruder is a good place to start. Then move right along to getting your okay for the sword swallowing act, and let's see—"

I cut him off. "No, on the sword business."

Creole covered his mouth and laughed. I reached out to slap his arm and came up with air.

"Where was I?" Doodad was doing a poor job covering how much he was enjoying relaying the news. "Cook's in a dither and wants to see you the minute you step foot in the door. I pointed out that you come through the kitchen more often than not and he should whistle. Didn't calm his feathers any."

Creole looked down, his shoulders shaking.

"Anyone die?" I asked. I guessed not, or he would've started the conversation with that tidbit, but better to ask than hear the excuse, It slipped my mind.

"Not in the mood for that today." Doodad grumbled unintelligibly. "I'd toe the body outside and lock the door. That's such a great idea that I'm going to keep it front and center in my noggin and use it should the sitch play out."

That wiped the smile off Creole's face.

"I'm thinking I need a second cup of coffee to deal with all your news. I'll be hopping over shortly. Won't that be fun? And if you have more tidbits, I'll be all ears." No answer. "I'll expect a repeat in case you missed pertinent details. And if you ignored me the first time, ixnay on the swords. I'm sure it's entertaining, but no. Hell no."

"I work hard to come up with these great ideas, and what do you do? Blow 'em out of the water in a blink," Doodad grumbled. "You could at least entertain a little back and forth."

Creole shook his head.

"I should get extra credit for not wanting to waste your time," I said and was rewarded with more silence. "You know I appreciate your endeavors to make Jake's the hot and happening dive joint it is." *But you need to tame it down* was the last thing he wanted to hear.

Doodad snorted.

"I'll see you when I get there."

He grunted and disconnected.

Creole leaned across the counter and brushed his lips across mine. "Since I know you're about to ask, I'd love to go along with you, but I have a meeting on the other coast."

If he thought the sad face was convincing, it wasn't. "Free tip for you: if you're going to be less than truthful—or as some might phrase it, trot out a bald-faced lie—you might want to practice. I'd offer to help, but not to use on me."

Creole chuckled. "I'm happy that you don't use your skills on me. Or do you?"

I stared down his squint eye. "Maybe a little. More like withholding. Good news: I fess up in the end." He shook his head. "I realize that you're broken-hearted about having some phony meeting hours away, so to ease your conscience about ditching me, I'm going to go lie to Fab to get her out of the house. I learned from you that I need to come up with something believable." I downed the rest of my water and handed the bottle to Creole.

He opened the trash compactor, stood back,

and slam dunked it, then came around the island and put his arm around me, steering me toward the entry. He hooked my purse over my shoulder, handed me my briefcase, and walked me to the SUV. "Do you think you can stay out of trouble?" He waited while I got in, then rolled down the window and closed the door, sticking his head inside to kiss me.

"I wouldn't put cash on it."

"Maybe I should —"

"Don't you worry your pretty self." I winked at him. "I'll finish dressing by the time I get to Jake's and be gunned up and ready." My Glock was in my briefcase, but I'd strap it to my thigh before getting out of the car.

Creole swooped in for another kiss and waved as I backed out of the driveway under his watchful eye and turned towards Fab's house.

Before getting out, I slipped my lockpick out of my purse; then I headed to the door, opening it in seconds. I closed the door quietly and turned to meet the hard blue-eyed stare of Didier, who'd been in the midst of refilling his coffee mug.

"You're lucky my wife is otherwise distracted." Didier pointed to where Fab sat on the couch talking on her phone. "I can't guarantee she wouldn't have shot you."

"You need to have a talk with her about neighbor relations." I tsked. "You might want to suck down your coffee and scoot out the door, or you're going to be late for that meeting in

Naples." I chose the first city I could think of on the west coast.

"Naples? How did I not know…" Didier picked up his phone and flicked through the screen.

"Also check with Creole; it would suck for him to drive over by himself," I said in a sweet tone.

Didier backed up and leaned against the counter to make the call.

Fab appeared out of nowhere in one of her ghost moves. "Did you knock?"

"Actually, I did something better." I pulled my lockpick out of my pocket and waved it. "So much more efficient." I blocked her attempt to grab it out of my hands. "Before you get all attitudinal, I need your backup services this morning. The same ones I extend to you, mostly with minimal grumbling." I clapped my hands. "Speed it up; we need to get going."

Didier finished his call and slid onto a stool. He shook his finger at me, a stern look on his face.

"You know, Frenchie, you're going to need work on your *behave* face, because it just makes you look hotter. Who knew that was possible?" That got a smile out of him.

Fab slapped her hand on the counter. "That's my husband."

"Good thing you told me."

Fab didn't roll her eyes, but she was thinking

it. "You're in luck, since I also need your services today. Gunz wants to meet at the office — another relative gone off the rails, I'm guessing, since he was short on details."

"I know I've suggested this six times already — and it's a good idea, so this time you might to want to listen up — the man doesn't even have to get off his oversized rear to send the deets in an email. You might also mention that his finger-snapping routine is old." I patted my lips. "Oh wait, then he wouldn't be able to dribble all over you."

Didier grinned.

"Eww." Fab glared at both of us. "It's a yes that we're teaming up today."

"My job is so easy in comparison that I'm thinking you'll owe me one. You smoochy it up with your husband while I head out to the car." I winked at Didier, then grabbed her purse and briefcase and waved them at her. "In case you're thinking of not showing up in a timely fashion."

"See what I have to put up with?" I heard her say before I closed the door.

Fab didn't drag her feet like I suspected she would and slid behind the wheel a few minutes later. She hit the gas, honked, and flew out of the driveway. "You going to input the address?" She pointed at the GPS.

"Jake's. I'm betting you can find it on your own. There're sixteen problems afoot, and Cook wants to speak to me. And since I know you're going to ask, no clue what he wants."

"Probably wants to sneak grilled rodent or some such onto the menu."

Fab flew south down the Overseas, past the center of town, and pulled into the parking lot of the block I owned. She slowed going past the lighthouse, payment for a job she'd done and currently unoccupied, which was about to change. Since Fab hated every one of my ideas for the place, I'd surprise her. Opposite was Junker's, an old gas station that had been converted into an antique garden store. They needed to be open regular hours—any, actually—and that was also about to change, since I was tired of fielding calls from people who were annoyed that there wasn't even a sign displaying the hours. She swung around the back and parked at the kitchen entrance.

We entered, and Cook was nowhere in sight. I waved to the line cook and continued down the hall to the bar.

Kelpie, our previously pink-haired bartender, had recently dyed it turquoise. "I was having a down day," is how she described the change. It matched her snug-fitting t-shirt, sedate for her, which advertised the Florida Keys in big letters.

"Hey Bossaroo. Your usual? No-alkie, since it's still morning." Kelpie shoved two sodas across the bar top, one with lime, and to the other, she added a stick of cherries at the last second. She tossed her head toward the open doors out to the deck. "You better pokey on out before you're late. Oops! You already are. You know Cookie hates to be kept waiting." She laughed.

Fab grabbed both drinks and headed outside.

"Spread the word," I said in a conspiratorial tone. "I'm the owner. I can be late and don't even have to come up with a good excuse." I caught up with Fab and sat next to her across from Cook. Like me, she wanted to know what he was up to.

"What's up?" I asked the man, who was staring us down, trying to ferret out any secrets we might be withholding. Good luck to that. "If this is about you venturing off the menu again, the answer is no."

"You really need to broaden your palate," he said with the start of a grin.

No, I don't.

Reading my mind, he laughed. "You know the Taco Bar that you cheat on me by eating at?"

"I'm not sure how you know that, so I won't bother to deny it. Sadly, we saw it burst into flames the other day. Is this where you tell me you're going to fill the void and put a mini taco platter on the menu?" I licked my lips.

Cook shook his head. "On the menu or not, you ask, and you know I'll whip it up. Back to the explosion. Thankfully, no one got hurt."

"How does this relate to you?" Fab asked, and engaged in a stare-down with Cook.

My eyes darted between the two, and I let out a loud sigh to break up the game of who'd look away first that they were enjoying.

Cook flicked his gaze between the two of us. "The Vickers, who are friends of mine, own the wagon. I'm sure some would be surprised to learn that it was a lucrative business. As you're aware, they always had a line of customers." He downed his water and sent the bottle flying into the trash. "The Vickers planned to turn the business over to their grandson, who recently returned from military service, but now it's a pile of rubble."

"What do you want Madison to do?" Fab asked.

Cook shifted his gaze to me. "I want you to investigate how the supposed accident happened. Was it really arson, as suspected? If so, the culprit needs to go to jail, but not until restitution is paid."

No point in telling him that the restitution part wouldn't happen until they were out of jail. And more than likely not in a lump sum, but as a payment plan. "Did the Fire Inspector rule it arson?"

"Not officially. But I have a friend... you know how that works." The brown of his eyes intensified and bore into me.

"Not sure arsonists have much money, and if caught, what they do have will go to attorney fees," Fab said.

Cook ignored her. "The Vickers have owned that strip of property forever—long before the million-dollar mansions were constructed around it. Travis West bought the neighboring land and finished building his mansion about a year ago, and from day one, he's been after them to sell him the land," he continued. "West harped on about the food truck being an eyesore and that, besides being bad for property values, he didn't want it next to his property, even though he can't see the wagon unless he's going in or out of his driveway. When the Vickers continued to turn West down, he backed off, and the code department started showing up on a regular basis. The first guy was a friend to the Vickers, and no reports were filed. They prudently cleaned up all potential violations so that when the next man showed up, he couldn't find anything to write them up for."

"Burning it down would be one way to get rid of the problem," I said. "Except that if he's caught, West is looking at jail time."

"Interestingly, a few days before the fire, he made what he called a final offer."

"That was stupid, if it was him," Fab said.

"A friend of the Vickers' told them they noticed West standing on the opposite side of the street while the flames leapt in the air and staying until the last of the fire trucks drove away. It surprised them when he had the gall to actually say he was happy that the land had been cleared. Later that day, West ran into the Vickers and snidely told them that his offer was still on the table but would be substantially reduced."

"It will be easy enough to confirm if it was arson, which would trigger a police investigation," Fab said.

"What about insurance?" I asked.

"They didn't have replacement cost, only coverage if someone got hurt, which thankfully didn't happen."

Being underinsured seemed to be a theme amongst those that didn't have an outstanding loan that made coverage mandatory. Most gambled, even knowing that they wouldn't be able to replace anything.

"I'm not certain how much help we can be." I flicked my finger between Fab and me.

"I've got a couple of ideas." Cook gave us a toothy grin.

I heard Fab's groan and was certain Cook missed it, since he didn't react.

"I'm convinced that West is behind the fire," Cook continued. "Rich guy isn't going to get his hands dirty and probably hired it done. Getting reparations could be a long, involved process, and I'd like you to shorten it and squeeze the most money possible out of the man."

What he was suggesting wouldn't be easy and might be impossible. A quick glance at Fab told me she was thinking the same thing.

"Do you have any idea how we're supposed to

accomplish that? Besides extortion, blackmail, or whatever you were getting at but didn't spell out," Fab said, echoing my thoughts.

"Verify that it was arson and pin it on West if possible."

"You've lost your mind," I said with a head shake.

"Another thought: you purchase the land and restart the business, then work a favorable deal with the grandson so that he can take over." After a pause, Cook added, "If he wants." He didn't sound certain that the idea he was pitching was something the family even wanted.

"Your hot idea is for me to buy the property and start the same kind of business that just got burned out? By probable arson. And what stops whoever lit the first match from doing it again?" I asked, knowing full well Fab wouldn't be partnering in a taco business. She and I exchanged raised eyebrows. Her smirk told me she'd been digging around in my thoughts again and agreed this wouldn't be a business we'd be partnering on.

"Madison has her talents, but running a roach coach business isn't one of them. What you really want is it resurrected, then sold off to the grandson, and that's without knowing if he's even remotely interested." Fab ignored Cook's raised eyebrows. "Don't try to sell me that you know the answer when it's clear you have no clue. You're in luck, though; I have an idea."

I clenched my jaw to keep from laughing.

Fab broke the stare-down between her and Cook. "Why not take the money out of your mattress and be all do-good-ery yourself?"

"If Madison's name is associated with the business, rich boy won't bother her. Unless he's stupid." Cook grinned.

"Here's what we can do." I flicked my gaze between Fab and Cook. "Fab and I will look into the circumstances surrounding the fire, find any potential suspects, and get back to you. I can't promise anything else until I talk to Creole, and I know for a fact that he'll be against buying into trouble." Not that I hadn't done it before, but he'd like a rest.

Cook's phone rang, for which I was thankful. "I have to take this." He jumped up, crossed the deck, and went back inside through the poker room.

"We'll get back to you," I yelled at his back before he disappeared. He waved over his head.

I sucked down the last of my soda and wolfed down the cherries, then picked my phone out of my pocket and called inside. "Where's Mr. Doodad?" I asked Kelpie after her sexually suggestive, "Can I help you?"

"Emergency trip to the dentist. I told him that, since the missing tooth didn't show, what the hell, he should wait and see whether he needed a new one to chew his food," Kelpie said cheerily. "I couldn't make out what he was grumbling about, but he beat it out the door when I pulled my fist back to punch him. Before you get in a snit, it was just for fun."

Good thing I'd hit the speaker button, so I didn't have to repeat any of this because Fab would never have believed me. "What do you know about the intruder?"

"He was asked to git, nicely of course. I went soft on him, since he spent the night with his head stuck in the urinal. Ouchy-pouch."

"Happy ending," I said before she could say it. "Tell your boss that if needs to speak to his boss, call anytime. In the meantime, no baloney going on."

"You're no damn fun."

"That's me." I hung up. "I'm thinking we make a run for it out the front, since it's the shortest distance to the outside."

Fab picked up our glasses and put them in the bus tray. She poked her head inside, then turned to me. "There's a clear path, so all you need to do is walk fast."

Fab and I cut across the bar with a quick wave to Kelpie, who was holding court, entertaining the "beer for almost-lunch" crowd, and out the front. We circled around the back and jumped in the Hummer. I hit the door locks. "I don't care that Cook directed the conversation at me; I made it clear to him, and now to you, that I'm your backup."

"Cook's not stupid; he knew we would show

together. His ploy of only talking to you is because he knows that I'm not a soft touch for any poor soul that wanders up. I'd have laughed. Problem solved."

Chapter Thirteen

"I'm going to avail myself of your investigator skills and ask that you swing by the remnants of the Taco Bar. You can have a look around, give me your expert opinion on what went down," I said. "While we're there, we might as well check out the neighborhood."

"If you only asked me so nicely all the time." Fab laughed. "You're the one who can come up with a good story in a second; you might start thinking up one for why we're knocking on Travis West's door and asking if he set the fire."

"I'm thinking that's too direct," I said. "Besides, if he's got dough to blow, makes sense he wouldn't risk a limb doing it himself."

"Put the word out that you're willing to pay for info on how the unfortunate incident happened." Fab turned off the highway and wound her way over to the Taco Bar... or rather, where it had once been, since the rubble had been cleared away.

The scorched strip of land was the only sign there'd been a fire. Fab cruised the block, which was a combination of new homes and lots available for custom builds, a number of which would remain vacant, as the buildable sections were the size of a postage stamp. She U-turned, pulled in, and parked in what once was the parking lot, the four spaces still clearly marked.

"I'm thinking it was only a matter of time before the builders of the spendy new mansions would have wanted the coach out of their neighborhood, since it's not a selling point." I stared out the window, checking out the neighborhood. "I'm surprised one of the developers didn't step up and attempt a deal."

"Or they did, and the Vickers turned it down."

"Even if I was remotely interested in this business venture, I'm certain that any attempt to get a business license would be met with a fight. The issue could easily bring the neighbors together and slow the process until it's not cost effective."

"Another option would be for them to sell the land and move the business elsewhere. A lot less hassle." Fab got out, and I followed. "Do you want my opinion now or after we walk around? Here it is anyway: you don't need this fight."

"There's something we agree on." I looked toward West's property. "The security gate is an impediment to our knocking on the door and catching him off guard."

A white Mercedes rounded the corner, cut across the road, and slid to a stop next to us. The window rolled down. "What are you looking at?" the driver yelled.

I stepped forward. "Checking out the property before I make an offer."

He laughed, his tone condescending when he asked, "And do what with it?"

"Margarita wagon, and I'm betting it won't take long before we have people lined up. Then we'll add tacos to the menu like the last people. They were very successful." I pasted on a practiced smile.

Fab moved to my side and nudged me slightly.

His face flooded with anger. "You'll never get a permit to operate any kind of business in this neighborhood."

"I had the same thought until I did a little digging, and with a connection or two, it's workable."

His face turned all shades of red, and he looked ready to explode. "Will. Never. Happen."

Fab hooked her arm in mine. "Nice meeting you." She waved and pushed me back towards the car. "You've had enough fun; I'm betting that we just met Travis West, and we need to get out of here before he expires behind the wheel." Good guess. Once we got in the car, the gates to the West mansion opened, and the Mercedes flew down the driveway.

I kept an eye peeled as we backed out. "I'm betting he wrote down the plate number, and now he wants to know who we are."

A few minutes later, Fab's phone rang, and

she pulled over to take the call. It didn't take her long to respond, "No problem. I'll get right on it."

"Let me guess, Gunz?" I asked after she hung up.

"His meeting is running over, and he'll text over the address of the place that needs the security system. It's not a rush, so it's not something that needs to be done today."

"You might want to point out how easy it was to make the call and forgo meeting at the office all the time," I said. "So we're headed home. Cool. I need to make a call myself, and you can eavesdrop, although probably not technically, since I'll have it on speaker."

"You should try to get to the point before you forget what you're talking about and have to start over."

"I'm thinking I might have forgotten to pass along a detail or two about another potential case. Freebie, so don't get in a snit." I fished out my phone and called Tank, telling her about Xander's friend while I waited for him to pick up.

"That will be a messy case."

When Tank answered, I said, "How's our favorite lawyer? And so you know, you're on speaker." Silence. "Disclosing upfront that this is a freebie."

Tank groaned. "You've sent me a couple of payers, so I can at least be gracious and hear the details. Know that I reserve the right to say no, and no complaining from you."

"This client is seventeen, and here's what I know of her story." I told him what Xander had confided.

"I'm happy to talk to Lena and inform her of her options, which aren't cut and dried. The mother risks charges if she kicks the girl out before she turns eighteen. After that, because Lena can prove she's lived there, the mother would have to go through an eviction process. As for belongings, you didn't hear me say this, but sneaking them out is probably the best way to ensure that she gets to keep them. If it goes before a judge, he's going to ask for receipts, which I'm guessing that neither has, and how he rules after that, who knows. Before it even got that far, there would be nothing to stop the mother from packing everything up and dumping it, which it sounds like she's in the process of doing."

"Maybe you can mediate a happy ending?" I said.

"You're not paying for my professional opinion, but here it is: highly doubtful that will happen if the situation has degenerated this far."

I sighed. "You're very swell. I'll have Xander call and set up a meeting."

"I'll do it myself — makes it easier to squeeze a favor or two out of him." Tank laughed, and we hung up.

"You turned the wrong way. We live that way." I pointed over my head.

"Those offers of free lunches that you complain I never follow through on... today's your lucky day. We're headed to the Crab Shack."

"Yum."

Chapter Fourteen

Creole and I spent the morning working together out on the deck, my cats, Jazz and Snow, asleep on my feet. Creole spent most of his time fielding calls and putting out fires. I sent off a slew of emails — Xander and Cook at the top of my list, requesting information on the Taco Bar. One to Doodad, who needed to put it out to his street snitches that there was money in turning over the name of anyone boasting about setting the fire.

"I think we should have more fun days." I leaned sideways and brushed a kiss across his cheek.

Creole had called in sick yesterday, and I'd heard him making threats if a certain person came banging on the door, then laughing at the response. It had been easy to deduce he expected Didier to keep a rein on his wife so we could have a fool-around day. We turned off our phones, dragged out the water bikes, and went for a ride out into the Gulf. The race was on getting back to shore. I couldn't compete with those long, muscular legs of his, and Creole had to wait several minutes on the sand for me, smirk in place. I demanded a rematch, and this time, we hugged the shoreline. I needed to save my energy and waited as he raced ahead and doubled back. The course hadn't been clearly established, so I cut mine short and got turned around and ready for him, then rammed his front tire, and as he struggled to keep from tipping, I sped off and barely made it back to the start before he caught up. He stored the bikes, threw me over his shoulder, and hauled me back to the house. I tried not to laugh all the way, but failed.

"And more mornings like this, working side by side." He pulled me to my feet. "Sorry that I have to cut it short, but I've got a lunch meeting." He led me back into the house and down the hall to the bedroom, where we showered and changed.

At the front door, I handed him his briefcase. "You've got company," he said before kissing me.

I looked around his shoulder and saw Fab headed in our direction. "Either she's got a camera on us or she's got impeccable timing."

Creole laughed. "I texted Didier that I was on my way out." He walked past Fab, and whatever he said had her lips quirking. Both he and Didier waved as the Mercedes roared down the street.

"Come in." I motioned to Fab. "I can cook you up a cup of swill."

"I've lost all hope of you expanding your tastes to include an excellent cup of coffee." She looked ready to laugh but would never let it happen if she could stop it. "You need to put something more professional on." She eyed my t-shirt skirt and top. "I've got a meeting with Gunz's nephew or something. You even try to weasel out, I'll call your husband and pitch such a fit, he'll ask you to go just to shut me up." Before I could say anything, she cut me off with a wave. "Then I'll be available to you for whatever you need."

"I thought it was a security system job, not a meet-and-greet." I picked up my laptop and paperwork and shoved everything in my briefcase.

"That was yesterday," she said, as though I should know. "You were deathly ill. Happy to see you've made a full recovery."

"Sarcasm..." I shook my finger at her.

"I gunned up Didier and took him as my backup. It was the most boring in-and-out job ever. Sorry you missed it."

"No, you're not." I laughed. "If you're going to be picky, you need to come choose something for me to wear. And hustle it up, or I'll pull the first hangar within reach out of my closet."

I was ready in record time, approving of the sleeveless black dress that Fab handed me, then going back and deciding on a pair of slip-on sandals.

On the way out to the car, I asked, "What's this latest family drama about?"

"Jimmy Jones…"

I rolled my eyes. "You need practice making up names."

"Are you finished?" I got the evil eye. "And just for that, you can wait until we arrive at the appointment to hear the details."

"If you need my personality to sparkle, a caramel coffee would give me the kick I need, and don't forget the whipped cream." I licked my lips.

"As it so happens… Well, just so you know, I didn't choose the meeting place. We've been there before, and neither of us was impressed. So be nice."

"It appears you've forgotten, Pot, that I'm always nice." At her raised eyebrows, I added, "Mostly."

It was a short drive. Fab turned off the highway and parked around the back of a brightly painted shack that advertised… Good one. If there'd been a sign, it was taken down, but I recognized the place. The gigantic coffee cup on the edge of the roof was a recent addition, and I guess the only identifier they thought they needed. The only other car in the parking lot was a bright-orange fifty-year-old hatchback Mustang in pristine condition. A motorcycle had been pushed up to the rear entrance, and in case anyone took a notion to wander off with it, they left the door open.

"I'm amazed this place stays in business," I said as we tromped down a gravel path to a seating area of picnic tables and benches. An upgrade from the folding chairs from last time? I'd disagree.

A slightly built man in his early twenties with dark hair swept to one side of his face dressed in his dad's roll-up jeans and plaid shirt stood and stuck out his hand. "Jimmy Jones."

I skipped the introductions and sat gingerly, trying to avoid getting a splinter in my butt.

"Gunz and I only had a minute to talk, since we were both headed into meetings, so why don't you start from the beginning?" Fab said to him and sat next to me.

I wanted to applaud her excuse for not getting Gunz to fill us in, although I suspected she knew more than she was letting on.

Jimmy plunked down across from us. "I got my masters in business and, right out of college, started working for a big property development company out of Miami."

Older than I thought. Okay.

"I'm taking night classes and studying to take the CPA exam, but all my hard work is about to be wasted, since I'm going to be charged with embezzlement unless I can repay the missing million dollars in five days." He oozed sadness.

"Did you steal the money?" I asked.

His brown eyes shot up and met mine. "I did not. Yesterday, I got called into my boss's office.

He informed me that the money came up missing during an audit, and after some digging, it was traced to an account with my name on it. I wanted to knock the smirk off his face but knew I'd get mine rearranged, since he's twice my size. He brushed off my denials, barely listening, then let me know what a great guy he was, giving me time to pay back the money before going to the CEO. He assured me that if I returned the money, it would lessen my prison time."

"I think he's overstepping his authority, keeping that kind of a loss from his boss," Fab said. "His job might be on the line for withholding the information, even for a few days."

"Going on the assumption you're innocent..." I said. Gunz must have thought so or we wouldn't be there. "You have any idea who would set you up to take the fall?"

"Milton Track—my boss. The only other person with access to all the accounts is the CFO, and he's an old man that rarely shows up at the office." He uncapped his water and about downed the bottle. "Milt seemed to be under the illusion that I could write a check. Even if he weren't wrong, I wouldn't pay back money that I didn't steal."

"Were you able to look at the transactions?" Fab asked.

"Briefly, and then I was locked out. It showed that the money was transferred to an offshore account. Whoever did this used me to cover their tracks."

"We've got a computer expert on call; he has the ability to track the cash," Fab said. "Is the money still sitting in the account and all it would take is transferring it back?"

"Milt said that the account had a balance of fifty thousand, asked what I blew it all on. I wasn't able to independently verify any of what he confronted me with."

"My first question to Milty would be, 'How do you know all this?' Because if his name isn't on the account, how did he gain access?" Fab asked.

"I pointed out the same thing, and he said, 'Unfortunately, you chose a bank where I have a friend.'"

"How convenient," I said.

"Are you still going into the office?" Fab asked.

"I've been asked to stay away until the meeting, which is on Monday. According to Milt, the theft isn't on the agenda, but he plans to break the news once everyone's assembled."

Even if Milt didn't have his sticky fingers all over the missing money, he would probably lose his job for bypassing the CEO, who wouldn't take the surprise announcement well.

"Since we're short on time, I'm going to make your case a priority. I suggest that you lie low and try not to worry." Fab smiled at him. "If all else fails, we can sneak you out of town."

"Do that, and no one would ever believe my innocence." Jimmy returned her smile, but barely. "I'll admit to the jitters. I keep thinking the authorities are going to descend and haul me off in cuffs."

"Both of us have worked for Gunz long enough to know that he takes care of his own and would never let you rot in jail," I tried to reassure him. "Even if you were guilty. And that's not the case here, so he'll be more motivated to see that you're not railroaded."

"Gunz has been around my entire life. Always looked up to him. When this trouble went down, I called him first. I need to tell my parents before it hits the news. Still hoping that everything gets resolved in my favor and I can tell them that as well."

"If they're anything like my mother, they're going to be annoyed," I said. "Only because they would've wanted to hold your hand through the process and reassure you it will all work out."

"It's hard to go from a kid that never got in trouble to big-time criminal, especially when you factor in that I didn't even do the crime. The thought of going to jail makes me sick." Jimmy hunched his shoulders.

"Trust me when I tell you I've got people who can help to clear you," Fab reassured him. "And we're getting right on it."

We ended the meeting and stood. Jimmy walked us back to the SUV.

"Nice car," I said.

"It's a 1965 Mustang and belonged to my grandfather. He loved it, and I was happy that he lived long enough to see it fully restored." Jimmy ran his hand down the door panel.

I reached in my purse and handed him a business card. "If you ever want to sell—and I don't mean for legal bills—I know someone who can get you top dollar."

"You can also reach either of us at that number," Fab said. "Don't worry, I'll be in touch. I won't leave you hanging out to dry, not knowing what's going on. You'll be getting a call from Xander Huntington; know that he works for me and can be trusted."

Jimmy took the card and nodded. He got in his car and roared out of the parking lot. We were right behind him.

"Mr. Jones needs a makeover," I mused. "Something more professional so he doesn't come across as a kid and he'll be taken more seriously. A self-defense class might give him some added confidence. Give him the courage to stand up for himself."

"Thinking the same thing, and I'll put that in my report to Gunz, along with a referral."

"Please don't let Xander hear you refer to him as your employee or he'll pack up and run out the door," I teased.

"I don't know why I'm the one with the scary rep."

"Maybe…" I tapped my cheek. "It's all the growling you do."

"I'll be telling Xander how much I appreciate him. That make you happy? He does a great job at getting us all the information we need for these jobs."

"I happen to know he likes sharing the office with us. Never a dull moment. Plus, we're not snore bores."

"What's next? You have some hokey client?"

"I object." I hit the dashboard and laughed. "It's afternoon, so margarita time. I need to make a quick stop at Jake's, and then we can go get our sauce on and I'll make drunken phone calls."

"You're going to have to put your tequila on hold. We need to go to the office and get started on Jimmy's case. If whoever set him up thinks someone is onto them, the cops will get called in that much sooner or the real culprit will run."

Chapter Fifteen

Fab turned into the parking lot of Jake's and parked at the front door for a change. We walked into the middle of a full-on brawl between Kelpie and another woman. The men at the bar were whooping and hollering, beer splashing.

"You break it up." I nudged Fab. "I don't want to get hurt."

Fab shot me a toe-curling smile, and I should've known I wasn't going to like her response. Before I could call her off, she drew her gun and put a hole in the ceiling. Another hole. It wasn't the first time a bullet had been lodged overhead. That brought the festivities to a halt.

I stared up, trying to assess the damage.

The women had initially rolled away from the other, but they tossed curse words back and forth and showed signs of launching themselves at each other again. "I'll shoot the next one that throws a punch," Fab yelled. "Now sit down." She pointed to the woman we didn't know.

I motioned Kelpie over. "You better have a good story or you're paying for the damage to the ceiling."

Fab stood over the other woman, silently

daring her to get up. The woman did a double take and stayed seated.

Kelpie roared, her words tumbling out over one another. "Stealing… short-changed… not on my watch." She twisted her turquoise leotard back into place, her matching hair shaking side-to-side. The men at the bar hadn't taken their eyes off her, not sparing a glance at the woman sitting on the floor.

"Kelp's telling the truth," one man yelled. The rest raised their beers in salute and nodded.

Kelpie gulped in several deep breaths. "That woman," she seethed, "came in with her friends and gave me a credit card so they could run a tab."

I looked over at the table where the woman's friends were seated. No one said a word as they stared wide-eyed.

"When my back was turned, she snatched the card from the side of the register and tried to beat it out the door. One of my regulars pointed her out, and I rounded the bar and grabbed the back of her shirt. One of her hands shot out in an attempt to dump me on the floor, the other came around with a closed fist. I don't think so." Kelpie heaved in deep breaths.

The bar stayed silent. Having heard every word, all the patrons nodded in agreement.

"You're a liar," the woman yelled. "I thought you'd charged my card when you handed it back. There was no way to know you were so damn stupid and had no clue how to do your job."

Kelpie leapt forward with an aggrieved shout. "Lying witch."

I grabbed hold of her arm, and she carried me a few steps before skidding to a stop.

Kevin strolled through the door, a huge grin on his face. "Got a call that mayhem was happening and hurried right over. Want to tell me what's going on? This time." He stared at the woman on the floor until she looked away. When she looked back, he pointed to an empty table, and she hauled herself up and took a seat. He motioned to Kelpie to do the same.

"You might want to have them sit at separate tables," I said, not able to hide my sarcasm.

"Thanks for telling me how to do my job."

I was tempted to offer him a soda, sugar him up a bit, but decided next time… and there'd be one. Instead, I whispered to Kelpie, "Stay calm when you tell Kevin what happened.'

"The first person to leave by any exit gets arrested," Kevin yelled.

It wouldn't be the first time, or last, that patrons beat it out the door at the first sign of the cops. The downside to having an outstanding warrant—you always had to be on the lookout to avoid getting arrested.

Another cop walked in, and the two exchanged words. Cop two walked over to the men at the bar, Kevin back to the women.

I pulled my phone out of my pocket and texted Doodad: *Where the hell are you?*

In my office. Let me know when it's all clear came the answer.

I walked behind the bar, smiled at the customers, and was ignored. "Round on the house." That got their attention, along with a once-over.

Fab came up to the bar. "I'm going out the back via the deck. I'll be waiting in the car."

"One step," I threatened, "and everyone on this block will know you're making a run for it."

A couple of the men laughed.

"Hop on a bar stool and get your freebie." I motioned to Fab.

"All clear?" Doodad poked his head out of the hallway.

"Cops are here. When you find out who called them, they're banned," I grouched.

Doodad asked what happened, and I told him.

"That's a popular scam that's going around," he said. "I think we should press charges. If word gets around that we're an easy mark, folks will come in to rip us off, thinking we're dumb stints."

"We've got security footage that will back up Kelpie's story, since I'm certain she's telling the truth," I said. "You can handle it however you want."

Fab answered her phone and grabbed her drink, mouthing *Xander*. Like me, she figured it would take a while before we got out of there. She went out to the deck and sat at our reserved table.

Doodad joined me behind the bar as I refilled the beers.

"The side job I contacted you about..." I said. "You get any good information on the demise of the Taco Bar yet? The arsonist's name would be way cool."

"These delicate issues take time."

"Whatever the going rate is, you decide and pay. Take the money out of the till and pay yourself a commission."

Bouff, one of our closing bartenders, walked into the main room from the hallway, looked around, and laughed. The broad-chested six-foot man moved with confidence on his prosthetic leg and didn't take guff off anyone. "Did I miss a chick brawl?"

"Kelpie was a smidge away from cleaning the floor with the woman," I informed him with a big smile.

"I wouldn't bet against her, no matter the challenger," Bouff said. "I'm here to talk to you. Word drifted down the pike that Cook got you involved with the Taco Bar explosion. That's what he told the Vickers. Anything new yet?"

"Do you have a contact number for them?" I asked.

"They're still reeling from the fire; the grandson is the one you want to talk to. Cook said to put the two of you together. He lives close by and can be here in five minutes, if he's got clothes on." Bouff grinned.

"I believe this place has corrupted you," I said with a shake of my head. "Call him. Might as well take care of this now. No nudity."

"Gotcha." Bouff took out his phone and backed up.

I poured a soda and went out to the deck, barely getting seated before Kevin came tromping out and pulled up a chair.

"It's a 'she said, she said,' so..." Kevin said.

"Excuse me, officer," I said. He looked faintly amused for a change. "We have security footage that will back up one story or the other. I left it up to Doodad to decide whether to show it to you."

"That will make my job easy." Kevin stood and headed back inside.

"He might be in the office," I called to his receding back.

As it turned out, he was standing in the middle of the bar, talking to the other officer. Kevin joined the two, and after a brief conversation, followed Doodad into the office. It took a while before the men came back out. Doodad slid behind the bar as Kevin put cuffs on the woman and walked her out.

Kelpie slipped back behind the bar and began entertaining her audience, who showed their appreciation by clapping and hooting.

I had one eye on the front door when it opened and a new face walked in—easy 6' 5", broad-shouldered frame. His intense grey eyes swept the interior of the bar. In the corner, two tipsy women engaged in a game of drunk darts leered as the man walked to the end of the bar to join Bouff, who'd beckoned him over and handed him a drink. After a few words, the two men came out to the deck.

"Mark Vickers," Bouff introduced him to Fab and I, then pointed to a seat.

"How do you two know each other?" I asked Mark.

"Bouff and I served together, then discovered that we lived down the road from each other."

I smiled at him. "Ass-kickers get the free-drink discount." Mark laughed. "Just know if word gets out, I suspect a few will get sauced to get their nerve up and pick a fight."

"Bouff has told me a couple of good stories about this place. Thought they needed work to be believable, but I guess I'll have to rethink that and give him credit for not being totally full of it." Both men laughed.

"As you probably know, Cook asked the two of us to investigate the fire," I said, indicating Fab with a wave. "Thus far, I've been able to accomplish a couple of things. I put out word that I'm willing to pay for credible information on who set the fire and ordered a background check on Travis West. Not sure what it will turn up, but you never know."

"I'm impressed. I didn't expect to hear that any progress had been made. Figured this would take months."

"Even if we're able to get the arsonist locked up, I'm not certain that solves your problem of re-opening, at least not in that location," I said.

"The last thing I want to do is disappoint my grandparents." Mark smiled at the thought of them. "I don't want to take over the family business but hadn't had that discussion with them. The fire has caused me to fess up, and like always, they were amazing."

"What is it you'd like to see happen?" Fab asked.

"I'd like restitution for the business and to sell the land so my grandparents can enjoy their retirement. It would give them extra money to go places they hadn't thought about." Mark sighed.

Fab stuck her head in the door and signaled Kelpie, flashing her fingers at the woman in a way that only they understood. It was minutes later when a busboy came out and served drinks, and not a one got sent back.

"I've been thinking we might need a backup plan," I said.

Fab rolled her eyes, and the three of us saw her. The guys laughed. I faux-glared. "One thing about Madison—she always comes up with a plan. Do they always work? No... but those are the ones that turn out to be the most fun."

It was hard not to laugh along with the guys.

"I need to run my idea by you because I'll want your okay and will need you to play along. Been thinking about the strip of land, and about the only use I can come up with for it—aside from a food truck location—is putting one of those tiny houses on it, which makes it a hard sell to Joe Shmo."

"Who?" Fab's look clearly conveyed that I'd lost my mind.

"He's not one of your Frenchy friends, so you probably haven't met." I ended with a phony smile.

Mark looked down. Bouff grinned, but he was used to the two of us.

"Where was I?" I gobbled down a cherry. "I'm thinking about approaching West and introducing myself as his neighbor-to-be, which I'm hoping will motivate him to up his original offer."

"I hate to suck the wind out of your idea, but West wants a fire sale price. Had the nerve to laugh when he said it," Mark said.

"That's because he thinks he's got the upper hand, having decided that no one will come along and offer on the property. Besides, you know what they say about never saying never?"

"What's your plan to get West to listen and avoid getting tossed off his doorstep, if you make it that far?" Mark asked.

"First off, I'm going to make him come to me.

When he does, I'll let him know that I've already submitted an offer and there's a slight hiccup due to a pending criminal investigation, but as soon as the file is closed, I'll be closing the deal. In the meantime, the rest of my assorted crew will show him firsthand how we can liven up the neighborhood."

Bouff laughed.

Mark looked confused, having no clue what kind of folks I could turn out.

"What I'm going to need from you is, when the police call—and I'm sure they will—to assure them I'm not trespassing. I promise that we won't be engaging in any kind of illegal activities, just offering a taste of damn annoying, so West knows that if my offer's accepted, the circus will never end."

"When Bouff mentioned you, he shared a few stories. I thought he was blowing smoke out his... Not sure how you challenging West will work out. If you pull off your plan, I'll be very appreciative."

"Ding, ding." Fab waved her hand. "Favors." She went on to explain that when a favor's called in, skip the excuses and put out. "Nothing illegal," she added at Mark's raised eyebrows.

"If I need to come up with another way to seal West's disgust, I could follow through on my margarita wagon idea and show up with one, complete with drunk friends."

"He's going to grind down his molars," Mark

said with a smile. "After my one conversation with the man, I couldn't get away fast enough or I'd have rearranged all his teeth."

"You know what the property is worth," I said. "West comes to you with an offer, double or triple it. No bargains for the man."

Fab handed Mark her card. "Or refer him to me, and I'll handle the negotiations." She trotted out creepy-girl smile.

Both men did a double take. Bouff laughed.

"It will take me a few days to get the guest list together for my little gathering. Then I'll call you and let you know when party day is happening."

"I can't thank you enough."

"No, thanks necessary. I'm just hoping to wangle a big check out of West."

Fab tapped her watch.

"I'll be in touch." We all went back inside and split up.

Chapter Sixteen

Fab headed straight to the office. We both needed to avail ourselves of Xander's talent for uncovering information. Lately, it seemed as though we were deluging him with requests.

"I originally wanted to figure out a way to force West to admit that he was behind the arson, but realized that had a minute chance of success. Now I'm thinking my new plan has a better likelihood of getting the Vickers what they want."

"I never doubted that you'd come up with something." Fab laughed. "Since you were light on details, you might as well run them by me, and I'll tell you if you've completely lost your mind.

"We know West thought the Taco Barr was an eyesore and not up to his standards. How about I bring in a different kind of drama and irk West's last nerve?"

"You declaring war?"

"In a friendly way." I ignored her groan. "I'm going to throw a property party and line up partygoers with never-ending antics. Entice locals with food and drink. I'm certain that word will spread and bring traffic. As long as everyone is parked legally — and as many in front of his house as will fit — shouldn't be a problem."

"Kevin will get the call, and he won't be happy."

"That's why everything needs to be legal. To that end, I'll hire a couple of Spoon's prizefighters for crowd control and make sure nothing gets out of hand. One look at their muscles, and people might behave. I'm thinking drunks, a few people showing up with wild animals, and as long as no one's doing it — or anything else — in the street, I might not get hauled off to jail."

"You know West will be hot on the phone to the cops, and if the first call doesn't get action, such as the guests getting dispersed, he'll call again and again."

"Party rules: Keep your clothes on and no illegal goings-on. I'll make the partiers sign an agreement so they can't claim ignorance. Remind me to double-check if there is a daytime noise ordinance."

"How are you going to get anything else done while you're planning this?"

"Translated: you want to make sure I'm available at your beck and call." I rubbed the middle of my forehead, which I knew irritated Fab. "Another idea coming on. I'm going to hire an antics coordinator. Who do we know that will do just about anything for a buck?" I tapped my chin. "Hint: he sure as heck doesn't need the money and has zero standards for turning down a gig."

"Make sure Crum's decked out in his tighty-whities and, if you're not around, introduces himself as your significant other. Blabber on about how excited the two of you are to be moving into your tiny house, which will show up in a matter of days." Fab could barely finish without laughing.

She turned into the warehouse and parked around the back. We'd barely gotten out when Arlo romped over and took a sniff, sitting for a head rub before taking off and going airborne in a flying leap, landing on the grass and rolling over and over.

We walked under the roll-up door and waved to Lark, who was on the phone.

Fab went over to Didier's desk and sat on the corner.

I was surprised to see Brad's desk looking neat as a pin, which meant he must be gone for the day. I walked over to Creole's desk and leaned down to kiss his cheek. "Where's my bro?"

"Brad called and said he had a personal issue to deal with and is taking a couple of days off." Creole pulled me into his lap. "Before you get all agitated, he said it wasn't anything serious. He knows we've got his back should he need it."

I turned so Didier could hear, and I knew Lark was listening. "I've got an announcement." Fab sent me a questioning look. I smirked in response. "I want all of you to hear it from me first. I may take on another husband — that's if he goes for it. I'll make it clear that the only benefit will be cash."

Creole laughed, clearly not believing a word of it and wondering what I was really up to. "A good place to start would be the beginning. Before you do, know that whatever you're up to, there will be no second husband. Period."

"Wait until who you hear who it is." Fab laughed and whispered in Didier's ear, and he also laughed.

I told the guys about the morning, starting with the bar fight, and moved onto my hot idea.

"How are you going to keep all those lunatics in line without ending up in jail?" Creole asked.

"Is this your nice way of saying you don't like my idea?"

"That question is in the same category as 'Does my butt look fat?'"

All of us laughed.

My phone rang, and I slid off Creole's lap to pull it out of my pocket, then sat back down. Brad's face popped up. I flashed the screen at Creole, and his brows went up. "Hey bro, you better be swell and all that or I'm going to come right over and kick your butt for not calling sooner."

"What are you doing?"

"Sitting on Creole's lap at the office, and you?"

"How about coming over? By yourself."

"You need me to bring chicken soup?"

Brad laughed. "One thing about the Westins, we can always be counted on for food. Now that I have a kid who loves to grocery shop, my fridge is full—can barely get the door closed."

"I'm on my way." I hung up and looped my arms around Creole's neck. "Brad wants to talk." I turned to Fab. "Do you mind hiking home? Or maybe…" I eyed Didier.

"I'll make sure Fab gets home." Didier winked at her.

After another quick kiss, I slid off Creole's lap and grabbed my briefcase.

"I'll walk you out." Creole hooked his arm around me.

Chapter Seventeen

The drive to Brad's was short, and I tried not to obsess all the way over about what he wanted. I ruled out sickness, since he didn't so much as sniffle during the call. Using my security code, I pulled into the underground garage and parked next to his SUV. I rode the elevator to the top floor, which consisted of two units, both of which he owned. He lived in one, and the other one, he rented to Allegra Kent.

Brad answered my knock, barefoot, in shorts and a t-shirt, and crossed his lips with his finger.

"Mila home from school?" I enveloped him in a hug.

"She's playing in her bedroom. I need a few minutes to talk." Brad led me into the kitchen, pulled out a stool at the island, and handed me a bottle of cold water. "Raise your right hand."

We'd been doing this since I could remember, and it was a given that you couldn't come back with any crossed-fingers nonsense.

"Whatever it is, I super swear." I stuck both hands in the air. "It would be appreciated if you could hurry it along with whatever you're about to confide, so the sick feeling in my stomach will go away." I did not want to hear bad news.

"Hmm… except, where to start?"

I reached across and took his hands in mine. "You're not sick, are you?"

"No. Sorry for letting you believe that for a second. I have a personal issue." He smiled weakly. "Frankly, I couldn't imagine telling anyone else. I'll need you to whip one of those plans out of wherever you hide them."

"You're in luck, bro-ski; I've been practicing lately, so I'm getting faster." I winked at him, which lightened the grim look that had taken over his features.

"So you know my neighbor, Allegra? Well, she…" He half-laughed and patted my hand at my annoyed reaction.

There was something about that woman. Chalk it up to overprotective sister… maybe.

"Don't go all lethal on me. I wasn't lying when I said we're just neighbors. Mostly, we just say hello in passing. But she has a friend, Layne, who came to stay with her for a few days, which turned into weeks. Anyway, Layne and I got very friendly."

"Is she in the next room?" I angled my head toward the hallway, where I could hear more than one voice.

"Layne's not here. What you're hearing is her three-year-old son, Logan. Mila adores him, and they get along great. Even though she's four years older, she never runs out of patience. She inspires me." Brad smiled.

A hundred questions ran rampant through my thoughts. *And what? She's crazy? You're getting married?* I stared wide-eyed, waiting. "It's nice of you to kid-sit."

"Layne and I hit it off, and we started spending time together. The four of us had fun times. In retrospect, I'm not sure what I should've done differently." Brad sighed. "Layne and Allegra got into a disagreement one day, and Layne moved in here temporarily while she looked for a place of her own."

"You've been living with a woman and her kid for how long?" I tried and failed to keep my hurt tone at bay.

Brad averted his eyes. "Just a couple of weeks."

I bit back my groan. "How is it that I was the one labeled the sneakiest?"

"Because that was in our younger days, and an apt description." His lips quirked. "It started out as a day or two, then time flew by... you know how that is." *Give me a break* on his face.

"Let me guess—you want me to plan a wedding when no one's met the woman?" He choked on his water. "Meet-and-greet, perhaps?"

"It's neither of those things and far more complicated." Brad stood and crossed to the dining room table. Opening his briefcase, he took out an envelope and came back, handing it to me.

I opened it and withdrew a legal document

titled Power of Attorney. I scanned the paperwork, which gave authority to make health and other decisions for Logan Winters to Brad Westin. Signed by Layne Winters and notarized. "This is… I don't understand why Layne would have this drawn up."

"She packed up and left. No goodbye. She left a brief note that I'd make a heck of a lot better parent for Logan, and she was off to get her life together. Couldn't guarantee that she'd be back." Brad heaved a huge sigh.

I heard a girl's voice that I recognized as Mila's scream. "I'm going to get you," followed by laughter.

"Noooo," a babyish voice squealed as it grew closer. A little boy barreled around the corner and into the kitchen, throwing himself at Brad, who caught him and kissed his cheek.

Hot on his heels, Mila saw me sitting there and launched herself at me. I wrapped my arms around her and tried not to squeeze the breath out of her. Then I held her away. "Happy to see you," I said and covered her cheeks in kisses.

"You two behaving yourselves?" Brad asked in a teasing tone as he opened the refrigerator and grabbed juice packets.

Mila, who'd settled on my lap, went into great detail about the game they'd been playing.

Brad picked up Logan and set him on his lap, and the little boy buried his face in his chest. He turned him to face me. "This is my sister,

Madison. And Madison, this is Logan." He
waved shyly.

"Very nice to meet you." I gave him a big
smile.

Brad turned his attention to Mila. "Do you
think you can keep Logan entertained for a few
minutes so I can talk to Auntie?"

Mila nodded, jumped down, and grabbed
Logan's hand after Brad set him on the floor. He
followed them into the living room, pulled out a
basket of toys, and turned on the television to a
kids' show, then motioned to me, and we sat on
the couch.

"Dude." I kept my low voice. "Did you skip
the part where Logan's your son and you just
found out?" The boy was Brad's spitting image.

"Layne noticed right away, and when she
introduced us the first time, we laughed at the
uncanny resemblance. But I swear to you, I just
met her a few months back. I've heard it said that
everyone has a twin somewhere; well, there's
mine." Brad inclined his head.

It was hard not to stare at the little boy. Brad,
Mila, and Logan were remarkably similar and
could easily pass as a family with their sun-
streaked brown hair and brown eyes. "What are
you going to do?"

"I have no idea. What happens if Logan's
preschool finds out that his mother took off? Do
they have a legal obligation to involve the
authorities? Last thing I want is to be caught off

guard, with Logan hauled out of here crying."

"First thing you do is enroll Logan in the same school as Mila. Cook told me his daughter expanded last year and is now accepting preschool to sixth grade. If she asks, you have the POA, and you have references from me and Cook."

"I'll give them a call." He smiled as he watched Mila handing Logan toys to throw into a pile.

"Better yet, I'll get Cook to put in a word for you before you talk to her. You know how that family works—if it's in their power to make it happen, it's a done deal. They're an accommodating bunch. What about...?" I inclined my head toward Logan, who was busy chatting it up with Mila. About half of what he said made sense. Mila didn't skip a beat and answered back.

"Are you asking what if Layne doesn't come back? I don't have an answer since I don't know what my options are, if any. I tried asking Allegra a few questions, and she was so evasive it made my head hurt." Brad watched the kids for a minute. "As you can see, Mila and Logan are more than a little attached."

I followed his gaze to the kids playing. "They're very sweet together."

"I need to know everything there is to know about Layne, and that's where you come in. Would you run a background check?"

"That's an easy request." I smiled at him. "If you could decide the outcome, what would you want it to be?"

"For Layne to walk through the door. Logan loves her. I thought we were building something, but I'm not interested in someone who'd leave their kid." Brad got up and stomped to the kitchen, coming back with more water and sitting down. "I did a little research this morning, and since I have no blood relationship to Logan, it's a toss-up if the POA would hold up. The other thing that bothers me is that there's probably family out there. And if so, they'll want him, and reuniting them would be the right thing to do. I never got the entire story on bio dad; Layne vaguely brushed the subject off. I'm thinking the grandparents are the best people to take him—as long as they're suitable and not crazy. I'd like to know what our options are before making any decisions."

"Then there's Mila."

"In hindsight, I shouldn't have let Layne move in. I told Mila back in the beginning that it was temporary while they looked for a home." Brad sighed. "How do I explain this turn of events to my daughter? I don't want her thinking I'd do the same thing to her."

"Here's what I'm going to do. I'll have background checks run on Layne, her family, and any friends that can be located," I said. "If I'm able to figure out where she disappeared to, you can be the one to make contact. Fab could force her back, but that would be awkward."

Brad half-laughed and shook his head. "You're right, it would be better if I was the one, and then find out for myself why she'd take such a drastic step."

"You could always call your cop friend, Kevin."

Brad shook his head. "No way. We both know he's by the book. What I found out online was that since I'm not related, if anyone were to report Logan staying with me to the cops, they'd call Social Services, and who knows what would happen to him. Sad thing is, because I'm not family, I'd never know. As you know, not all the stories you hear about foster care are good, and I'm not doing that to Logan. I'm sure once we locate his family, they'll be eager to have him."

"I know you think you can keep this a secret. Mother—remember her?—will be caught by surprise, but she'll be there for you. You could collect kids off the street and she'd be all, 'More grandkiddios.'" I attempted to mimic Mother's excited tone. The kid's heads popped around, and when they saw me laughing, they laughed too.

"I suppose it would be rude to have someone else tell her." Brad looked hopeful that I'd volunteer.

"The only thing Mother will be annoyed about is that she didn't know first. Remember that she's shown herself to be great in a crisis. More than once."

"Must be where you get it from." Brad looped his arm around me for a hug.

"I'm going to jump on this and help you figure out Logan's options. I'll keep you updated on anything I find out and email you a copy of every report. I want you to be able to make the best decision." I pulled out my phone, asked Brad a couple of questions about Layne, and typed the answers into a text to Xander, with a "step on it" to my request for information. I got back an answer that he'd start immediately. He added that everyone had left for the day and he was locking up and heading out.

I called Creole, and when he answered, I said, "I'm bringing dinner, you got a preference?"

"Got it covered. At the mention of food, a couple of others invited themselves, so…"

"You going to keep me guessing?" When he laughed, I said, "I hope you have enough for three more. And it's a surprise."

We hung up. "Got this last-minute great idea. Come to dinner. Creole just told me that 'a couple' of other people are invited." I made air quotes. "You can bet it's probably twenty. Bring the kids, and I promise no one will ask any personal questions." I waved off his *maybe some other time* answer. "The kids will have a great time, and by the time you get them home, they'll be half-asleep and ready for bed."

"Do you want to go to Auntie's for dinner?" Brad asked.

"Yes." Mila jumped up, hands in the air. Logan mimicked her.

Chapter Eighteen

I asked Brad to give me a five-minute head start so I could put the fear into people if they didn't do as I asked. I called Creole on the way home. "Has Mother been invited to put in an appearance?"

"They're headed to another Key for a romantic dinner."

"My original number of three has now grown to five, and if there's not enough food, you need to light a fire under Fab and tell her to hustle to the store."

Creole laughed. "Good thing we have plenty. You know she'd shoot me."

"I'm on my way." I knew if I didn't call Mother, I'd get grilled later on.

"This is your favorite daughter," I said when she answered. "You're so going to owe me when I tip you off to this tidbit."

Mother laughed. "I don't know what you're up to, but put it on hold; the husband and I are having an evening out." She made a kissy noise.

I gagged, loudly.

"Madison Westin," she admonished.

"Mother dear, you get lover boy to turn your

buggy around and head to my house or you're going to grouch for nigh on ever about missing the evening." That was met with silence.

"I'll talk it over with the husband and see if he's amenable."

"Spoon lives to please his honey, so I'll see you two later."

I took every shortcut I could remember and sped to the house. When I opened the door, I saw several people in the kitchen, a couple with their backs turned as they headed out the sliders to the deck. Why invite one when ten will do?

Creole and Didier were prepping food, which I assumed would be barbequed. Fab tipped her martini glass in my direction.

Before I took another step, a ball of fur skidded to a stop at my feet and sniffed my shoes, then worked its nose up my legs. "What the hell is that?" I pointed, knowing the what. More importantly, where did it come from?

Fab shook her finger and, in a snooty tone, informed me, "Bad words aren't allowed."

The guys looked up and grinned.

On the heels of the dog came Alejandro Famosa, arms crossed, his brown orbs every bit as intense as his father's.

Before he could launch into whatever was sitting on the tip of his tongue, I said, "Try not to get your shorts in a bunch when I know darn well your sensibilities haven't been one bit offended." I wanted to hug the high-schooler but knew that wouldn't be on his list of favorite things.

"Let me introduce you to the latest Famosa family member," Alex said with a smirk. "Larry. Madison. Try not to bite her."

"What kind of —"

"Australian Shepherd. Highly trained. My dad claims he behaves better than we do."

"It better be cat friendly or it needs to hustle outside." I pointed to the door.

"No worries. The cats took one look at Larry and hightailed it down the hall. He didn't chase them. He's better trained than that," Alex said with a snort.

"Where are your siblings?" I asked.

"When you get the food on the table, whistle, and they'll come running," Alex said in a stern tone. Only the quirk of his lips let on that *he* thought he was funny.

Creole came up behind me and enveloped me in a hug. "We're having a 'welcome to the family' dinner for Larry."

"Larry was the best name you could come up with?" I asked Alex, who wasn't amused.

"My sister named him." His tone dared me to comment.

"Sweet Lili." I smiled. "I suppose those thug brothers of yours are around." I'd nicknamed Cisco and Diego One and Two, since I couldn't tell them apart.

"They're playing on the beach with Dad."

"Okay, everyone listen up." I pointed to Alex. "I'll need you to spread the word to any adults, along with the warning that if they don't follow my edict, they'll be in hot water with me." Alex looked happy with his new task. "Brad is about to come through the door, and not one personal question or I'll sic Fab on any offender with orders to put a bullet hole in their butt. Kids excluded, of course."

"This is going to be fun." Alex whistled for Larry, and the two ran out the door and down to the beach.

"I'll be right back." I hustled to the bedroom, threw my purse and briefcase down, and changed into a comfy dress, then bent down to kiss Jazz and Snow, who were asleep on the end of the bed. I padded barefoot back to the kitchen. "Do we have enough food?" I asked, going into hostess mode, knowing that we didn't this morning.

"Casio brought the steaks, and between Didier and I, we've got the rest covered." Creole handed me a margarita.

It took a lot of effort not to gulp it all the way down, but I managed to stop halfway.

Before Creole and Didier disappeared outside with the two trays of food they were holding, I said, "I know you're all eager to hear about my chat with Brad, but I'll let him tell you." I turned to Fab. "We both have a lot going on. I'm thinking a morning meeting to get on track is called for. Let's do it at the office; I'm more than happy to bring food."

"Good idea." Fab nodded. "So you know, Larry was a surprise to me, as I met him right before you arrived. When Casio asked about getting a dog, I didn't realize he was telling me that he'd already gotten one. Larry's got a great resume: guard dog, well-trained, good with kids, and won't eat other animals."

"When Mila meets Larry, she'll be back to burning Brad's ears off for a pet." I crossed to the cupboard. "I think I have enough plates." I did a mental count. "I need to do some shopping."

Fab groaned. "Real stores or flea markets?"

"I'm thinking the out-of-the-way stores that I love and you hate."

Fab's nose went in the air. She didn't need to know that when I had a minute, I planned to sneak off on my own. Non-stop knocking saved me from a response. I knew it was the kids. "I'll get it." I raced to open the door.

I bent down, and Mila threw herself into my arms. I opened my arms wider to include Logan and kissed them both on the cheek.

"Thank you for inviting us," she squealed. Logan mimicked her: "Tanks."

My brother stood behind them, a big smile on his face and two infamous pink boxes in his hand from everyone's favorite bakery.

I stepped back as they all trooped inside. Mila grabbed Logan's hand and dragged him over to meet Fab, who enveloped them both in a hug without hesitation.

"Mila's going to be over the moon—the Famosa kids are lurking outside. Logan will fit right in, and they'll have a great time."

Brad craned his head around. "Does everyone…"

"I ordered everyone, under threat of dire consequences, not to ask a single question."

Brad laughed.

Fab took Mila's and Logan's hands and led them outside.

"Beer or something stronger?" I asked Brad as I took the boxes and set them on the counter, taking a peek and licking my lips.

"I got it." He headed to the refrigerator, helping himself. "The bakery had slim pickings left, so I cleaned them out of everything they had."

I picked up the other half of my drink and slugged it down. "I put the word out, so there won't be any weirdness."

Brad set his beer down and pulled me into a hard hug. "You're the best."

"So you know, Mother and Spoon are joining us." *They'd be on their best behavior; I'd make sure of it.*

"Most boring dinner ever is what you're saying," Brad teased.

"I'm going to help you figure everything out, but for tonight, screaming kids will keep all of us from having a single rational thought."

I pulled out an enamelware tub, filled it with ice, and stocked it full of beers and sodas. Brad picked it up and carried it outside, sitting it on one of the side tables next to the railing. Looking down at the beach, I saw the kids and Larry running wild from one end of the sand to the other, Casio's arms waving around in an attempt to steer them away from the water.

"Casio looks like he could use some help," Brad said and, with a nod, headed down the stairs.

No one questioned me, which made me happy, but I did catch a couple of questioning stares from Creole and Didier. I kept my focus on setting the table.

"Anyone home?" Spoon boomed out.

I craned my head to see him and Mother in the kitchen and went to meet them. I gave them the same admonishment as everyone else, which earned me quizzical looks but no questions.

Fab had come back from the beach, and when the food was ready, she unleashed a whistle loud enough to wake the dead. The kids trooped up the stairs, followed by Casio and Brad.

Brad hugged Mother, and the two talked for several minutes. She patted him on the cheek. Spoon, Mila in his arms and Logan on his shoulders, brought them over, and they exchanged kisses with Mother.

The food had been set up buffet-style, and

everyone was directed to grab a plate and help themselves. Brad and Casio helped their kids and got them seated. A few stares were sent Logan's way, but no one said a word. The kids kept up a constant chatter, relaying what they'd done in school.

I leaned sideways and asked Fab, "What kind of activity do you have planned for the kids after dinner?"

"I say we move the fun back down to the beach and let them continue running in circles until they fall asleep on their feet."

"When I was a kid, I always wanted to stay outside and milk every last second of daylight because going inside generally meant bedtime." I made a face and Fab laughed.

Once we finished eating and the dishes cleared away, we moved down to the sand, Brad and Casio taking balls and frisbees. Larry staked out his position on the beach, Mother at his side with Logan in her lap, and the three kept an eye on the action.

Spoon organized everyone into two teams for beach ball kicking. It appeared to be the adults' job to make sure no one took one to the head.

"How long has Brad known he has a son?" Creole asked me, Didier and Fab in hearing range. "And how long have you known?"

"Do we congratulate him?" Didier asked.

I hurried to relate what I knew. "If you have more questions, you need to wait until he's back at the office."

"It would be easier and a more clear-cut course of action if Logan were his son," Fab said.

Casio had come up in time to hear bits of the conversation. He punched Didier in the shoulder. "You're up, dude." He jumped up and ran down the beach to change places with the man.

"I can hit up a cop friend of mine, who can check to see if there's any active reports on the mother," Casio offered.

"Is there any chance that Brad wants to keep him?" Fab asked.

"He wants what's best for Logan." Reuniting him with his family needed to come quick, before Brad and Mila got really hurt.

The kids yelled for Creole, who jumped up and answered the call.

"What's your plan to find this woman?" Fab asked.

"Layne has to want to be found. If not, it could be difficult, but hopefully not impossible. I've got Xander working on a background check and sent him her last known phone number. I tried it, but no answer. Then I'll locate her family. If it comes to that, the three of us can show up, introduce ourselves, and won't that be awkward?"

Casio grunted. "That would be the last job I'd sign up for."

"If it were me and the mother reappeared tomorrow, I'd have a hard time handing the boy back over, wondering when she'd take off again," Fab said.

"I don't get it myself," I said. "I just want a happy ending all around."

"Good luck to that one." Casio snorted.

Chapter Nineteen

For two days, Fab and I worked from home — her house, since she had the largest island space and we could spread out. We used the time to catch up, read all the reports we'd requested, and sift through the latest information Xander had emailed over.

Fab's phone rang constantly with calls from Gunz, demanding to know the latest on his nephew's case. During the last call, he told her he'd be handling it himself.

It was the first time I'd ever heard her yell at him. "You need to stop this and let me do my job. Your beating the hell out of the man you think responsible won't prove that Jimmy didn't embezzle the money."

That calmed the man down, and the two spoke civilly after that. She hung up with a frustrated sigh. "Jimmy was on the call too, although he barely got in another word after hello. The looming threat of prison is turning Gunz into the crazy one, and it's not his big butt on the line. I was happy when Jimmy made the point that if the missing money wasn't located, this would always hang over his head."

"Once the CEO is informed, I assume he'll call the cops, though he probably won't want it to make the news," I said.

"Xander has more information for me." Fab pointed to her laptop screen. "I'm sending you a link to join our meeting, so don't dawdle."

"I'll try." I made a face, and she laughed. I opened a new window on my computer and, after a couple of clicks, waved wildly at Xander, who waved back.

Fab opened a file and scanned the screen while Xander began his report.

"Milton Track, Jimmy's boss, was terrible at covering his tracks. The man didn't know what he was doing and left a clear path back to himself." Xander snorted.

"This attempt to extort Jimmy into repaying money that he didn't steal is clumsy. Even if he had the money, which he doesn't, why would he pony up... a million, is it?" I asked.

Fab nodded. "You did a great job, Xander. You got proof that Milton had his sticky fingers, and only his, all over the account he set up in Jimmy's name."

"I don't know how this works," Xander said. "Won't the District Attorney want to know how you procured the information before dropping any charges?"

"Tank is Jimmy's lawyer, and he knows that you've been attempting to track the money, so he'll know how to present it to the court. Since you've done other jobs for him, he doesn't have to worry that the information is bogus," Fab said.

"Wait until Gunz's best friend, Cruz Campion, finds out he's been replaced by a lawyer that doesn't have billboards all over South Florida boasting of his courtroom prowess." I shot a smirk at Xander, who winked. I'd questioned the BF status in the past, but one thing I didn't have the nerve to ask was, "How the heck did you two become besties?"

"Cruz took the family to Greece for a month, apparently without Gunz's permission." Fab laughed. "He was beyond irked to find out he was not only not in the office but not even in the country."

"You're sending the file to Tank and case over?" I asked.

"Maybe... or not. I'll let you know," Fab said.

Swell. "Speaking of Tank, what's happening with your friend Lena?" I asked Xander.

"She spoke to him, and her only option if she can't work it out with her mother would be to sue her. She said that would start a war and her mother would immediately set fire to her belongings."

Yikes. "Surely Tank had some good advice."

"He offered to mediate a sit-down between the two, which Lena turned down, fearing the same result." Xander half-laughed, not amused. "He was in favor of Lena continuing to stash away personal items that she wanted to keep. I've been helping with that. We've been replacing the items with junk, and her mother hasn't noticed."

"If I were in Lena's shoes, I'd be doing the same thing," I said. "But you could be arrested, and who knows what charges her mother could level against you in her anger over being bested."

"Tank told her to remove her own belongings and not involve anyone else, as that wasn't a crime," Xander said. "I've rounded up items from the thrift store and several times gave her a ride to her friend's house, where she has everything stored. Lena's gotten almost everything she wants boxed up and out of there. She's just hanging onto everyday items that she needs until her eviction on her birthday."

"The two still have time to fix the relationship…"

"Slim chance of that," Xander huffed.

"Lena has another month of school after her birthday — where's she going to live?" Fab asked.

"There's one thing that worked out great. She's been invited to stay with the same friend who's storing her stuff until college starts in the fall."

"Happy to hear," I said.

Fab ended the conference call, assuring Xander that we'd be in the office in the morning.

* * *

Fab demanded that I be ready to leave early the

next day, as she planned to wrap up the Jimmy Jones case and needed the element of surprise — annoying people before they had time for coffee was her plan. When she informed me that she needed to stop by the office to pick up a file, I told her I'd be riding in with Creole, since the guys had an early meeting.

"I got the barest of details about today's job," Creole griped as he cut across the highway to the office. "This is where I remind you again that you're not to go traipsing off without a heads up, and before, not after."

"Fab's winding up a case, and I'm the ride-along. Not planning on messing up my do." I tugged on strands of my hair and hoped it hadn't frizzed between the house and the car. It could easily be one of those days, with humidity threatening to zoom through the roof.

Creole snorted. "Uh-huh."

"On the off chance I have to get out of the car, I know it will give you peace of mind to know I'm gunned up." I pulled my skirt up all the way. Creole laughed. "This new tidbit should make you happy: I've been led to believe that we'll be hanging out at the office more, which I'm totally in favor of."

"Sounds good in theory, but Fab can't solve her client's problems sitting behind her desk."

"I've got a solution: get rid of Lark and hire Fab to run the office. She'd be great with the clients."

Creole groaned overly loudly. "We took a vote, and we like Lark, eccentricities and all. We'd also miss Arlo; he's good for a game of fetch when we take a break and go out to the patio."

"What you're saying is that I did a good job in hiring her?"

"Maybe." He laughed.

We arrived at the office and barely got parked before Fab squealed up beside us, parked, and laid on the horn. Didier must have told her a time or two to slow down or she'd have beaten us here. Fab and Didier headed into the office, parting ways at the elevator.

"Fab's got something that needs her attention upstairs, and while she's doing that, it will give me time to update Brad," I said.

"Hoping that no one gets hurt with the Logan situation." Creole got out and walked around his truck, helping me out.

"Hopefully we can reunite him with family that he knows and loves," I said. "The alternative of letting the situation play out is fraught with potholes."

We walked around and went through the side entrance. Creole opened the door, and I waved to Brad, who was drinking coffee at the conference table. I walked over and put my arms around his neck, kissing his cheek.

"Xander is investigating Layne's background, and once I pull together all the information, I'll go over it with you and we'll decide what to do next."

"Appreciate all you're doing." Brad patted my hand.

Creole and Didier grabbed coffee and sat down at the table.

"Can anyone listen in?" Creole asked.

Brad laughed. "Anyone has a secret, it doesn't stay that way long." He turned to me. "Thanks for the tip on using Cook to expedite getting Logan into school. He didn't hesitate, and the next thing, his daughter was calling. Mila was excited to be walking Logan into school this morning. It was just sweet."

"Cook is one of those people that never says he can't do something," Creole said.

I nodded in agreement.

"Madeline looked a little put out that she was under orders not to question you the other night at dinner." Didier half-laughed. "I'm assuming she caught up with you."

"You know, Mother. The next night, she showed up with food, played with the kids until bedtime, and got them tucked in without a single whine." Brad's smile disappeared. "She was really disappointed when I told her Logan wasn't my bio child. She showed up ready for him to call her Gram."

"I love that about Mother—always room for one more."

Fab blew through the door and came running

into the room. "You ready for the shootout?" She only had one hand to gun up the room; the other was filled with files.

I stood and imitated her.

Not one of the guys appreciated the humor.

"We're Miami-bound, and by the time we get there, Madison will have a plan worked up." Fab winked at me.

Creole and Didier rolled their eyes.

"Now, now, none of that." I shook my finger at them.

The guys stood and walked us out to the Hummer, both of us getting kisses.

Chapter Twenty

"First stop, Milton Track's house. I want to verify that this is a good address before handing it to his boss." Fab turned onto a palm tree-lined street in South Beach, several blocks from the water and adjacent to a heavily trafficked road. She cruised slowly past a rundown mustard-yellow house with banana trees growing rampant around the entry. She circled the block and turned down the alley. Coming back to the front, she parked in the only available space, ignoring the sign that clearly stated, "Permit parking only."

"It's unfortunate that the house has been neglected," I said.

"It's a three-plex."

I scooted up and looked again. "It's hard to believe that there's million-dollar real estate a few blocks over."

"Xander was able to forward me great pictures. Inside the arch are three doors. Milton lives in number three, which backs up to the parking lot of the apartment building next door." She pointed to the left.

"I've got a pretty good idea what you're

doing, but since you weren't forthcoming with details, I've got nothing for you." I eyed her with raised eyebrows. "You're here for more than address verification. Scaring the pee-dawdle out of him isn't illegal. Just remember to stop before crossing that line—the one where you get arrested."

"That's why, Ms. Bail Money, you're going to stay in the car, and should I need it, you'll snap your fingers and have me out of the joint pronto."

"Don't think so." I reached behind the seat and grabbed a tote I hadn't dug around in in a while but knew would produce a trick or two. I pulled out a handful of pamphlets and waved them at her. "If your plan is to squeeze a confession out of Milty… here's a freebie to get him to open the door. Although I doubt he'd confess unless you were pointing firepower at him, and I wouldn't recommend that course of action. As for me, I'll be in the background, ready to dispense a commiserating smile if you get hauled off."

"You've lost your mind."

"This is another of those Pot situations. Before you start an argument that won't result in a winner, you might want to hustle your bum to the door before Milt heads out to work." I tapped my wrist. We both got out, and I followed her up the cracked concrete pathway. "I'm going to try one more time—forget about Milton and hand over what you've collected to boss dude. He can check Milton's personnel record should he need an address. That brings the case to a close. On your part anyway."

Fab ignored me as she hustled to the door and knocked politely. I hung back in the archway.

The door cracked open, and Milton (I presumed) stuck his head out. Apparently liking what he saw, he opened the door wide, and the smell of weed wafted out. "Come on in, babe." The skinny shirtless fifty-something was wearing a matted brown toupee that he was attempting to get to stick on the top of his head. He gave up and let it hang lopsided. It was hard to determine whether he'd slept in his suit pants or they were always a wrinkled mess.

"You and I are going to have a talk." Her tone held a hint of malice that I only heard on rare occasions.

Fear flooded the man's face. "What the hell?" He attempted to shut the door in Fab's face, but she stopped that with a hard shove. "What do you want?" He jumped back a step.

"You won't get away with setting up Jimmy Jones. He's not going to take the fall for a crime you committed." Fab leaned forward, almost nose to nose.

"I don't know what you're talking about." He pulled his phone out of his pocket. "I'm calling the cops."

"That's a great idea. I'll wait right here." Fab

snickered. "I'm certain that they'd like to hear why I'm camped on your doorstep."

Milton shoved his phone back in his pocket and lunged forward, his hands out.

Fab twisted to one side and managed to grab the back of his pants in a wild yank.

I stepped off the porch and into the dirt with the overgrown plants.

The two stumbled through the arch. Then Milton jerked free and raced out to the sidewalk, tripping over a gaping crack. He righted himself and took off in a mad dash down the street.

Fab and I moved out to the sidewalk to watch his flight. He turned into another parking lot two apartment buildings south. To my surprise, Fab motioned to me, and we got back in the car.

"Milton went that way." I pointed. "I'm surprised you didn't run him down and kick his butt to the ground."

"Except that would get me arrested for assault." Fab collapsed back against the seat. "This will surprise you, but I was hoping he would call the cops and I could tell them about the case I was hired to investigate since Gunz forbid me to call them myself."

"Wouldn't they say that's a judge's decision to make?"

"Several things need to happen before it gets in front of a judge. I'm guessing, since Milty's on foot, that he's hiding, waiting on our next move, and when we leave, he'll go back to his apartment. Not that I had any doubt, but his running shows his guilt." Fab pulled away from the curb and drove slowly, checking out where we'd seen Milton turn in. Surprisingly, she kept going.

"Jimmy would probably like to face him in court and see the man get his due."

"I asked him, and he told me that he just wanted it over." Fab pulled a piece of paper out of her pocket and handed it to me. "One more stop."

I keyed it into the GPS, and when it came up Star Island, I knew she could find it without help. "The security guard won't bother to stop you, if he's even in his little house; I think he's more for decoration. Once you're on the island, what's your plan for Mr. Bigwig's house?"

"Wing it, same as before, since that worked out so swell." Fab grimaced.

It was always a beautiful ride over the Causeway, and the brilliant blues of the water that surrounded it on both sides glistened today.

Fab took the turn for Star Island and cruised past the guardhouse, where the man inside was drinking his morning brew from a local coffeehouse. She waved, turned to the right, and was just pulling up at a security gate at the far end when it rolled back and the pool people came driving out. I counted three men crammed into the front seat of the truck. The house wasn't visible from the street.

"I should mention to Mr. Allen that he might want to have the 'don't let anyone else in the gate' talk with his contractors." Fab cruised down the brick driveway and pulled up in front of a two-story Mediterranean villa with a garage on either side that could easily park ten cars.

"If this mansion were for sale, would it be one of the cheaper ones on the island?"

"At eighteen thousand square feet, it's at the top end, with a value of forty million, minus a buck or two."

"Happy I don't have to clean it." I made a face.

"You'd have staff," Fab said in her snooty tone and pointed to the door. "You're going with me, no arguments."

I got out and smoothed down my dress, happy that I hadn't gone for obstinate and shown up in sweats. I knew full well she'd have driven me home to change.

A foot from the door, I tugged on her arm. "Go all sexy and charm the pants off the man. Not completely off, but you get what I mean."

"Can you behave yourself?"

"No worries. I'll take a deep breath and trotted out the party manners."

Fab laughed, which surprised me. She rang the bell, which couldn't be heard from outside, so we'd have to wait patiently to know if anyone heard it. Didn't take long before a harried housekeeper threw open the door.

"Mr. Allen is expecting us. I thought I was

going to be late, and look, a couple of minutes to spare." Fab oozed magnetism as she muscled her way in, sticking out her hand and introducing herself without a word about me. She continued to charm the woman right into a seat in the living room and sent her happily scurrying away to announce Fab to her boss.

"Wow," I said in a low tone. "Quite the performance. I'm impressed."

"Few people are nice to the help, and that's plain stupid."

Mr. Allen stormed into the room. The grey-haired, sixty-ish man had an aggravated look on his face and exhaled anger after checking the two of us out and realizing he'd never met either of us before. No sign of the housekeeper. I hoped she wouldn't be fired.

"I don't know what kind of scam you're running, but you need to leave now. I'll be turning your license plate number over to the cops, and they'll deal with you," he snapped, spitting flames. Not quite, but close.

Fab stood and wiggled over to the man, her choice of a black dress that molded to her hips a good one. "One minute of your time, Mr. Allen." She held up a finger. "I promise that you won't be sorry. Then, on the off chance that you're unhappy, you can have the pleasure of tossing me out."

"You're a confident young woman." He scanned her from head to toe. "You've got one minute." He tapped his watch and continued to stand, arms across his chest.

I stayed seated out of embarrassment, not knowing what to do. If Mr. Allen tossed Fab, he wouldn't have to ask me twice.

"Milton Track embezzled one million dollars from your company and set up Jimmy Jones to take the fall, and I have the proof."

"Have a seat and tell me what you're talking about from the beginning." He held out his hand and ushered her back into the living room, where he shot me a quick glance but didn't say anything.

Fab introduced herself as a private investigator and handed him her card, which he pocketed with barely a glance. "Jimmy was referred to me after Mr. Track confronted him about repayment and claimed that criminal charges were forthcoming. I put my team on it. It was easy to track the money and who did what, and it was all Mr. Track. He did an amateur job of setting up my client."

"Milton has been a loyal employee for over fifteen years."

"When you put your people on it, it won't take them long to come up with the same information that I did." Fab handed over a manila envelope that she'd slipped under her arm. "Milton knows that I'm onto him and have proof. Wouldn't surprise me if he's leaving town as we speak."

"Where did Track stash the money?" Allen opened the folder and pulled out the report, thumbing through it.

"An account in Jimmy's name was set up in a local bank, and there's still fifty thousand in that account. The rest was moved to another account, and on that one, Milton used his mother's maiden name. If there's any attempt to move it, my man will know, and that information can be forwarded to you."

Mr. Allen leaned back and studied Fab. She met his stare without blinking. "You vouch for this information and that you're not wasting my time?" He gritted his teeth, jaw rigid, as he scanned the report. He looked back to Fab, black thunder filling his expression, and shot a few questions at her.

Fab dropped a couple of high-profile names, which had him scrutinizing her once again. He relaxed somewhat, and the two schmoozed over people they knew and places they'd hung out.

"I want to hire you to stop Track from leaving town." Allen stood and crossed to a side table, opening a drawer and handing Fab a business card. "My legal team will be on this today and will also speak to the DA, who's a friend." The two shook hands. "We'll talk. If this turns out to be true, anything I can do for you, I owe you one."

Since they were both ignoring me, I made my way over to the front door. I wanted to slip out but figured that wouldn't go unnoticed and instead waited quietly.

Allen opened the door and turned to Fab. I slipped out and kept going. Fab and he stood on the front step and chatted. Thankfully, she'd left the car doors unlocked, and I got in. I was tempted to honk and had to laugh at the mental image of her pure shock at that.

Finally, she came back and slid behind the wheel, backed out, and waved to Mr. Allen.

"How do you plan to keep Milton in town? I can already tell you that your husband — remember him? — is not going to like this new job one bit."

"I shouldn't have confronted Milton, but can't undo that one. I'll hand the job off to Xander, who can track him through his cell phone and credit cards." Fab scooped up her phone, called Xander, and told him to immediately put an alert on Milton's accounts.

Chapter Twenty-One

The next morning before leaving the house, I went through the meager information I'd collected on the Taco Bar fire, as though it would feed me a clue, I hadn't ferreted out the numerous other times I'd read it over.

Knowing that Fab planned to stay home and get her files updated, I drove to her house and laid on the horn. Satisfied that I'd made enough noise, I got out and went around to the passenger side. The front door flew open.

"What?" she yelled, arms crossed over her chest.

I powered down the window and got in, sticking my head out. "Hustle it up. You can't take all day; we've got places to go. Chop, chop."

"I'm not going anywhere."

I laid on the horn again and didn't let up until she poked her head back out the door.

"Don't make me call Mother and have her lay on the guilt." I interpreted the door slam as meaning she'd be right out.

I entertained myself on my phone until she stormed out and slid behind the wheel. "This better be good."

"If it looks like it's going to be a snore bore, I'll hop right in and sauce up your experience. First stop: Taco Bar. Before you get all snitty, I can't promise there won't be more stops, because if I do, my phone will explode with emergencies."

"This is where I remind you: no tacos. It's a vacant strip of land that will take us two minutes, if that, to foot cruise." Fab hauled out of the gate and over to the highway. "Has Doodad been able to buy any good info?"

"It's all quiet on the streets. If anyone had information, they'd sell it in a hot second. A few came sniffing around in an attempt to scam a few bucks, but Doodad ran them off." He had excellent radar for BS and put up with a lot until that line was crossed, which I suspected depended more on how he felt that day than reaching his threshold for being fed up. "I can answer your next question—the background check on Travis West came back squeaky clean. Turns out he's a lawyer; his office is in Miami."

Thanks to light traffic, it didn't take long before we were cruising the neighborhood, and true to form, Fab drove slowly, checking out every property twice before parking. "There's a woman puttering in her garden across the street. It would help if I knew what information you're looking for."

"I'm thinking we wing it and let our outgoing personalities do all the work."

Fab laughed.

We both got out and paused at the bumper, checking out the street. I tried to stay behind her — she could be the bossy one today — but she wasn't having any part of it. Fab hooked her arm in mine as we headed across the street and dropped it as the woman caught our approach, giving me a slight shove in front of her. I pasted on what I thought was a friendly smile, and the woman laughed.

I'd gotten a few words out when I realized I was sounding like a used car salesman and took a breath to change course.

The woman sat back on her heels, an amused smile on her face. "Spit out whatever it is you want. I have a short attention span, so..." She rolled her hand.

I officially liked her and plopped down in the dirt next to her. Fab stood off to the side, and I was surprised she hadn't decided to check out the property. "I've got a few questions about the Taco Bar."

"You a cop or something?" I didn't answer. "I'm surprised no one showed up sooner. Except there's not much to tell. Boom and the trailer exploded in flames. By the time I hustled outside, the fire was sending out plumes of black smoke. Quite the show, if it weren't so dangerous. One by one, the residents came out of their houses and congregated over there..." She pointed down the street.

"Anyone around here have an issue with it

being parked in the neighborhood? You know, thought it was an eyesore and should be hauled away?" I asked.

The woman laughed. "There was only one neighbor that had that opinion. He went so far as to circulate a petition—said that when he presented it, it would motivate the city to evict them."

On what grounds? It would take more than a petition, but I didn't say anything.

"Only a couple of people signed; the rest of us not only liked the Vickers, but ate at the Taco Bar quite often. Word spread, and I kept an eye out and didn't answer the door. Not that I do that anyway. But it took three attempts before he got the message."

"Did he get enough signatures for the city to take notice?"

She shook her head. "And he wasn't happy."

"Would that be Travis West?" Fab asked.

"He's a dick neighbor." The woman nodded and laughed. "He got into a dispute with the owner of the lot that borders the other side of his property over a new fence they planned to put in and demanded a survey. They already had one, but he said it was old. He didn't want to be told that property lines don't change."

"Were they able to work out the dispute?" I asked.

"When he threatened legal action, they got the survey. I tend to mind my own business and not get caught up in any drama on this block. West, in particular, has shown himself to be unrelenting. Everyone's got a smile for him, but no one has a nice thing to say behind his back."

I decided to put my cards on the table and see where that got me. "I'm asking questions on behalf of the Vickers and have no intention of telling anyone we talked."

"Free advice?" The woman gave me a sweeping once-over. "I'd be careful before you go door-knocking, asking questions. First, you'll be wasting your time, as most won't want to get involved. And there's a couple of neighbors that can be guaranteed to hop on over to West's doorstep and tell all before you've even cleared the block." She put her tools back in a canvas gardening bag.

I stood. "Thank you for speaking to us; you can be assured I won't say anything."

She extended her hand for help up, which I provided. I grabbed the bag and handed it to her, then pulled a business card out of my pocket and put it in her hand. "If West bothers you again, give me a call. I'll send a friend or two, both built like brick outhouses, to have a chat. Can promise you he won't look your way after that."

She laughed. "If you go head-on with West, watch your back."

"Nice to meet you, and should we meet again and you don't want anyone to know that we've met, we're good at pretend." Fab nodded in agreement. "We'll follow your lead." I waved as she rounded the side of her house, and the two of us walked back to the car.

"So we've learned that West likes to get his own way and isn't terribly friendly about it," Fab said as she once again circled the block.

I was disappointed that nothing we'd learned could be used as leverage against him.

"Before I ask what's next, I'm going to need coffee," Fab said.

"That sounds good." It didn't take her long to cut across the highway and through the drive-thru, after which, she pulled up under a tree.

"What did you hope to accomplish?" Fab asked.

"I wanted to figure out how to get the best price for the Vickers. It appears that regular blackmail isn't going to work. Also ixnayed rent-a-thug, as I'm certain he'd go to the cops."

"Agree there."

"I'd like to help the Vickers not have to reduce the price *and* avoid having Crum and his friends involved, but I haven't come up with any way to do both, so I'm left to pull every juvenile trick I can come up with."

"Meaning what?" Fab demanded.

"I think pretending to be his new neighbor and being as annoying as possible is my best bet." I smiled as she laughed.

"That plan needs work." Fab drank her coffee in record time and snapped the lid back on.

"Now that I've had an infusion of caffeine, where to?"

"The Cottages."

Fab turned out of the driveway and cut through a residential neighborhood.

"You get an update on the Jimmy Jones case?" I asked.

"Eerily quiet. I do know that Jimmy's not in jail, which is a good thing." Fab braked for a mama duck and her six babies crossing the street single file. "Jimmy was put on immediate paid leave. There's a meeting next week, and he's been ordered to attend."

"They've probably got their security guys checking everything out. They'll find out that everything you handed to Mr. Allen is true," I said.

"I'd do the same. Let's face it, they don't know me." Fab waited for the last duckling and continued. "Since I know you're going to ask about Gunz, he's called a couple of times and I had to talk him down from confronting anyone. Told him he couldn't expect a quick response and to take it as a good sign that Jimmy wasn't in jail."

Chapter Twenty-Two

Fab pulled into the driveway of The Cottages and parked in front of the office. She nodded toward the rearview mirror. "Something must be going on, since Mac and Rude rarely hang out in the barbeque area." It was the best place to watch any action going down on the property, as long as it wasn't in the pool area.

I scanned the driveway, checking out the porches of every cottage, and breathed a sigh of relief that all appeared to be quiet. That could change in a hot second. "If someone jumps out of the bushes... you can handle it."

"Bad idea." Fab laughed, sounding maniacal.

We got out and crossed the driveway.

Mac unleashed a shrill whistle. "What brings you two here? Checking up on us?"

My attention was focused on the pink plastic pool that the two women had their feet in, filled with enough water to cover their legs to mid-calf. "What is that?" I pointed, knowing the answer but not the why.

"Got it at a yard sale around the corner," Rude said, proud of her find. "Had to haul it back by myself, and it smacked me in the head a couple

205

of times. Good thing it's not heavy." She brushed at her grey doo, which had a mind of its own today.

Fab poked me in the back, her way of letting me know she was laughing. The two of us sat on one of the concrete benches across from the women.

"We have a much nicer pool around the corner." I pointed, not that they didn't already know.

"It's a busy place these days; can't hardly catch a quiet minute unless you get up at the crack, and who does that?" Not her, Mac made it clear.

"How was the funeral?" Fab asked Rude. "My condolences."

"It was quite the sendoff. We were invited on this amazing boat, which cruised out into the Gulf, the water blue and calm. Once we were away from the shore, they handed out biodegradable balls filled with old Felix's ashes, and we got to pitch them into the water." Rude demonstrated. "I was a bit surprised, since I'd originally heard that they'd sprinkle the ashes directly into our hands for us to disperse." She didn't appear happy with the change of plans. "Cootie was relieved, since he worried that he wouldn't be able to get the ashes off his hands unless he leaned over the side of the boat and washed them off. He was afraid that, after tipping a few, he'd fall in. He can swim but doesn't like to."

"You should call the funeral guys. They're always looking for new ideas; maybe they'll name this new option after you," Fab said.

I turned and gave her a *Why are you being so nice?* look.

She answered with a smirky smile.

Rude clapped her hands. "That's a great idea. I'll do that."

"Any more wildlife issues?" I asked as I gave the driveway another quick scan for anything four-legged I might have missed.

"Got them all bunked down the road," Mac said, her tone conveying relief. "Nix has already had a first visit with her offspring. Before you ask how it went, I wasn't about to go there for fear she'd tell me and the conversation would never end."

"I asked, and she shared pictures with me," Rude said excitedly. "The animals have fit right in and even made friends."

Swell. "Any more issues before I get to why I'm here?"

Both women shook their heads, suspecting I was about to kill the joy for the day.

"Last count..." Mac waved her finger around. "Most of the guests are out by the pool. The regulars are sleeping off their drunk-on, which I prefer since they're easier to keep track of."

"Where's Crum?" I craned my head towards his cottage, knowing that I didn't have a clear view. "I need to talk to the man. I've got a job for him."

"You know he'll take it." Rude nodded. "Unless he's got to be fully clothed. If so, better be a short gig. He gets testy if he has to be covered for too long. Claims it makes him itchy."

"No worries there. He's going to love the uniform I have in mind," I said.

"Fair warning…" Mac held up her hand. "I'm hoping you don't shut down the fun when you get an eyeful of the pool action. Makes my job more difficult. Before you start complaining about my lack of rodeoing up the guests, the new offerings have been well-received, and it shows, since we're booked until oblivion."

"I can see you're overworked."

My sarcasm didn't slow her down. "Free tip: pull your sunglasses down off your head—wouldn't want you to burn your eyes." She made a sizzling sound. "Now that you've been warned, you should be able to fake your enthusiasm."

"I'm in the process of making a cutesy calendar for guest activities," Rude said, clearly loving her idea. "I'll email you a copy so you can keep track. You could stop by once in a while; the guests are always asking about you and would love to hang out."

"That sounds like fun." Fab smacked me in the back and traded smirks with Mac.

Rude didn't appear to notice that Fab answered for me.

"Since we're talking about social activities, there's one coming up that I may have failed to mention," Mac said, a sneaky smile on her face.

"No," I said emphatically. "You can blame everything on me since, knowing you as I do, you've already spread the news of this idea of yours and gotten everyone excited. I'll be the meanie. Won't be the first time."

"Just hear Mac out," Fab cooed sympathetically.

Mac and Rude both smiled at her. Leaning slightly forward, I flashed her the stink eye.

"I wouldn't want your hair to permanently frizz, but it's a done deal," Rude said, then attempted to flatten hers down; it still wasn't cooperating.

"I'm certain that you're mistaken, because Mac and I have an agreement not to jump the gun without running it past the owner first." I turned a fierce stare on Mac.

Thoroughly amused, Fab had a big grin on her face.

I squeezed my eyes shut, arms across my chest. "I've been known to be open-minded."

I don't know who snorted. Maybe all three. My eyes shot open.

"We've planned a weekend welcome event." Mac wiggled her finger between herself and Rude, then cut me off with a hand wave. "A boatload of Cruz Campion's relatives are all landing on the same day. You remember him—

the criminal lawyer you call when your butt is in the clink or about to be dragged off in cuffs?"

I groaned.

"Anyway, being an accommodating manager and always willing to give a hundred percent..." Mac preened.

"You're giving me a headache." I rubbed my forehead, which gained me no sympathy.

"The Campion relations — those that speak to one another — have planned a family reunion. All of them have stayed here in the past and, of course, loved it."

I was expecting a fist pump, but it didn't happen.

"Cruz actually made the call himself. He requested that I personally see to the details, knowing that I can bring the fun. You know I like to accommodate."

I caught Fab's garbled noise and looked down.

"Cruz's not asking for a freebie. No ma'am, and I didn't even have to strongarm him, which I wouldn't." Mac's cheeks pinkened at the idea. "The fun kicks off with the relations being picked up at the airport in the short bus, which will be tricked out into a party bus."

"I don't know how many are on the guest list, but is the bus big enough to accommodate them all?" I asked.

"Don't be a pooper." Mac reached down, cupped water in her hands, and splashed it across her face. "It seats twenty with some creative arrangement. They're not all arriving at the same time, but I'm sure I could shove them all in if they were. I also lined up a trailer to haul the luggage. If anyone's real drunk, I'll bring an air mattress, and they can lie out in the fresh air on the trailer, sober up some."

"That's illegal."

I was ignored as Rude added excitedly, "I wish we could turn it into a double-decker. Imagine the fun!"

"I think that's done at the factory, not after the fact." Imagining the guests falling off the second level into traffic had me wincing.

"And for the all-day tour of the Keys, we're renting a full-size bus," Rude continued, still ignoring me. "That way, we don't have to turn anyone from the neighborhood down."

That would be a shame. "How long is the Campion brood staying for?" I asked.

"A month," Mac said.

"Cruz ordered you to plan events for all thirty days?" Fab asked.

"He didn't specify, just told me to make sure they have fun. We've got plenty planned, and those that don't want field trips can stay here and sit out by the pool. Crum, who's a favorite, has been recruited to lifeguard—in addition to his classes, which he's ramping up—and hired a friend of his from Custer's to share the hours."

"This man, whoever he is, knows that he can't drink on the job, right?" I asked and was ignored again. "Make that very clear," I said, loud enough to finally catch everyone's attention.

"Both of you are invited, and bring the husbands," Mac said. "They'll be added eye candy."

"Why don't you call and extend the invitation?" Fab said, smirk in her tone. "While you have them on the phone, enlighten them as to all the sneaking around you've been doing. You know how they love that."

"Let's see if we can stay on track, since I'm now asking the question for the third or fifth time." Maybe not that many times, but all eyes were finally on me. "What is this event going to consist of?"

"Month-long fun and games, maybe not every day but close. I've got activities planned on and off the beach and here on the property." Mac smiled and nodded as she relayed her plans. "The weekend they arrive will be a special extravaganza. The driveway will be cordoned off, a guard will be stationed out at the entrance, and neighbors and any lookie folks will be told to scram, that this is a private event. Besides firing up the barbeque, there will be an open bar."

"What could go wrong in two days of partying?" Fab shook her head.

Drunks crowded around the pool, encouraging each other to do what the heck ever. Just great.

"If you're going to be inviting guests, send me

the names," Mac said to Fab and me. "I'm outfitting the guard with a clipboard so he'll look professional. I thought about a uniform, but wouldn't want him to sweat to death."

"What—"

Mac cut me off. "Before you tell me you're busy or whatever excuse you'll use, you're expected to put in an appearance so I don't have to come up with something sincere-sounding as to why you're so unfriendly."

"I thought you were talking about me, but you really meant Fab." I grinned at her.

"I'm expecting both of you to show up," Mac said.

"We're instituting a dress code for the month—bathing suits all day and night." Rude grinned. "If they're going on one of the road trips, all they'll need to bring is a cover-up or a shirt. That way, there's no problem getting into a restaurant or bar. Another option for fun is to hit the liquor store and drink on the beach out of a bag."

"Let's hope you've got a bondsman on speed dial." That earned me a couple of testy looks. "Also, remind the men not to forget their pants or they'll be sitting on the curb." Rude nodded, so one in my corner.

"Don't forget why you came," Fab reminded me.

I jumped up and adjusted my sunglasses. "Sorry to break this up, but I'm headed to the pool to talk to Crum."

"Do we get a heads up first?" Mac asked. "Run whatever scheme you've concocted by us for a vote?"

"Nope." I side-bumped Fab as she stood. "Let's make this quick. I could use something cold and tasty to drink." I waved as we cut across the driveway and rounded the corner to the pool.

Rock music wafted over to us. The oldsters were lined up, swinging and swaying, all wearing scraps of material covering just enough to keep them from getting arrested.

I skidded to a stop and stared, and after a minute, a slow smile formed on my lips. A tweak or two, and my plan instantly came together. I elbowed Fab. "Since my whistles are lackluster, can you unleash one and wave the professor over?"

Fab released one that was shrill and loud. Someone shut off the music, the pool area went quiet, and all heads turned our way. She jabbed her finger at Crum and motioned him over.

His feet slapped the concrete as he trotted over to the gate to meet us, a squinty look on his face. He stopped to adjust his bright-green sling bathing suit and, at the last second, pulled a t-shirt out of his backside and tugged it over his head. It would've spoiled any goodwill if I'd had to snap cover yourself up.

"Yes, ladies?"

"Would you mind joining us out here?" I

asked. Fab unlocked the gate and held it open. "I have a proposition for you." My motive for moving the conversation away from the guests was not wanting anyone to eavesdrop.

"Back in a few," Crum yelled to his groupies in and around the pool.

They watched him walk out, and once the gate slammed shut, the music went back on and they went back to yelling over one another.

"I have a job for you, not related to The Cottages. While I was planning it, your name came to mind as someone who could pull it off." I pitched my plan, wiping the suspicious look off his face and replacing it with a calculating grin.

"What's in it for me?" Crum asked.

"Name it, as long as you don't try to hold me up. If you do, that would put you on my s-list and I'd seek revenge," I said.

"To keep things a lot simpler, I'd just shoot you," Fab informed him.

The guests in the pool started yelling his name. "I'm in, and we can negotiate terms later." He turned and hustled back to his fans.

"You've lost your mind," Fab said as we turned to leave.

"If you have any better tricks to trot out, now would be the time to speak up."

We walked back to the SUV and waved to Mac and Rude, who were still hanging out by their pool and barely glanced our way, too busy kicking water all over one another.

"Aren't you going to..." Fab pointed to the women.

"Nope. The only thing either woman will hear is blah, blah, blah, and they'll be back to splashing one another before we get out of the driveway."

Chapter Twenty-Three

Fab's phone dinged with an incoming text. I snatched it out of the cupholder, not feeling the least bit bad about being nosey. "It's your gardener. Says there's a problem and wants you to come home. Waiting on your input. Urgent."

"Text him back: 'On the way.'" Fab made a U-turn.

"I wonder what's up." I sent the text.

"He's never done that before, so it must be important." Fab pulled up to the security gate, where a sedan neither of us recognized was pulled off to the side, a woman behind the wheel. We both kept an eye on her.

The gate opened. Fab pulled in and came to a stop, giving the gate just enough room to close. Long ago, we'd made a rule that anyone coming in would wait until the gate closed to discourage intruders. The sedan roared up behind us and honked. When Fab didn't move, the woman continued to lay on the horn.

When the gate was more than halfway closed, the woman jumped out of her car and made a run for it. Too late.

"Wonder what that was about?" Fab mused. "No time to find out now."

"I'm sending you a text to remind you to call Tank, since he's your friend." I smile shiftily. "Find out if we can shoot intruders."

"He's your friend too. Name one time he's refused to take your call." Fab sniffed. "As for wannabe uninvited guests, the standard is that we have to be in fear for our lives, not brushing up on our shooting skills."

"I'm thinking we should have a sign." I tapped my cheek. "'Trespassers will be blown to bits.' Or we could get a dog and not feed it; let it hunt for its own chow."

"When Casio approached me about getting a dog, I waffled. Now I think it should be allowed to prowl around and go anywhere it wants."

"Thanks for sharing when the dog subject first came up," I said in a faux snit. "I guess my input wasn't needed."

"What is it Mac says? Calm down before your hair frizzes."

I patted my hair and laughed despite not wanting to.

Fab pulled up to her house and parked. The head gardener dude and his guys—all brothers, cousins, or some such... family members anyway—were leaning against the side of a truck with a trailer attached that was chock-full of work equipment. They were loaded up and ready to go, except they'd never finished this early before — ever. It took his crew most of the day to keep the compound looking green and weed-free.

I was wracking my brain trying to remember his name; I didn't ask Fab, as chances were fifty-fifty or better that, even if she did remember, she'd prank me with the wrong name. We got out, and I pasted on a friendly smile, one that had worked for me in the past.

"What's going on?" Fab asked and looked around.

He motioned her to follow him to the street side of the truck. He stopped suddenly and pointed across the compound to the wall nearest Fab's house. "The reason I called you first..." He lowered his voice. "I don't want to be involved with the cops and hope you won't involve me." He gave her a squint that told her he expected that favor.

I followed his finger and couldn't figure out what he wanted us to see at first, then gasped. A man was nestled face down between the fronds of one of the small palm trees, bending the branches down. He wasn't moving. Bad sign. I suspected the news wouldn't be good.

"I don't want to be involved either," Fab snapped and took out her phone. Pictures from this distance wouldn't be the best.

The two engaged in a stare-down, communicating some shifty speak that I didn't understand. Finally, he asked, "We're good?" He didn't wait for an answer but beat it behind the wheel of his truck. The rest of his bros didn't need to be told and vaulted over the sides of the trailer. One got in the passenger seat.

I stepped up to the open window before he could roar off, and judging by the way he revved the engine, he was planning on doing just that. "There's some chick at the gate. Don't let her or anyone else in. Ever."

Both men nodded, and they took off.

"Hey, sweetums," I said to Fab, almost laughing at her raised brows. "Yes, you. I'm telling you now that we're not getting involved either." I edged my way toward my house. I'd fetch the SUV later.

She pointed at me. "Don't you dare…"

That trick got me to pause, at least, but wouldn't work for long.

"As soon as you report dead dude to 911, we're in it," Fab snapped.

"Nice try. I'm not the owner of this swanky piece of property, which just dropped in value thanks to whoever that is." I waved in his general direction, not wanting to take a second look, and took another step backward. "Do you want to hear my idea for foisting or not?"

"Oh, for Pete's—"

I cut her off. "Now, now. That sounds mean."

"What's your well-thought-out plan?" She sounded halfway amiable, except for the fierce glare, stuck-out chest, and hands clenched at her sides.

"When we came in, I noticed Casio's truck parked in his driveway. I volunteer to go roust him out and delegate." I didn't wait for an answer, and instead turned and ran down the road. Fab's screech was clearly audible as I veered into his driveway, bounded up the steps, and pounded on the door. Just in case he hadn't heard my first attempt, I kicked the bottom of the door. I was about to play on the doorbell when the door flew open.

Casio's enormous frame filled the doorway, smoke coming out his ears. If he had hair, it would be standing on end. "Whatever it is, I don't want to know. If you don't mind..." He had the door half-closed.

I stuck my leg inside and screamed out of frustration, not pain. "Your son just walked in the gate, and I was worried something was wrong, knowing it's a school day." I'd apologize and feel bad later. It would be easier to pawn the dead-body situation off on him once he was out of the house.

"What the..." He threw the door open—surprisingly it didn't hit the wall. He didn't bother with shoes, cleared the three steps in a leap, and ran down the driveway. He skidded to a stop and scanned the street, then hopped from one foot to the other as the cement started to burn the bottoms of his feet. "Where?" he bellowed.

I pointed in the opposite direction, quite certain he wouldn't see the body without closer scrutiny. "Sorry, I wasn't completely upfront." Okay, not at all. "The reality is that you're better equipped to handle a dead body than either Fab or myself."

Casio continued to scan the corner of the property, and once he spotted the body, he moved forward a couple steps, stopped, and turned tail, running back to his house. He reappeared wearing a pair of rundown tennis shoes half on his feet, phone in hand. He came up beside me and snorted. "How long has it been there?"

The better question was, how did it get there? Fab had moved closer and snapped more pictures.

"No clue." I shook my head. "Fab would be the one to ask; she could give her expert opinion."

I waved like a lunatic at Fab, who tromped through the grass back towards us. I hung back but could still hear their conversation.

"Another palm tree bites the dust," Fab said, and he responded with a silent, *So?* "Not quite sure how his body landed in that position. The gunshot wound makes it certain he didn't fall off the wall."

"You need to stand back; no more messing

around in a crime scene," Casio admonished her with a grin.

"I'm thinking, since you're the hotshot here, you can make the 911 call," Fab shot back.

He nodded and skirted around the area, getting a closer look before approaching the body and getting on his phone.

"I'm going to go hide in my house," I whispered to Fab and turned away. She grabbed my shirt and wrenched me to a stop.

"You're not going anywhere," she growled. "The cops and the dead-people unit are going to converge, and I'm not handling it by myself."

"That would be the coroner."

I ignored her eyeroll, and she ignored my *you should know that* tone.

"Our story is exactly what I told Casio. If you didn't get it all—"

I waved her off. "I got it. I'm thinking we don't have any reason to hedge on any facts. Unless that's your handiwork and you dumped him earlier in the hopes that the gardener would take care of it."

Casio's approach cut off her response. "What's on the other side of the wall?"

"It's an empty lot covered in trees and weeds. Not sure who owns it, as I never checked," Fab told him.

Fab's phone alerted us that the cops had arrived, and she opened the gate. Two cars drove in. Casio waved them down, and they parked in front of my house.

I moved out of the street, standing at the end of Fab's driveway. She joined me, and I nudged her and tossed my head back towards the front gate. The woman who'd been waiting outside in the sedan had followed the cops inside. She parked away from the houses, farther down the road, got out, camera in hand, and started frantically snapping pictures. Before I could stop Fab, she took off at a run and came to an abrupt stop in front of the woman. They attempted to shriek over one another, Fab pointing to the gate. I hotfooted it after Fab before fists started to fly. The woman didn't stand a chance.

The two were doing a dance, the woman attempting to skirt around Fab but being cut off at every turn. Suddenly, the woman yelped and bent down, then came back up, cradling her camera between her hands. It hadn't survived contact with the asphalt.

"Bitch," she hissed.

Fab got in her face. "You're trespassing."

I gently touched the small of her back as a reminder not to do anything felonious. "She's right; you need to take a hike before we press criminal trespass charges." I wasn't a hundred percent about that charge sticking, but it sounded good.

"Dense chick didn't react the first time, or the second, or even the third time I told her. She either wasn't listening or she's stupid. I bet on the latter."

I stepped closer to Fab. "Get in your car and leave now, or I'm calling the police."

The woman backed up and leaned against her car door, arms crossed. "There's two cops here already. Call one of them. I'm filing assault charges. Before I'm done, besides buying a new camera, you'll be writing a hefty check for emotional distress."

"You really are stupid. You trespass and you're the victim? Good luck selling that story to the cops." I turned to Fab. "Who is she?"

"We skipped introductions. It took great self-control on my part not to shoot her, but I'm out of patience."

The woman threw open the driver's door and hopped behind the wheel, hitting the locks.

"That's one way to get rid of her." I nudged Fab.

She started the car and hit the gas, leaping across the road, up and over the grass, and beelining it to the crime scene. Casio intercepted the woman as she got out her car. Not one to let a good fight pass her by, Fab ran after the car, and the threesome had a heated discussion.

I took my phone out and called Creole. "Are you back from one of your phony meetings in nowhere?"

He chuckled. "Would you believe that I just walked in?"

"No," I said, and he chuckled again. "There's a

dead body at the house, and if you want to be in the know, you better hustle your backside in this direction. The cops are here, but the coroner hasn't made an appearance, so there's still plenty of action to be had."

"What in the hell is going on?" He yelled for Didier.

"That's my ear. If I go deaf, don't whine when I tell you over and over, 'Can't hear a word you said.'"

"Are you done?"

Creole didn't sound terribly irked, so that was good. "You know I can keep it up."

He sighed. "We'll be right there."

"Woah. Before you hang up, heads up that we have a trespasser. A squatty blonde with a permanent snotty look affixed to her face. Thank goodness I was able to restrain Fab from beating the smack out of her, or worse." A little added drama to the retelling never hurt anything. "Don't be speeding; I've got my Glock to help me keep control. That should give you peace of mind."

Creole mumbled something, and then he and Didier laughed. I'd need to give him a reminder about telling me before putting me on speaker. "Do not shoot anyone," he said and hung up.

I turned and went to find Fab, who'd planted herself in a position to observe everything going on. "The guys are on their way," I called out and crooked my finger for her to join me, which she ignored.

Casio escorted blondie to her car, even opening the door. He crossed his arms and glared, conveying, "Beat it." She lost the flirty look and wrinkled her nose. She U-turned and drove slowly out of the compound, checking out the houses as she left.

Hopefully, he'd suggested that she not come back without an invite that she wouldn't get.

Fab waited for Casio to join her, and the two walked over. "That was a freelance news reporter," she said.

"She claimed to know about the dead guy, having gotten a tip," Casio said. "Carol Sand is her name. Wouldn't divulge her source. I suspect she was lying about how she got the information. She's looking for a high-profile story to parlay into a job, since she's not affiliated with any particular news outlet."

"Why didn't you shake the information out of her?" Fab demanded.

"I'm an ex-cop, and the current ones would not appreciate me meddling in their case. Carol claimed to be investigating the two bodies that were tossed on the dock. She got a local to do a drive-by from the water for a few bucks. Back on land, she cruised the strip of highway until she caught a break, driving by as the pool guy drove out from between the trees. Otherwise, she wouldn't have known that the turnaround was actually a road."

Fab shook her head in disgust. "How did you leave it?"

"Told her that it was an ongoing investigation and if local cops got wind of her interference, they'd arrest her. Probably not the first time she'll get a warning. Also warned her that if she ever came back, or I heard her name again, I'd press charges and had the clout to make them stick."

"This is a reminder that we need to be on alert, driving in and out," Fab warned.

"You got any info on John Doe over there?" I asked. "How he died? How he ended up in the palm tree?"

"You need to be patient, since the investigation just got under way," Casio said. "Once I find out anything, I'll keep us all updated."

Chapter Twenty-Four

I got up early and spread paperwork across one end of the island, reading the last of the reports that Xander had sent over. After yesterday, I'd be requesting more.

More cops had converged on the compound, and it took what seemed like forever before they dislodged the body and hauled the man off. Creole and Didier had arrived home and stayed outside until the last officer left. After one of the officers questioned me, Creole told me it would be okay to go in the house. I didn't hesitate and, on the way through, grabbed a cold drink and my laptop and headed out to the deck. Fab had stayed back with Didier, his arm hooked around her.

Creole finally came in the house, slamming the door. "Everyone's left. Didier and I hung out at the gate until the last vehicle went through. A couple more reporters showed up, but couldn't get past Casio. He made certain that no one else snuck inside and warned them that if they came back without an invitation, he'd rearrange their faces."

"If they're that stupid, they better hope they

don't run into Fab. Dead dude?" I grimaced.

"Didier and I were the ones to ID him — Rick Pierce, our previous trespasser."

I gasped.

"Feel bad for the man," Creole said. "I told him when we walked him back to his car that lying to whoever hired him would be bad for his health, and if he had anywhere to go, he might want to head out. But I figured a beat-down, not murder."

"I was sure he gave us a phony name, but Xander ran a check on him and it was real. He had a couple of misdemeanor arrests, but they were years ago. I can have him do more checking."

"I'm going to do a little digging of my own, starting with that scumhole bar. Hopefully, someone will remember him and talk."

"You need backup?" I flexed my biceps.

Creole's brows went up. Clearly he wasn't going for my offer. "The last place I want my wife hanging out is at a bar where trouble breaks out regularly."

"Management generally routes it out the rear exit and lets the brawlers finish it up in the alley."

He didn't give me an eyeroll, but close.

* * *

Creole came trudging down the hall, dressed for

the office. I slid off the stool and poured him a cup of coffee, setting it in front of him and leaning in for a kiss.

"What's on your agenda today?" I asked.

"I've got a meeting later. Before that, I'm going to get with Casio and see if his contacts have any updates about Rick Pierce."

"Three dead bodies and no connection to any of us. That leaves a big why unanswered."

"I won't stop digging until we get answers to all our questions, and I know Didier and Casio feel the same." Creole eyed my paperwork. "What are you up to? Can't be anything I don't know about, as that would be a violation of terms."

I laughed. "That sounds so... official." He hated non-answers. "I like to think of myself as flexible and able to adjust to the demands of the day."

"I can tell that I'm going to need more coffee." He grunted and crossed to the opposite counter to fill his mug.

I picked up my phone off the top of the stack of papers, scrolled through my screen, and made a call. "Hey babes." I tried for a husky sound, and it came out like I had something stuck in my throat. "The husband is getting ready to leave, can you come over?"

"What are you up to?"

"Stop by the Bakery Café and bring a box of delicacies to get me in the mood."

He groaned. "I know he's listening, and you're going to feel bad if we get into mutual body harm."

"I'll be waiting," I said, back to the husky tone that fell short of sexy.

"On my way." He laughed and hung up.

Creole banged his cup on the countertop and leaned in, nose-to-nose. "You auditioning my replacement?"

"Hmm…" I scrunched up my nose as though giving the idea some thought. "Wouldn't be easy." I slid off the stool, rounded the island, and kissed him. "You have a good day, dear."

He took out his phone and made a call. "What's going on?" After a minute, he ended the call with, "Later." He hauled a stool around and sat down. "Not going anywhere. I don't want to accuse you of being up to something, but you are, and I mean to find out what it is."

I laughed and made a fresh pot of coffee and didn't squawk when Creole flicked through my paperwork. "Xander does a good job." He looked up at me. "You're lucky I have a flexible morning or I'd be hauling you out of here to keep an eye on you."

"I'd enjoy the day more."

It wasn't long before the front door opened and Brad entered with two large pink boxes in his hands and set them down on the island.

"Just pretend I'm not here," Creole said. "I hung around for the food."

Fab came barreling through the patio door, out of breath. "What am I missing?"

"What are you doing?" I said back, ignoring her question.

"I saw Brad's car come through the gate and figured you forgot to call me," Fab said in an irked tone, her annoyance escalating.

There was a knock on the front door. Creole stood and headed that way.

"Your next guest isn't going to be happy," Fab whispered.

"Who?" I mouthed.

Brad, who'd been listening, lifted a mug and held it out to Fab. "Coffee?" he asked with a grin. She shook her head. He poured himself a cup.

"Didier's here," Creole announced as he came back into the kitchen, Didier two steps behind him. "Can you believe that Frenchie actually knocked and waited for someone to answer? Didn't use a lockpick or whatever." He glared at Brad and then turned it on Fab. "Or come barreling in the back way."

"All this drama is making me hungry." I patted the empty stool next to me. "I know I started it, but I just meant to tease you a little," I said to Creole. "And here we all are. I have an update for Brad, but we can do it later."

Creole grabbed a stack of dishes, silverware, and a roll of paper towels, which he tossed to Brad, who caught it and set it on the island.

Didier made another pot of coffee.

Everyone served themselves.

"No one has secrets in this family," Brad said. "You can share my personal life while we eat."

I winced. "That's not how I planned for this to go."

"Saves me from repeating everything." Brad sent me a reassuring smile.

"I don't have as much information as I'd like on Layne, but I do have a proposition. Before everyone's hair stands on end, and you know who I mean by that—" I glanced at Creole. "—I'm in the creative stage. I assure you that Fab is coming out to the Everglades with me as backup, as you all know I need someone who knows how to drive."

"I've never said that you don't know how; I'm just better," Fab said with a smirk.

"Happy we got that cleared up." I winked at her.

"Now, back to whatever it is you've got cooked up," Brad said.

"Layne Winters on paper is kind of a bore. No arrest record, which makes your sister happy." I made a face at Brad.

"Guess what? Me too."

"She doesn't have much of a credit report—no long list of credit cards—and I'm thinking it's because she pays cash. Another plus is that there's no record of her being committed."

Brad locked his eyes on mine. "There must be something."

"Nothing exciting. I did get an address for her family. Everglades City. Hence the road trip."

"Before handing over Logan, I'd like to meet them," Brad said. "Although it probably doesn't matter whether I like them or not. Probably won't have any other option."

"This is where my awesome plan comes in. Fab and I drive out to the Glades and do a meet-and-greet and check the situation out for you. That way, no weirdness. If the family is close, they must be concerned about not hearing from Layne and worried about their grandson."

"Or maybe they have heard from her and will be able to tell us how to get in contact," Fab said.

"As soon as we're out there, I'll call and give you a report. Then you can set up a meeting," I said.

"Truthfully, I'm fine with shoving it all in your lap," Brad said. "I'm not sure what I would say to her family. What if they think I had something to do with her disappearance?"

"We'll disabuse them of that notion. Besides, in addition to a note in her own handwriting, you have a notarized power of attorney," I reminded him. "Anyone else with an opinion, raise your hand."

"I want you to check these people out before you visit, and then plan your trip if there are no red flags," Creole said. "You're good at friendly and getting people to share most anything."

"If anyone in the family has any kind of

criminal record, we'll reconvene and decide on another plan of action," Didier said.

"All Xander found out so far is that the family owns a large parcel of land out in Alligator Alley. Surprisingly, like Layne, not a lot more information."

"I know Xander's thorough," Creole said, "but I'd appreciate if he'd double-check so you two aren't walking into any surprises. Even the most thorough of background checks can't apprise you of everything. But the more you know, the better."

"That's my update," I said, da-da-da in my tone.

"I've got one on Jimmy Jones, my client, who was being set up for a crime he didn't commit," Fab explained for anyone who didn't know. "The CEO turned my report over to his own investigation team, and they verified what I submitted. A couple of days ago, there was a meeting in the CEO's office after hours. Milton Track, Jimmy's boss, must have thought I didn't have the goods on him and that he was in the clear because he showed and, in fact, showed up at the office every day after I'd confronted him, like he'd done nothing wrong."

"I'd have thought he would've hightailed it out of town," I said.

"Track was presented with the evidence and given a chance to explain, and he choked his way through a partial explanation, realized that no one believed a word, and then changed course and threw himself on their mercy." Fab shook her head. "What he didn't know was that two of the men seated at the table were detectives, and they hauled him off in handcuffs."

"And Jimmy?" I asked.

"He was offered favorable terms for his resignation — in exchange for a signed non-disclosure agreement, he got a large severance package and a glowing reference."

"Why not keep him?" Brad asked.

"The CEO didn't want anyone associated with a theft on the payroll. Innocent or not, he didn't want to risk word getting out. Maybe he thought it would encourage others? Not sure. Another interesting tidbit is that two other people in accounting were fired. They weren't offered a sweet deal, but they also didn't leave in cuffs."

"What's next for Jimmy?" Creole asked.

"He's currently studying to take the CPA exam, which will get him an even better job," Fab said. "Gunz has great connections and can get him in the door of highly sought-after firms. Jimmy's smart enough to sell himself and seal the deal."

"One thing about Gunz, he does take really good care of his family," Didier said.

Chapter Twenty-Five

Fab and I put off our trip to Everglades City by a day, taking the time to re-read the latest information that Xander had dug up and make sure there were no red flags that I might have missed. It was a perfect day — baby blue skies with barely a cloud. We got off to an early start. We took Highway One out of town and cut over to another road that cut through the Everglades over to the west coast.

Eventually, I directed Fab to take the next exit. "Try not to fly down this road. In a mile or so, we need to be on the lookout for a turn-in," I said. There was one other car on the two-lane highway, going in the opposite direction. Thick rows of green bushes lined each side of the road, giving no clue as to what lay on the other side, if anything.

"Who lives out here?"

"People who want to commune with nature and do it with some privacy." I turned in my seat and craned my neck. "You missed the turn. Maybe. It was definitely a road, and we should check it out before looking for the next one. That's if there's one to find."

"This kind of privacy makes me wonder how this family is going to take to two strangers showing up on their doorstep. I think we should be careful not to let our guard down." Fab waited for a car that came out of nowhere and blew around us. She barely braked before making the U-turn and managed to stay off the grassy strip.

"That's why we're both going to trot out our charming and friendly selves." I pasted on a whacked-out smile that she caught out of the corner of her eye, judging by her smile. "We're leaving badass in the car. You are listening, aren't you?"

"I'm hanging on every word." Fab slowed and hung over the steering wheel. "Your turn to listen. Keep your gun handy. At the first sniff of trouble, we're going to jump in the car and skid back down that road, if that's what it is." She inclined her head to the other side of the road.

"It looks like the road's been upgraded with gravel over the dirt on the other side of the ravine."

Fab turned, cut across the grass strip, and eased into the dip, then back up onto flat land. The road disappeared into the trees, and we couldn't see where it led. "This is creepy."

I agreed with her.

The road slithered through the trees, past an open gate, and into a wide-open cleared space, a large modern farmhouse off to one side. The wrap-around porch overlooked a small pond with a dozen or more ducks hanging out on the banks. In the distance was a huge red barn surrounded by a fenced pasture, with three garages on one side that could easily house a dozen cars each. The rolling green land went back as far as the eye could see.

"This is a heck of a lot nicer than I expected. In fact, it's impressive," Fab said as she pulled up and parked.

We got out and walked over to the plant-lined brick path that led to the front door. The door opened, and an imposing man in short overalls, tufts of white hair sticking on end, stood in the opening and checked us both out. A yellow Labrador scooted around the man and skidded to a stop, sitting at his side. The man and his dog moved to the top of the six steps up to the porch. "You lost?" the man grouched. "How did you get in, anyway?"

I wanted to suck in a deep breath and instead pasted on a friendly smile and nudged Fab, murmuring, "Old men are your specialty, so you're up."

"Nice try." Fab stepped behind me.

"I hope we're not trespassing," I said. "There wasn't a sign. We're hoping this is the Winters residence?"

"Someone forgot to close the gate again," the man huffed. "Who are you anyway?"

He didn't deny that we had the right address. I took a step closer and continued to smile, hoping my cheeks didn't cramp. "I'm Madison, and I'm looking for Layne Winters."

The man continued his snooty appraisal of the two of us — how-to lessons from Fab wouldn't be needed. Unable to help myself, I returned the look.

"You've got some gumption; I'll give you that." He hawked spit into one of the three potted plants next to the railing.

"When the plant dies, you'll know why." I inclined my head towards the pot.

Fab knocked me in the back.

The front door opened again, and an older woman waltzed out in a tent dress splashed with paint, some would say a work of art. One arm was weighed down with an overloaded charm bracelet and several more bracelets, and her platinum hair was fashioned into a twist. "What's going on, Herb?"

That answered my question, as Herbert and Ines Winters were on title to this property.

"They're looking for Layne." He spit again, maintaining eye contact as he did it.

"You're a little late..." Ines Winters sniffed. "By two years. Dead and buried." She flicked her hand toward the acreage off to the side of the barn. "If you're a bill collector—" She gave me a once-over, as thorough as her husband. "— although you don't look like one—we're not responsible."

Dead? What the... "Are you certain?" I was

shocked and sounded it.

"I bet you're here about Cassie." Ines nodded knowingly and moved to stand next to her husband.

"If that's all, you two can leave." Herb pointed back toward the highway.

"Actually, I'm here about your grandson, Logan." I turned to Fab and telegraphed, *Help*.

Fab—who'd hung back, reluctant to move closer—stepped up and stood at my side. "We originally came here to locate Layne. I'm sorry to hear that she's passed on and we want to offer our sincere condolences. Logan is living with a friend, and we're here in the hopes of reuniting him with his family."

The couple stared as though dumbfounded. Ines finally broke the tension. "Come up and have a seat." She claimed one of the oversized chairs on the deck, her husband next to her, the dog never leaving his side.

"Did you have any questions about your grandson?" I was about to show them a picture, but stopped myself when neither said anything. Weirdness crackled in the air.

"Should we be contacting Logan's father?" Fab asked.

"He died in the same car accident as Layne. Our other daughter, Cassie, stepped up and took over the care of the baby," Ines informed us. "If there's an issue, you'll need to contact her."

I forced back anger at their lack of curiosity.

We were talking about their grandson. Didn't they want to know what was going on? It also hadn't escaped my notice—and I was certain Fab had also noticed—that neither had introduced themselves, nor were they interested in our names. If I had to guess, I'd say they were up to their earlobes in illegal. For that reason, I curtailed my interest in the rest of the property.

I decided at that point that I had nothing to lose by being direct—see where that got me. "Cassie and Logan were living in the Keys, and she befriended a neighbor, who also had a child and kid-sat on occasion. Several weeks ago, she left a goodbye note, leaving Logan with the neighbor. We're here to reunite him with family if that's possible."

No longer interested in making intimidating eye contact, Herb shifted his attention to the packet of chew he took out of his pocket, shoving a wad in his cheek. He licked the tips of his fingers and wiped them on his bib.

Ines reached out and patted Herb's hand, a calculating look in her brown eyes. "As you can see, we're both older and... have health issues. We're unable to care for a small child."

Both appeared damn healthy to me.

"We only met the kid once or twice," Herb grumbled.

"Do you have any interest in raising Logan?" I asked, hoping that I was wrong about the answer.

Fab broke the silence that hung in the air. "Do you have any way of contacting Cassie?"

It seemed more and more like Cassie wasn't coming back. The note she'd left had indicated the same thing, but I knew Brad still hoped she'd walk in the door.

Herb unleashed a loud snort. Except for the few noises that the man made, he was content to let his wife do all the talking.

"Cassie is what you'd call a free spirit," Ines said. "If she ditched the kid, that means she ran out of money. Probably cut off by the bank."

Fab shook her head. "We don't know anything about that." *But we'd like to* was left unsaid.

"Logan had a small trust fund, and regular payments were made to Layne, but one of the provisions was that those payments would stop if she died and the money would be transferred into another account that Logan can't access until he reaches eighteen. The bank must've found out that Layne was dead and cut off the cash."

Herb grunted. "Cassie assumed Layne's identity, as it was the easiest way to keep the kid and fewer questions would be asked."

I was surprised that they were sharing all this information, since what Cassie had done was a felony.

"Do you have another family member that would be interested in raising Logan?" Fab asked. "One that knows the boy would be helpful. How about Logan's father's family?"

Herb shook his head. "Don't know anything about them. We'd never met, as they weren't close."

"It's not that we're not interested; we're just not able," Ines purred. "It would be wonderful if Logan found a family to care for him."

"Just so I'm clear…" I started out testily and had to dial it back. "You have no interest in Logan, and there are no other family members that would be interested. Are you okay with him ending up in foster care? Possibly being adopted by strangers?"

"I'm sure they'd be able to find him a good home. That's what they're trained for." Ines smiled blandly.

"Would you be willing to sign papers releasing any claim on the boy?" I asked, catching Fab's look of surprise out of the corner of my eye.

"That would probably be for the best," Ines answered without a second thought.

Fab nudged my elbow and stood. "Thank you for your time."

Herb stood. "Now's the time to ask all your questions before you go skirting off," he said gruffly. "This is private property and the last time you'll find the gate open."

What the hell's the matter with you would end the meet-and-greet unsatisfactorily.

"Can I get your phone number, to give to the lawyer, so he can contact you when the papers are ready?" Fab asked.

That question set Herb off. Anger sparked in his eyes. "We really don't want to get involved in whatever trouble Cassie's got herself into. We'd appreciate your leaving. And remember we don't cotton to trespassers." He held his hand out to his wife as she stood.

"Nice meeting you," Ines said as she walked back into the house.

Herb and his dog stood in the doorway, a fierce glare on his face.

The last thing I wanted to say was "thank you," and when Fab tugged on my arm, I turned and left. Neither of us said anything as we walked back to the car under Herb's watchful eye.

"I couldn't bring myself to say 'nice to meet you' or some such," I said in an exasperated tone. "It never once occurred to me that they wouldn't have a scintilla of interest in their grandson. Not a single question about him. Just their 'don't bother me' attitude."

Fab U-turned and headed back to the highway. "We're being followed." She nodded to the rearview mirror.

I looked in the outside mirror and saw a younger man on a three-wheeler approaching our rear bumper. I pulled my Glock. "I don't know what he's up to, but he's not going to catch us off guard."

Fab maintained a slow, steady speed as she

cleared the trees. The highway was a few feet ahead of us. Once we crossed the ravine, the man got off his bike, pulled the privacy gate across the road, and attached a lock.

"Whatever they've got going on there is illegal, and they don't want anyone, including their own grandson, around," Fab said as she made the turn that would take us to the highway that cut through the Glades and back home. "As much as I'd enjoy a good snoop around, we're not coming back here. It wouldn't be good for our health."

"I agree with everything you said." I turned and looked out the window. "What am I going to tell Brad? He's not going to call Social Services."

"You're going to tell him the truth. Then suggest that he talk to a lawyer and figure out his and Logan's options. Not to be a killjoy, but I bet they suck."

I pulled out my phone and texted Xander: *Find out everything about Cassie Winters. ASAP.* I read it to Fab and hit send.

Almost immediately, I got an *On it* text back.

"You should also ask Xander to track down Layne's husband's family. Maybe they'd like to be involved with their grandson, although based on what Herb said, they had no relationship with the boy either," Fab said in disgust.

"Sounds like the only one interested in Logan was Cassie, and that was just for the money. I was hoping for a happy situation for him." I sighed. "Assuming everything we heard is true, who could make that up?" I called Xander instead of texting. "Sorry to be burning up your phone." He laughed. "Logan's situation just got way more complicated." I told him about Layne being dead. "Would you expand your search to outside Florida?"

"As soon as I've got anything, I'll call," Xander said, and we hung up.

"I need something super cold to drink." I flashed Fab a pitiful smile that earned me a laugh. "If you really want to be a good friend, let's go shopping."

"Sorry." Fab faux pouted. "No room in the schedule."

Chapter Twenty-Six

As Fab jetted down the highway back to the Keys, I whined enough that she finally pulled into a drive-thru and ordered hamburgers and my favorite strawberry lemonade. Just to shut me up. We ate in the car, which was something we rarely did. As I balled up the trash and got out to dump it, my phone rang.

Fab answered for me and handed it to me, already on speaker, when I got back inside. "You're not going to be happy."

I glanced at the screen — Xander. "Tell me Fab's full of it and she's just being mean."

"Don't get me in trouble with her."

We both laughed.

"Turns out Cassie Winters has a long arrest record under her married name, Field," Xander said.

I let out a long sigh. This day just kept getting better.

"She's been arrested for drugs and guns, and a couple of times, she had large amounts of cash on her that was confiscated. Here's the interesting part — all the charges were eventually dropped, except for a couple of really old ones. It's hard to believe, with so many charges, that there's not one conviction. Another interesting tidbit is that the other people involved did prison time."

"For my brother's sake, I don't want to think this, but I need to know. Can you check for a death certificate for Cassie?" A woman with that kind of track record could easily have ended up dead since she took off.

"I already made a note to myself, figuring you'd want to know," Xander said. "How did Brad meet Cassie/Layne?"

"Allegra Kent," I snapped. "The ex-FBI agent who's currently working for the Chief."

"Ran into her once. She looked pained to say hi, so now I ignore her and she's fine with that." Xander chuckled. "Be interesting to run a background check on her, see if there's anything interesting that's not classified."

"I wouldn't mind knowing the answer, except I don't want it to trigger some kind of alert that gets you in trouble." I hissed out my aggravation. "I hope I don't regret asking, but is there anything interesting going on at the office?"

Xander hesitated. "I've been sworn to secrecy. I overheard a conversation and was caught and told to mind my own business. I pretended like I hadn't heard a word, grabbed a snack, and lit out of there. In exchange for the hint I gave you, you need to keep my name out of any drama."

"No worries there." We hung up.

"That was rude of someone," Fab said. "What do you suppose Xander was talking about?"

"One way to find out. We'll use my needing to update Brad as the reason for a surprise visit to the office and, while there, find out about the other. If Lark knows, she'll tell us."

"Didier told me that he didn't think Lark would last a week, but now they really like her. The other day, she told someone, 'You should be nicer or I may never put your calls through,' and hung up. Didier clapped."

"Survival in Florida is not for the weak. A hint of niceness, and the locals will see it as an invitation to walk all over you. Learned that fast."

"Thanks to me and those badass lessons I gave you, and now look at you." Fab laughed.

"I'm positive that I've said *merci* for that six or seven times. Maybe more. And thanks to you, I'm bilingual."

"Don't blame that on me."

I laughed.

Fab morphed into her Queen of the Road attitude and burned it back to The Cove. She hit the Welcome sign, took a shortcut or two, and cruised into the parking lot of the office, opening the security gate from a half-block away. Because why wait? She parked, and we got out and were halfway across the parking lot when Arlo flew out from under the roll-up door and skidded to a stop for a head scratch. We both complied; then he beat it over to the fence to check for squirrels and other bugs.

"What's new?" I yelled, walking into the Boardwalk offices and eying Lark, who waved and then pointed to the guys, who were gathered around the conference table.

"That's subtle," Fab whispered.

I wandered over and kissed Creole's cheek, then leaned over his shoulder to read his paperwork. Boring. I smiled at Brad and sat next to Creole.

Fab kissed Didier and claimed a chair next to him.

"We went to Custer's this morning," Didier told us, indicating that he meant him and Creole.

I leaned down and looked under the table. "Dressed like you are now?" Both had on jeans and dress shirts. Neither were amused. "I bet you didn't get squat in the way of information." It would be mean to say *I told you so*.

Didier shook his head. "There's always something positive to be gleaned from any situation."

"Didier's been brushing up on self-help advice on the internet again." Creole laughed.

Didier unleashed a flood of French on him. Creole and Fab laughed, so I knew it was a good one.

"Custer's a condescending, uppity pain-in-the-ass, and it surprised me when he turned down cash," Creole said. "Once we asked about Rick Pierce, his attitude turned downright frigid. Claimed not to know the man and said if we weren't drinking… get out."

"I assured the man that we were trying to find Rick's killer," Didier said. "He snorted and shot back, 'Sometimes you need to mind your own damn business. I wouldn't tell you even if I knew, which I don't. You should heed my words; it's healthier.'"

Fab shook her head. "One look at you two, and Custer knew that neither of you were regulars. Probably had you pegged for cops. Him, anyway." She raised her eyebrows at Creole.

"Creole disabused him of that notion." Didier laughed.

"Threatened to sic the cops on him, and he laughed. I leaned over the counter. That wiped the smile off his face. He reached for something, and I told him, 'I wouldn't if I were you.' That stopped him." Creole was clearly aggravated.

"That's when he pointed to the door and ordered us out, threatening that he'd be the one to call the cops," Didier said.

"I told you Custer was tetchy and wouldn't take kindly to strangers wanting information, especially in light of a murder," Fab said.

"I didn't like your idea of confronting the man yourself."

"You underestimate your wife's charm with

crotchety old men." I smiled at Didier.

"Listen up, you two." Creole smacked his hand on the table. "If my instincts are right about where you two think the conversation is going, neither of you is to go confront that man."

"Look, surly…" I winked at him. "You just don't want us to show you up."

Creole snorted.

I mimicked Creole and slapped my hand on the table, but not as hard. "A little wager? Dinner? On the water, yum food, and no paper plates or plastic."

Creole sniffed the air. "I smell a setup, so no."

"Bawk, bawk."

"It's better when you flap your arms." Lark demonstrated, leaping around the room.

Everyone laughed.

The side door opened, and Allegra came swooping in with a nod to the room and went over to Lark. She lowered her voice so we couldn't hear.

I glared at her.

Fab nudged me with her foot.

I stood and kicked back my chair. "Allegra," I said in a surly tone, louder than necessary, "your mooching days are over. Next time you need something, go to the store."

The guys' mouths dropped open.

Allegra nodded and, without a word, moved toward the door.

"Hold your horses, girlie," I barked. "Before

you trot on out of here, I've got a couple questions."

"Maybe another time; I need to get back upstairs." Allegra's hand was on the knob.

I drew my Glock and put a bullet in the wall. Oh well, needed to be christened at some point. "I won't miss if I have to take another shot."

"Bitch," she hissed.

"You bet I am," I hissed back. "Why don't you tell us all what you know about Cassie Winters? I'm betting you knew that she was using her dead sister's identity when you introduced her to my brother. As if that's not bad enough, no warning that she's got a criminal record a mile long." Convicted or not, no one gets arrested that many times without being hip deep in trouble.

"How would I know any of that?" Allegra returned my glare.

"How indeed? You may be a bitch, but you're not stupid. Ex-FBI and all, or are you? No way are you going to let someone live with you, however temporarily, when you don't know their background. Or is Cassie part of some case you're working, and Brad was just a handy tool?" I'd long lost the struggle to dial back my anger and ended up shouting at her.

"I honestly—"

"Honest," I cut her off. "That's a laugh."

Creole stood and put his hand on my arm, and I pushed it away. "I don't know what's going on between you two, but you need to leave," he told

Allegra, pointing to the door. "We'll figure this out when everyone is calmer."

Everyone? He meant me. "If you were any kind of human being, you'd tell Brad what you know," I yelled as she walked out the door and it clicked shut.

Brad pointed to my chair. "Sit. Tell me what happened today." He walked over to the fridge and grabbed cold waters, bringing them back and setting them on the table, handing one to me.

"Thanks." I unscrewed the top and downed half the bottle in an attempt to calm my temper. I told him about the trip to the Glades, then paused to drink more water. Fab picked up the story and filled in a few more details.

"What's going to happen to Logan?" Brad demanded.

That was a first on the day — someone asking about the boy and his welfare.

"Get an appointment with Tank, and he can go over your options and recommend whatever kind of attorney you'll need," I said. "Xander's going to attempt to locate Cassie. You should have that information before making any decisions."

Brad nodded. "I talked to Tank a couple of days ago, but now we know that Cassie had no authority to do what she did. My options were slim at the time and are probably nil now. The state will step in and take custody."

"I'm guessing that Cassie didn't get legal

custody of Logan. Not with her record. Another thing I can have Xander check out."

"The Winters are not the least bit interested in raising the boy," Fab told him. "And the other grandparents are who knows where."

"Do they know about me?" Brad asked.

"They didn't ask a single question about who had their grandson. Fab and I are in agreement that they're doing something illegal and don't want to be bothered because they'd come under scrutiny and whatever they're up to might be discovered."

"Have you decided what outcome you'd like to have happen?" Fab asked Brad.

"This morning, I wanted Layne to come back. Now I find out that she has no more claim to Logan than I do. What a mess." Brad looked sad and overwhelmed. "I'll be having a talk with Allegra, and if she was using me, or worse Logan, having her next door will be damn awkward."

"Say the word. I have movers that can box her junk and have her out by the end of the day." I trotted out my demented smile.

"You behave yourself." Brad shook his finger at me. "Allegra might shoot you just because, so stay away from her."

"We're going to figure something out." I stood. "I need to go upstairs and talk to Xander."

Creole stood. "I'm escorting you. I don't want you stopping on the second floor and getting in a shootout. I don't want to visit you in prison."

"Allegra's gone," Lark informed us. "She was upstairs long enough to grab her purse and then flew out to the parking lot."

I walked around the table and put my arms around Brad, who'd stood. "Call me anytime. Don't worry."

"You're the best." He hugged me hard.

Chapter Twenty-Seven

I had my day all planned out. Creole had gone to the office, and I took a bottle of iced tea and my laptop out to the deck, hoping for a few hours of peace to get some work done. Hopefully, no dead bodies would turn up. It wasn't long before I caught movement out of the corner of my eye and looked down the beach to see Fab taking her aggressions out on the sand, kicking it everywhere. I continued to watch as she got closer and climbed the steps.

"If you want something to drink, help yourself before you sit down. I'm not getting up." I added a smile to my snarky tone.

"Some hostess you are," she said and threw herself down in a chair next to me.

"You're hardly a guest; more like a fixture."

"We need to go back to morning meetings." Fab kicked her feet up on the railing. "Good food is a distraction from any less-than-pleasant news."

I groaned. "You must be up to something. We updated our husbands on yesterday's trip, and nothing has happened since then."

"We've got a busy morning, and it's important

that we leave ASAP to make our meeting on time."

"You must be mistaken about this 'we' business, since I don't know what you're talking about."

"You know I'm not supposed to go out on a job without backup, and that's you. Not to worry. I'll update the guys... but after. We can point fingers, saying we each thought the other called with the update."

Fab's smile alerted me that she was up to something, but that radar had gone off already. "Apparently, you've forgotten the part where you're expected to pony up details before you venture off or it could get you locked in the house. Not that I'd mind being under the watchful eye of Creole for a couple of days with no interruptions."

Fab rolled her eyes. "Focus." She snapped her fingers. "Don't take away my great enjoyment in dancing those two around."

"How do I put this and sound nice? What the heck are you up to?"

Of course, she ignored me.

Fab gave my t-shirt dress and bare feet a once-over. "Put something cute on, gun up, and don't forget your tennis shoes."

So much for my quiet morning. Tennis shoes was code for the possibility of running for our lives. "I want you to learn from my example." I stood and gathered up my paperwork. "Look at me—no whining, no complaining, just going to where the heck ever and trusting we'll get back in one piece." I had a pretty good idea where we were headed and hoped it wouldn't be a time-waster.

"I'll pick you up out front, so don't drag your feet."

I turned and went into the house as she headed down the stairs. Back in my bedroom, I decided on a full skirt and a short-sleeve top that would cover the Glock at the small of my back and, as requested, slid into a pair of tennis shoes. I shoved a pair of flip-flops into a tote and went out to the front, where I knew Fab would be waiting—somewhat impatiently, even if she hadn't started to honk yet.

"How about rewarding my cooperation with some details about where we're going?" I said as I slid into the passenger seat. If I was wrong, I still had time to jump out of the car.

"We're going to go hit up our friend Custer for information."

I knew it. "Friend, huh? I could pick him out of a lineup, if that qualifies as a friend; you're the one that can chat the man up without risking bodily harm. It didn't escape my notice that you didn't share that tidbit with Creole and Didier."

"The best way to approach Custer is with zero expectations. However, it turns out, you won't feel like it was a wasted trip."

"Do you have a game plan? It's been a while

since we put in an appearance at that hole-in-the-wall. I don't remember if we left on good terms the last time. Though I do know we didn't shoot the place up." I'd already come up with an explanation for Creole—a sweet smile, and an "I didn't know what she was up to until we were on the road." I didn't need to mention we were pulling out of the driveway at the time.

Custer's had a reputation for fistfights, not exchanges of bullets, so being gunned up was just an added precaution.

Fab pulled out to the highway and cruised in the direction of the bar.

It surprised me when she blew past it. I pointed over my head. "You missed the driveway."

Instead of making a U-turn, Fab turned into the neighborhood. "I'm thinking we park a block or two behind the place, cut across a couple of properties, and use the kitchen entrance off the alley."

"Better yet, we could stick to the sidewalk."

"You know there aren't any. Our only other option is the middle of the road." Fab easily found a parking spot.

We got out and hiked down the block, cut down a path belonging to a four-plex, and ended up in the alley. It surprised me to see the kitchen door propped open and no one in sight. Fab led the way into the bar, where we found Custer watching television—a bickering family drama.

He caught sight of the two of us and hit the remote.

After a once-over of the interior, I ascertained that nothing had changed since our last visit. The odd assortment of furniture was clearly more worn, and nothing matched. The floors hadn't been cleaned since the last time we were here. Three locals were sitting at the outside bar nursing beers.

"What do you want?" Custer growled. His gaze ran over the two of us, stopped briefly on me before dismissing me, and zeroed in on Fab.

"Information." Fab put up a hand as he opened his mouth. "Before you launch into some diatribe about not knowing anything, you and I know that's a lie. What we do know is that in the unlikely event that you didn't know, you could find out."

He actually preened at that. "Here's a tidbit for you. You can lengthen your lifespan considerably by keeping your mouth shut."

"Let's make this quick so you can go back to working hard and we can get out of here." Fab reached into her pocket, and his brows shot up. She held up her hand, stuffed with cash. "Rick Pierce. What do you know about him and his murder?"

"He's far more popular dead than he ever was when he sucked air. You're not the first to come in here asking questions. What's up with that?"

"Your friend Rick told more than a couple of

people that all he had to do was hang out here and he could pick up odd jobs."

"You and I have known each other awhile, though we don't tend to acknowledge the relationship, and it's in our best interest to keep it that way. You want it plain and simple? Don't stick your nose into that man's death. He was a braggart, hanging with dirtballs, and thought himself invincible. Look how that turned out."

"I'm not paying for 'mind your own business' advice. I hear that all the time," Fab told him in a snooty tone.

Custer smirked and held out his hand. Fab slapped the cash in his palm. He thumbed through it, counting, and when done, shoved it in his pocket. "It all has to do with the old Theodore Roberts case. You might want to do your homework. Several guys formed a criminal enterprise and did what they wanted for a couple of years until the cops brought it down. Roberts took the fall. The others turned state's evidence. Roberts got a life sentence, but recently got out, after which his associates met untimely deaths."

Just great.

"So you'll feel like you got your money's worth..." Custer smiled at Fab. It was smarmy and made me happy I wasn't the recipient. "After he got out, Roberts had plastic surgery, so don't expect him to look like his mugshot. It's not all fun and games behind bars."

"Are you telling me that this Roberts character

had something to do with the dead bodies piling up?"

Custer shrugged. "I would never speculate." That smile again. "I'd offer you a drink, but I know you're in a hurry."

"Was Rick part of this group to begin with?"

Custer ignored me, his eyes not leaving Fab's face. "Word has it that he got paid for a job and didn't deliver."

"Does Roberts still frequent your establishment?" Fab asked.

"On occasion. If you come in and confront him, don't say you weren't warned. Why would you anyway? I never heard of a relationship between you and Pierce."

"His sister hired me to check out his death," Fab lied.

Let's hope the sister news didn't get back to Roberts, because if had one and went looking for her, he might kill her.

"Thanks for the information." Fab waved.

Custer grunted. "Where are you parked?" Fab told him... sort of, pointing in the opposite direction. "Good. You never know who has an eye on the parking lot. You ever bring the cops here, you're no longer welcome and will be booted out the door next time you show your face."

"We'll just show ourselves out the same way we came in." Fab grabbed my arm, and we hightailed it to the exit. Once outside, we turned in the direction Fab had indicated and walked a bit; then, after a quick scan of the alley and adjacent properties, doubled back. We didn't run the entire way, but close, in agreement about getting out of the neighborhood as fast as we could.

"Pierce got himself killed for a hundred dollars," I said once we were in the car. "Let's hope he didn't brag that he talked to us."

"I'm thinking the body dump was a warning to mind our own business." Fab turned onto the highway and headed toward home. "Let's hope this Roberts character hasn't figured out who lives in the compound. It wouldn't be easy to get the information from public records."

"The conversation you just had leaves us with more than a few questions." I picked up my phone and shot off a text to Xander for a report on Theodore Roberts, his crimes, and where he was now. "Now what?"

"You can be the one to inform the husbands that we won the bet and got information out of Custer."

"They're not going to be happy. I say we pick the restaurant and trick them into showing up, then stick them with the check."

"I'm suggesting a little tweak to your idea — we hold off until you get the background check back on Roberts, so we don't have to say 'I don't know' over and over."

Chapter Twenty-Eight

It took Xander a couple of days to complete the report, which surprised me. He was excited when he asked for the extra time, so I didn't squash his enthusiasm with "Hurry up." I told Fab to lay off scaring him, as he was the best at ferreting out information, minus the stuck-up attitude of those we'd used in the past.

We decided it was a good time for our surprise dinner, since we knew that Creole and Didier were coming home early. Fab chose The Shrimp Company, a restaurant located in a marina, which hung out over the water and boasted outside dining.

On the drive down, I asked, "What's the ruse going to be to get them to drive down here without asking questions? Besides yelling fire." It was the next town down, and although it was a short drive, they would want some kind of explanation.

"I did the hard part and found us a new restaurant. The rest is up to you."

I laughed. "So nervy. Let me guess, you exerted yourself and called Mother?"

"You know, she's the best for a

recommendation. Says the food is excellent."

"Nothing so far." I tapped my temple, enjoying Fab's smirk. "If your plan is to claim ignorance—'I had no idea what she was up to'—the guys aren't going to buy a word of it."

"Don't look at me." Fab half-laughed. "Let's hope this is one of those fun-and-games scenarios that ends well." She winked.

Fab easily found the square turquoise cement building and pulled into the parking lot. The bottom level of the two-story building was a bait store with a drive-up ramp for boaters. The restaurant was on the second floor, with seating wrapped around the deck that overlooked the water, where customers could watch the boats going in and out of the marina.

Fab had shown up at my door in a black dress that molded to her body, and I'd chosen something similar from my closet. Where we differed was Fab had on heels and I'd slid into wedge sandals.

"Let's go upstairs and snag the table with the best view, order drinks, and I'll call and request a ride, since we've been drinking. If Creole hesitates at all, I'll tell him, 'No worries, the nice man at the next table can drive us home.'"

"This is a really stupid idea."

I agreed, but we were here. "Two or three drinks from now, it'll be the best idea we've ever had."

We laughed as we climbed the stairs and

scanned the deck, asking the hostess for a corner table with a view of the water. A hottie server grabbed up menus and seated us himself.

"What would you like to drink?" he asked.

"I'll take a pitcher of margaritas, and she'll take a pitcher of martinis," I ordered. "With a side of olives and cherries."

He laughed. "Be back."

Once our drinks arrived, I downed half the glass, then took my phone out, called Creole, and hit speaker. "I'm going with the truth."

"You're no fun." Fab shook her head with a laugh.

"Hi, babes."

"Didier and I were just wondering where you two were. Headed home?"

"You know that bet that you wouldn't agree to... not in so many words anyway."

"You better not be at Custer's," Creole grouched. "You're on speaker."

"So are you. Anyway, did we fail to mention that little meet-and-greet was a couple of days ago?" Creole and Didier both groaned. "You want the juicy info? Go to the address Fab is texting Didier." I nodded at her to do just that. "Be prepared to pay up."

"This is underhanded, and Didier and I aren't caving to blackmail, so we'll see you when you get home."

"Fine. We're going to finish up our pitchers of drinks first. Then I'll hit the guy at the next table up for a ride. He's been flirting heavily; he'll jump at a twofer." Fab shook her head. "See you later, hon." I hung up before my cheeks caught fire.

"When they get here and there's no one sitting at the tables on either side of us, then what?"

"We had to turn down the sweet man, and he left." I downed my drink. "Liquid courage," I toasted to Fab's raised eyebrows. "I'll drink the next one slower, so I don't slur my words, relaying all the information we've compiled."

We sat and sipped our drinks, watching the boats come and go.

"So, have you finalized your plan for dealing with Travis West?" Fab asked. "The taco people must be getting antsy."

"I'm going to start squatting on the property, become a nightmare neighbor, worse than the Taco Bar, and hope he makes a good offer," I said. "I'm kicking my plan into action with the help of Crum this weekend. I hope you're going to stop by and lend your support."

"Probably not." Fab turned up her nose. "But then, if I don't show, something good will happen and I'll have missed it. So maybe."

Creole and Didier walked out, beers in hand, and crossed the deck.

"Nice glares, you two." I gave the men a thumbs up.

"Didn't we tell you not to go question Custer?" Creole asked.

Didier nudged Fab.

She turned a seductive smile on him, which he clearly enjoyed. "I didn't hear any such thing out of either of you. What about you?" Fab asked me.

I shook my head. "You two are just irked that the sexy one got information out of the crusty man. If I could take credit, I would."

"How do you know him?" Didier asked, staring down at her, surprise in his voice.

"I'll admit to me and Custer being acquainted." Fab sniffed. "What I've done a time or two in the past is buy information, and the other day was the same. If he trusts that you're not going to bring the cops around, he'll take the cash." She stared Creole down.

"Obviously neither of you has a sense of humor about being tricked into dinner with your wives, so how about we just enjoy the food?" I said. "This was my no-so-hot idea, so direct your surliness my way."

"Enjoying the food is something we can agree on," Creole said.

Didier pulled Fab to him and whispered in her ear, and she smiled at him.

"You're going to be a little less surly when you hear what Custer had to say, or rather, what he told us to look into." Fab raised her eyebrow at me, a signal to impart the details. That was a surprise.

"Okay, I'll start. Although Custer only had eyes for Fab." I winked at her. "He dropped a name—Theodore Roberts—and told us to do our own investigation. Xander really got into this search request, donned his PI hat, and investigated every person linked to the man." I telegraphed *your turn* to Fab and finished off my drink. Creole refilled my glass with a wink.

"Turns out Roberts headed up a group of criminals that trafficked drugs through the Gulf from Mexico. The Coast Guard caught wind and busted their boat. The driver, in exchange for a deal, gave them names. And the two guys that were dumped on our dock were picked up by the authorities and made the same deal. They all turned on Roberts."

"I don't like where this is going," Creole said. "It's not a name I recognize, but I can hit up some law enforcement sources and find out more."

Fab nodded. "I scrutinized the pictures of the dead men that Xander sent over. I may be bad with names, but I'm good with faces, and I haven't met a one of them before. I never knowingly took a case that had anything to with drugs. One case, a couple tried to pull one over on me, having me transport coke, and I dumped them."

Didier covered Fab's hand with his own.

"The quick version, since I'm planning to send over the mammoth report so the two of you can peruse the fine details—" Fab eyed Creole and Didier. "—is that the two tossed out of the boat were apparently his right-hand men and testified to everything they knew in exchange for lenient sentences. As it turned out, they got a slap on the wrist."

"They must have had some damn good information," Creole said. "I don't know a district attorney that likes those kinds of deals."

"A number of people ended up going to jail, but not for the same fifty-year sentence Roberts got."

The server came and took our orders.

"There's more. The three dead men found in the house that Gunz had his eye on also worked for Roberts and, at the time of their death, were associates of the other two men. They'd regrouped and were back to running drugs again, but on a smaller scale," Fab said. "That last tidbit came from a cop source via a friend of a friend of Xander's."

"The cops put one drug operation out of business and, unfortunately, more established ones take up the slack," Creole said.

"Are you in any danger?" Didier put his arm around Fab, pulling her head to his chest.

"Hard to know," Fab said. "I'm going to give Casio a heads up, and all of us need to stay on alert."

I nodded.

"How did Roberts get out of jail?" Creole demanded.

I patted his arm, and he took a breath.

"His conviction got overturned on appeal — his legal team was able to prove the witnesses lied about some events."

"Roberts gets out of jail and kills off his associates, guaranteeing that not only will he go back, but he'll get the death penalty this time," Didier said in exasperation. "You'd think he'd know he'd be at the top of the list of suspects."

"That many dead bodies... it wouldn't surprise me if there were more." Creole shook his head.

Fab nudged me under the table. "Interestingly enough, there were no follow-up news articles on any of the men that turned up dead," I said. "As for Roberts, he disappeared after getting released from prison. Custer says he's had plastic surgery, so even though Xander sent over his mugshot, we have no idea what he actually looks like now."

"Did Rick Pierce also work for Roberts back in the day?" Didier asked.

"Xander didn't find any record of that. According to Custer, he didn't deliver on the job he was hired for and Roberts wasn't happy," Fab said. "I'm only guessing, but it wouldn't surprise me if, under the threat of death, Pierce told the man everything he knew about where we live... then died anyway."

"Why dump the body in the compound?" Creole asked. "Normally it would be a message, but since none of us have had any dealings with any of these men, it makes no sense."

"The news did say that a woman witnessed the bodies being dumped," Didier reminded him. "If Roberts thinks he was seen disposing of his victims…"

"I'll get with Casio and make sure he's not withholding information," Creole said.

"Xander has an alert if anything pops up in the news, and so far, nothing." I turned a smile on Fab, silently asking, *Did I forget anything?* A slight shake of her head told me, *No.*

At last, our food arrived, and it not only looked good, it also smelled yum.

"One more thing before we table all this unpleasant talk," Didier said. "Can you two raise your right hands and swear to stop looking for trouble?"

"We'll do our best. How about that?" I gave him a sneaky smile.

"Don't be shocked when we're forced to resort to underhanded tactics." Fab smiled up at him. Game on for those two. They'd both enjoy every moment.

"I've got my eye on you," Creole whispered in my ear.

Chapter Twenty-Nine

Fab and I had been on our best behavior the last few days, reassuring our husbands we weren't out looking for trouble and, in a show of good faith, maintaining a low profile.

That was about to end. It was party day at the old Taco Bar property. My plan was to make such a nuisance of myself that Travis West would make a generous offer on the land. I'd spoken to a real estate agent about putting it up for sale and was informed that it was a useless strip that couldn't be built on and basically, "Good luck." I checked with a friend who worked in the office of the County Code Department, and he said it was unlikely a building permit would ever be issued. I ran Plan B by him, and he laughed. "Mind if I stop by?" The more the merrier.

Fab never mentioned the big day, and I figured that was her way of saying, "Thanks, but not going," without actually having to say it.

Creole kissed me before going out the door. "Know that I'm always good for bail money."

I made a face, and he laughed, getting in his truck.

I wasn't far behind, arriving at the property after Crum, who'd arrived early, parking a motorhome on loan from Spoon. A customer had garaged it at his business and gave permission to use it for a few days. Less would make me happy.

Crum had set up large umbrellas, tables, and chairs, all lined up to overlook the strip of water, then set up a makeshift bar and hauled several ice chests out of the motorhome.

I parked across the street and got out, then stepped back as the short bus rounded the corner and cruised to a stop, Cootie behind the wheel. He opened the door, and a line of scantily-clad men and women stepped off, drinks in hand.

Cootie U-turned and pulled into Travis's driveway, using it to turn around, then parked in front of his house.

Mac arrived in the hearse and got out, along with more barely-clad people. I recognized a couple from the neighborhood. Not certain where she recruited the others. She let out a shrill whistle for help, and a couple of men hustled over and offloaded several more ice chests that I knew held a variety of beers and soft drinks. Two surprises: Mac was driving, and who knew the hearse was available to borrow? When Rude found out, she'd be planning a death tour.

I didn't see where the boombox came from that now sat in the middle of one of the tables, blaring music. The guests grabbed drinks and swayed around, clinking beer bottles — the official start of the party. They'd all been told to make a spectacle of themselves, but not to venture into anything illegal.

Last but not least, the lime-green food truck that I'd hired to cook up greasy food on demand rumbled up and shared the parking lot with the motorhome.

The party atmosphere was in full swing. A few of the men gathered around one of the tables and got a card game going. Wearing his tighty-whities, which weren't on the banned list for the day, Crum started a conga line. The revelers sang at the top of their lungs and danced around the perimeter.

I had to admit that I was in awe of how quickly everything came together. I crossed the street and joined Mac, who was leaning against the hearse, which I refused to do, instead standing about a foot away.

"Next time, I'm borrowing a casket, making it the centerpiece for the table and loading it up with drinks. Once the funeral guys hear that idea, you can bet it will debut at the next send-off," Mac said, proud of her idea.

"Do you worry about your mental health when you come up with one of these ideas?" I asked.

"You've got some nerve." Mac laughed, her girls jiggling around in her *I'm hot* t-shirt. "You apparently need to be reminded that you organized this fun fest."

"Fingers crossed—" I demonstrated. "—West gets a look at the fun and frivolity, flips his stick, and hustles to the Vickers with an offer. Creole already warned me that this gig has a time limit. I don't relish the thought of coming back here day after day, and I'm not certain how much the antics can be ratcheted up to keep folks interested."

"It's nice what you're doing, since most people would tell the Vickers to deal with their own problems."

"I'm just hoping it works."

"I was just about to ask after your cohort." Mac pointed to the Porsche that screamed around the corner and squealed up to park behind the Hummer. "How do I get a ride in that pretty damn awesome sportscar? I'd want to cruise through town, hanging my head out the window, waving like a madwoman."

I conjured up a picture of that and laughed. "I dare you to ask her. If Fab's nose shoots in the air, the answer is no." The two of us walked over to her car. "I guess she listened when I warned that she might miss a shootout."

Mac pulled her imaginary six-shooters and shot up the street, then blew on the ends of her fingers and reholstered them. "You know—"

I cut her off. "If I didn't think it would land us all in jail, I'd have at least entertained the idea of a faux shootout." I shook my head. "Creole would kill me."

"If Creole's going to put in an appearance, I'm happy to keep him entertained while you smoochy it up with your other husband for the day... Crum." Mac made a choking noise.

"Creole got a good laugh when I told him who his replacement was."

"I better not have missed anything," Fab said, getting out of the car and pocketing her phone.

Mac cleared her throat and nodded towards something behind us. Fab and I turned as Travis West stomped in the direction of the property, his hard glare examining every person in sight.

Fab nudged me forward. "I don't think we introduced ourselves the last time. I say we don't bother this time, either."

"I'm thinking we hang back, see how this plays out. Crum assured me he can hold his own. I'm sure there will be an opportune moment to hop in and be friendly to the neighbor—offer him a greasy burger," I said as the three of us moved closer.

West began to yell, which was drowned out by the music. He swept out his arm and sent the boombox airborne; it crashed into a nearby boulder. No more music. He was now the center of attention, all eyes on him.

Crum stormed over, got right up in his face, and yelled, "What the hell are you doing? This is private property." He fisted the man's shirt and shoved him backward.

"We need to make sure this doesn't escalate." I went running over. "Honey…" I grabbed Crum's arm and stepped in front of him, in case he was thinking about taking a swing. "I don't want you getting hurt." I hooked my arm in his and stood at his side.

"You've got two minutes to pack up and leave, or I'm calling the cops," West thundered.

"We have every right to be here." I pasted on a phony smile. "The Vickers have given me permission to use the property while my loan for the purchase is under review."

"To do what?" West looked around, his eyes landing on the food truck. "That's illegal," he roared.

"Actually, it isn't," I said sweetly. "This is private property, and the truck has the appropriate licensing."

He attempted to glare a hole through me, and I pretended not to notice. "You didn't answer my question about what you're going to do with the property."

"My hub and I plan on living here." I patted Crum's forearm. "It's legal to park any vehicles we please in the parking lot; the county zoned it for five. And there's plenty of on-street parking for our guests." I waved my hand around to the various vehicles. West followed my wave and did a double take when he got an eyeful of Crum's idea of suitable outdoor attire, which he'd apparently missed when he stomped over.

"Don't tell me that barely covered is legal, because it isn't," West grunted.

"You don't know the law very well." I stepped closer to Crum as steam blew out West's ears. His face reddened with anger. "Once we've signed the papers, if there's still a problem, we can take it to court and let a judge decide. How about that?"

Crum smirked openly, and West's face turned redder, the veins on his neck sticking out.

"You're getting too much sun; you should have a seat under one of the umbrellas," I said. "I'll get you a burger, and we can get to know one another. You can also meet a few of our friends, who'll be around all the time." One of the women found music on her phone and turned up the sound, and she and several of her friends started gyrating around and letting their assets shake.

West watched for several seconds before storming off.

"Come back anytime," Crum yelled after him.

"You need to watch out for him," Fab said and nodded in West's direction as he disappeared.

The woman had turned off her phone, so Mac hopped in the hearse, rolled down the window, and turned on the radio, letting it blare. Fab, who'd followed her, inspected the inside.

The drama over, everyone turned their attention to dancing, drinking, and cards.

"West isn't used to having someone tell him to

take a hike," Crum said. "I wouldn't put it past him to do whatever he has to to make sure you don't become his neighbor."

"He's a smart man. He needs to get hot on the phone and make an offer on the property. Problem solved."

Fab and Mac wandered back over.

"Are you disappointed that there's not a body in there, waiting to be transported?" I asked Fab.

"Raul approached me once about picking up bodies when they had an unreliable guy who called in all too frequently with some excuse or another."

I remembered that guy; he was a flake. "And you answered, 'Thanks for thinking of me, but no'?"

"I don't know what I said, but it was no." Fab wrinkled her nose.

"Uh oh, hope you're ready to talk to the law," Mac said. "You're about to get an 'it's time to break it up' speech."

Fab and I turned as a cop car pulled up and parked. Kevin got out, his face not giving away a thing.

"Let's try to be nice," I said to Fab.

"You first."

Kevin had me in his sights. Mac went and sat with the card players.

"Hello, Officer," I said with enough sweetness that his lips quirked on the sides. "Would you like a burger and a soda?"

"You're not allowed to bribe me while I'm duty."

"Sucks for you, since the food's good."

"Give me a straight answer as to what's going on and why you two are in the middle of it." He turned and looked over his shoulder as Mac turned up the music. "Some of your friends don't surprise me."

"You know how you try on a hat, see how cute it is before you buy? That's what I'm doing with this property — testing it out as a party place. Doesn't that sound fun?"

Fab tried to disguise her laugh with a cough, but I knew her too well.

"Do the Vickers know you've appropriated their property and brought over your, hmm, friends to make complete asses of themselves? Not to mention a blight on the neighborhood? Police switchboard lit up when you arrived."

"I'm in negotiations."

"Sure." Kevin snorted. "A number of these so-called friends, I met when they checked into The Cottages, and I gave them the speech — 'A cop lives on the property, so you might not want to break any laws.'"

"I appreciate that."

"I'm still waiting on the straight answer I've been asking for from the beginning."

"As you know, the Vickers were burned out. I don't suppose you've arrested the arsonist?" No answer could mean no or none of my business.

Probably both. "Where was I? Straight story. The Vickers need to sell to move on to a comfortable retirement."

Kevin stared as though trying to read my mind. Good luck to that. "I'm going to go talk to West, chief complainer when the Taco Bar was here, and let him know that as long as you abide by noise ordinances and keep your fun, or whatever you're doing, on the property, there's nothing I can do. I will suggest that he make an offer better than yours, which would solve his neighbor issues and keep him off the phone to dispatch."

"That would be very sweet of you."

"Don't be saying that where anyone can hear." Kevin's humor leaked out once in a while. "I'm good friends with Mark and like his family a lot. When he shared your plan with me, he had doubts that you could pull it off. I reassured him you had nerve to spare and if you couldn't get it done, no one could. If you do manage to pull it off, there will be lots of happy folks. Won't that be nice?"

"So you knew the whole time what we're doing here?"

"Just wanted to be sure." Kevin grinned.

"Over your right shoulder," Fab whispered.

Not sure how West knew that law enforcement had arrived, but here he was. Kevin intercepted him, and the two men talked.

I waved to Mac, who came running. "Could

you get Kevin a to-go bag? Reinforce our good standing. Or yours anyway."

"Already done."

"That's why you're the best." I smiled at her.

Chapter Thirty

It turned out to be a long week of sitting at the property day after day, the only goal to annoy West. I was ready to give it up and accept defeat, as much as I hated that idea. Fab had gotten called on a couple of minor jobs for Gunz and took Didier as backup.

The neighbors got into the spirit and stopped by to partake of food and drink, and a number of them joined in the dancing and games. Crum managed to keep the bus arriving at regular intervals with an assortment of odd folks—a number of whom I'd never met before. Others I recognized as regulars at Jake's. I fished for information on Rick Pierce from those that showed, and all pled ignorance. One man pulled me aside and warned, "It's best to not ask questions when someone is murdered. Especially when there are no suspects." He nodded and expected the same from me. It was good advice, and I didn't ask anyone else after that.

On more than one occasion, West was seen standing on his property, glaring at anyone who glanced his way. The second day, he lurked around with a camera and filmed the comings and goings. It set off Crum, who wanted to confront him, but I managed to talk him down, reminding him, "We don't want any trouble." It was then I began to think that my idea wasn't going to work.

On the fifth day, about to be the last, I arrived late to find that Crum and West had squared off and several people were gathered around, hooting and hollering. I got out of my car and dashed over. Crum was spitting mad, his right eye swelling up.

"You hit an old man?" I shrieked at West, stepping closer to Crum and peering up into his face.

"He hit me first. I had to defend myself."

"You lying turd." Crum cut around me, about to advance on the man.

I grabbed his arm and tugged him to a halt.

"I'm calling the cops," West growled.

Crum straightened to his full height, nose in the air like the man let off a fierce smell that was atrocious, his condescending stare firmly in place. I didn't appreciate it when that was leveled at me, but was enjoying it in this moment. "You go right ahead. The only person going to jail is you. You want to know why, asshat? I've got proof you hit me first. After you get out of jail for assault and battery, I'll sue your socks off. It will please me to see a 'For Sale' sign go up on your house to pay the judgment. You can bet I'll take you for all you're worth for attacking an old man."

West was on the fence as to whether he believed Crum or not, looking around suspiciously. "What proof?"

"You were recorded." Crum pointed to the back window of the bus as a cop car breezed around a corner and came to a stop. "If that's not enough, there were witnesses, dimwit. It'll be interesting to see what comes out of that dumb mouth of yours when that cop gets to us. I'm not one to mix it up with the cops, so unless you lie, I'm fine with brushing it under the bus, so to speak." He laughed, a squeaky sound suggesting he didn't do it often.

Kevin strode up, irritation written on his face as examined Crum. "What the hell happened?"

Crum turned to West, who said, "We were fooling around, and it got a little out of hand. We're both okay, aren't we, pal?" He clapped Crum on the back.

"What he said," Crum told Kevin, barely making eye contact.

"Yeah, sure. If that's the story both of you are going with, then that makes my job easier. Know this—if I have to come back out, I'll arrest you both." Kevin motioned to Crum to follow him, and to West, he said, "Stick around." He and Crum walked over to the bus and had a brief conversation. When they finished, Crum was about to join his friends, but I motioned to him. Kevin walked over to West. Another conversation I couldn't hear.

"I'm sorry. Do you need a doctor? I know one that makes house calls."

Crum shook his head. "The conversation was heated, mostly West bellowing what a-wipes we all are. Didn't see his fist until it was too late."

"This is where I throw in the towel and admit this little idea of mine isn't going to work," I said.

"Hold your shorts, girlie. Once copper leaves, I'm going to have a quick conversation with West. I'll stand back this time, make sure there's plenty of space, and offer him some good advice. Give him a day or two to ruminate on my words of wisdom, and he'll want to be done with us, if he doesn't already. I'll throw in the advice to offer double whatever the asking price is, since it's cheaper than getting his behind sued off by an esteemed college professor that's old enough to be his father."

"It's so nice of you to want to confront him one more time, but I don't want you getting hurt."

"Like I said, I'm standing back. Besides, if it works, I want more favors to salt away."

It had surprised me, when I offered to pay him for his time, that instead, he wanted favors. He planned to hoard them and use them in case I threatened to kick his butt to the curb again.

"Here comes Kevin." Crum practically sprinted off.

Kevin beeline straight for me. "You know

they're both lying."

"I wasn't here when it happened, and I heard the same version of events that you did."

"I reminded West that he once wanted to buy the property and he should follow through — that way, he could control the traffic. Then, the next time a grease wagon shows up, it can be gotten rid of in short order."

"Was he receptive to your suggestion?"

"I guess we'll find out." Kevin glanced over the property.

"You'll be happy to know that I'm only giving this gig one more day."

Kevin nodded and waved as he walked over to one of the tables and grabbed a soda before going back to his car.

As soon as he rounded the corner, Crum headed toward West's property.

I ran up alongside him, and he stopped. "If you're not back in five minutes, I'm calling the cops again."

"Calm your curls; I'm only going as far as his gate. I'll ask him nicely to come out for a short talk. You can watch everything go down."

My offer of five minutes was generous. Once West got to the gate, he stayed on his side, and the two spoke through the wrought iron. The conversation lasted all of two minutes.

When it was finished, Crum walked back over to where I was standing. "I told him I didn't want to live here with my wife but didn't know how to tell my little darlin'."

I wanted to laugh but bit it back.

"That would be you, in case you've forgotten," Crum continued. "The only way to prevent that was if he put in an offer that the Vickers couldn't turn down. As far as I was concerned, we could keep it between the two of us. My honey would never have to know."

"How did that go over?"

"Not a word. West nodded and walked off."

"Another day, and we're calling it quits."

"Patience, chickadee." Crum patted my shoulder and went back to his friends. I hopped on the bus and got out my laptop for a little work.

* * *

A few hours later, I got a call from Mark, the Vickers' grandson—West had made an offer with the condition that the property be vacated immediately. He requested anonymity. Under no circumstances was his name to be mentioned, as he didn't want any trouble. Mark didn't disclose the specifics about the offer, but did say that his grandparents were ecstatic.

I hung up, gave brief thought to vaulting off the steps of the bus, and laughed at myself. I jumped sedately to the ground and attempted a whistle that went nowhere. I yelled, "Crum," waved him over, and told him about the call.

"About time." He laughed. "I'm ready to pack in the fun and take it back to The Cottages. My ladies have been complaining; they miss their stretching classes."

I reminded myself no grumbling and would go so far as to ignore the near-nudity for a few days, then sic Mac on him. "If West ever bothers you, let me know; I'll have someone talk to him about manners."

His hearty laugh conveyed that he liked the idea.

Chapter Thirty-One

I had the foresight to tell Fab I was taking the morning off and kicking up my feet. Instead, what I really had planned was to sneak off for a morning of shopping—hit up a few of the local shops and see what they had new in beachy items. I'd confided my plans to Creole the previous night. He wasn't happy, reminding me that the murderer of Rick Pierce hadn't been apprehended. I promised that I would stay in the Cove and wouldn't venture very far down the highway in either direction. I mentioned at least six times how much Fab hated some of these stores. He gave in easily enough, laughed it off, and extracted a promise that I'd call if anything out of the ordinary caught my attention. That would be an easy promise to keep—I'd get hot on the phone at the first sign of trouble.

I dressed casually and comfortably for the day, choosing a cotton skirt, t-shirt, and a pair of designer wedge flip-flops I'd scored on a deal. For those that thought they weren't "real" shoes, tough; they were, and they were comfortable. If I lucked into a good find, I'd bring another pair home today.

Creole, in jeans and a button-down shirt with the sleeves rolled up, scooped me up and twirled me around, giving me a big kiss and setting me back on my feet. "You know how much I love you?"

It was the sheepish grin that had me doing a double take. "You know I feel the same way about you. Did you forget to make breakfast or something?"

"You know," he teasingly admonished, "we should get into the habit of having breakfast together every morning. Not just a quick cup of coffee."

"Are you wanting me to start drinking that green muck you like to suck down to get your day started?" I imitated a hairball noise that had Jazz looking up from the end of the bed; neither he nor Creole were impressed.

Creole hooked his arm around me, and we headed towards the kitchen. I skidded to a stop when I saw Mother and Fab sitting at the island. I turned and looked up at Creole, lowering my voice to say, "I knew you were up to something."

He cut me off with a kiss. "You're going to have a great time. If not, one word from you, and I'll deal with the two culprits, and so you know, they've been warned."

I wished I'd been there when Creole strong-armed Fab. I turned and gushed, "This is a fun surprise." I almost laughed at Fab's eyeroll. I waltzed over and hugged Mother, who also caught the sarcasm and remained amused. When I spotted the bakery box, I licked my lips. "Yum. It's been too long."

The front door opened, and Didier came in. "I got the text about breakfast, and here I am." He crossed the room and stood next to Fab.

Creole made coffee for everyone.

We tabled talk about our plans for the day until after we'd eaten; I was certain everyone knew but me. We filled our plates, sat around the island, and ate as Mother regaled us with stories about Mila and Logan.

"I know you three have a busy day planned, so Didier and I will clean up," Creole said.

"Whatever you think you have planned here won't go as smoothly as you'd like." I raised up on tiptoes and kissed him. I turned away, linked my arm in Mother's, and with the other grabbed my purse and headed out to the car.

Fab drove out to the highway and turned north.

I scooted forward in my seat and asked, "Didn't Creole tell you this was a local trip?"

"That didn't sound like as much fun as what I have planned."

"We're going to have the best time." Mother nodded at me to agree with Fab.

"Maybe. Depending on what the Queen of Shopping has planned."

Mother grinned and shook her finger at me.

"You don't need to reconfigure your entire

plan—toss in one beach store and yummy food, and I'll be happy. Then you won't have to answer to Creole for not holding up your end of the bargain." Whatever that was, but I'd find out later.

"I promise fun," Fab said. "Or we'll just have to have a redo."

She pulled into the gas station we used most often, as Fab and I liked the old guy who owned it. It was one of the few independent ones left. Just as she pulled up to a pump and cut the engine, the young guy at the next pump over jumped a woman and started pummeling her, keeping it up even after she fell to the ground. Fab and I jumped out of the car and raced over.

"Knock it off," Fab bellowed and stepped forward, her hand raised.

"What are you going to do?" I jerked on her shirt, which barely slowed her forward momentum.

She shrugged me off and leapt into the middle of the beat-down, wrestling the young man off the woman and flinging him to the ground. He rolled over, and it turned out he was a teenager.

Mother, hustled over to the woman, who'd stumbled to her feet and was gasping for breath, hunched over, her hands on her knees.

A number of people stood a few feet away and stared, but none offered any help.

Noting that Mother was talking to the woman and had the situation under control, I moved closer to Fab. The kid jumped to his feet, fuming with anger. He clenched his fist, and his arm swung back and shot forward. Fab curled her fingers around his fist and sent him flying. This time, he landed on his butt on the concrete. He yelled a couple of filthy names at Fab and bounded up, both fists in the air.

"Come at me and you're going to lose, you little cretin," Fab yelled and took a militant stance.

His anger apparently dulled his other senses, as he didn't heed the warning and charged.

Ready for him, Fab kicked his feet out from under him, and once again, he landed in a heap. She put her foot in the middle of his chest. "Don't get up," she growled.

Someone had called 911, probably the clerk inside the store, who had her face pressed to the window. Two cop cars rolled into the gas station. It surprised me that Kevin didn't get out of one of them. One cop headed to Fab and the kid and the other over to my mother and the woman. An ambulance rolled in and parked. The medics jumped out and headed over to the woman. Mother stepped back. It wasn't long before they had the woman loaded onto a stretcher and pulled out.

The kid calmed down in a blink and became the picture of innocence when approached by the cop. He sat up straight and answered all the cop's questions respectfully. From the anger etched on Fab's face, I guessed he was lying.

The other cop, after questioning Mother, came over and had a few for me. I told him what had gone down, and that there were a lot of witnesses, even though a few had jumped in their cars and roared off the second the cops arrived. A handful of stragglers had wandered over and weren't going anywhere, a couple with phones in their hands.

Mother sidled up next to me when the cop went to confer with his partner. "That was a family beatdown," she confided. "Here's the worst part: it's not the first time the kid beat her up."

I gasped. "Is she going to be okay?"

"She was a heck of a lot calmer than I would've been. Turns out she has asthma, and in a fit of rage, her son tossed her inhaler out the window. That's why she was bent over; she couldn't catch her breath, and as you can imagine, it was freaking her out. I about lost patience when she was more worried about her son than herself. I told her she needed to calm down." Mother shook her head. "You'll be happy to know that I didn't offer my parenting advice, which would've been to kick his ass down the street."

Ass, I mouthed with a shocked face, reminding her of her longstanding rule: no bad words allowed. "There's my mother; she was hiding for a second."

Mother made a face.

"If the kid doesn't get control of his anger, he's going to land in prison. I'm not sure how the cops will handle this case, and I guess it depends on whether the mother presses charges. It's probably not the first time they've responded to a call regarding those two." I gave Mother a side hug. "It was nice of you to rush to her side and lend support."

The one cop cuffed the kid and put him in the back of his car, and after an exchange of words with his partner, he drove off.

The other cop walked back over to Fab, and they talked. After a few, he walked back to the SUV with her, and she pulled out a business card and handed it to him. He went inside the convenience store.

Fab waved Mother and I over in an impatient gesture—hustle it up—as if we were kidlets and had been the ones to irk her last nerve.

"Did you know they're mother and son?" Fab demanded in a frustrated tone once we were all seated and the doors closed.

"I told Madison," Mother said.

"Here's something you didn't know: the mother doesn't want to press charges—it was all a misunderstanding. My you-know-what," Fab said in disgust.

"The cops pretty much know that's baloney, and they did arrest him," I said.

"I asked what they planned to do. I got a 'none

of your business' look, although he was nice about it." Fab laughed. "Curtis, the youthful offender, was excited to be going for a ride in the back of the cruiser. Didn't seem the slightest bit worried about being hauled off to jail. I suspect, from his blasé attitude, that it wasn't his first encounter with the cops, and if he walked the other times, he probably figures he'll be doing the same today."

Fab's phone started ringing, which she ignored. It stopped. And started ringing again. She hit the connect button and handed it to Mother, who didn't skip a beat but hopped into the role of Fab's assistant. I groaned and leaned back against the seat, hoping it wasn't one of her more outrageous clients.

"This is Madeline Spoon, Mr. Gunzelman," Mother said in an overly sweet tone. "I'm Fab's occasional assistant, and she's told me several times you're one of her best clients. And favorites," she added conspiratorially. "At the moment, she's busy with another client, but the second she's free, I can have her call you. Or I can help you." It was clear she preferred the latter option.

I covered my face. I didn't want to listen, but leaned forward to make sure I didn't miss a word.

"What time is convenient for you?" Mother asked.

If she was going to play assistant, she needed

to use the speaker button.

"Don't you worry; she'll be waiting on your arrival." Whatever he said, she giggled, and the two hung up.

"Just a little reminder, Mother—you have a husband and shouldn't be giggling with the likes of Gunz," I said. "Spoon will dispose of him faster than you can blink."

"Mr. Gunz was one hundred percent professional." Mother grinned.

I'll just bet.

Mother turned her attention to Fab. "Gunz is on his way to your office; he's got an important case he needs your input on." She turned to face me. "We can reschedule this shopping trip for another day. I'll plan it and make sure we all get a little of what we want."

"That sounds nice." I didn't have to see Fab's face to know she was smirking.

"This has been fun." Mother rubbed her hands together. "And more to come."

"If it's fun you're wanting, Mother, how about we ditch Fab and hit up all our favorite in-town stores?"

"We can't hurt Fab's feelings by leaving her out." Mother smiled at her. "Since I haven't seen your new office or met Lark, now would be the perfect time."

I nudged Fab's shoulder. "It would make Mother's afternoon if you showed off a couple of your shortcuts." I gave Mother a couple of days before she was back on the streets trying to retrace the route. She'd find out it wasn't as easy as Fab made it look.

I leaned back and closed my eyes.

Fab jetted us over to the office, and we all got out and stopped to watch as Lark tossed a frisbee to Arlo, who was more than willing to run and fetch. She waved and ditched her play partner, walking over. I introduced Mother to Lark and was pleased at the look of approval on Mother's face.

The four of us trooped inside, and I took drink orders. It was an easy one—we all wanted water—and I retrieved the bottles from the fridge and passed them around. I sat at the conference table with Mother and Fab, and Lark rolled her chair over at Mother's insistence.

"I thought you were, ah…" Creole said, coming out of his office. He eyed us, sitting around the table, and stopped.

I stood and yelled, "Gather around, gentleman."

Didier appeared right behind Creole and brushed Fab's head with a kiss before sitting down.

Brad was the laggard. He kissed Mother's cheek before sitting.

"You were supposed to be shopping." Creole's intent expression told me he was trying to figure out what happened without having to be told. Too bad that almost never worked.

"Stuff happened." I smirked at him. "Listen up, everyone; it's a good story. Fab and Mother were the stars of the morning. Thankfully, Mother didn't put herself in a position to get her butt kicked. As for my part, I corroborated everyone's story, and if the little bastard had tried to jump me, I'd have nicked his butt with a bullet."

"Really, Madison," Mother admonished, then grinned.

Now that I had everyone's full attention, I flourished my hand at Fab. "You're up, girlfriend, and you need to sauce up the details after this introduction."

Fab stood and bowed, then sat back down and launched into the events of the morning. She ended her recitation with, "If the kid had been a man, as I originally thought, I'd have given him an extra kick or two. I got caught off guard by him being a teenager and then finding out that he and the woman were related. That bit of good sense probably saved me from a ride to the police station. We haven't had need of bail money of late, and I'd like it to stay that way."

Didier hugged her. "You okay?" She nodded.

"I'll ask Xander to keep an eye out for any news items, so we can find out what happens with sonny boy," I said.

"I'm surprised you ladies stopped by to tell us in person." Didier smiled at us.

"You can thank Fab's assistant." I pointed to

Mother. "Fab foisted a business call off on Mother, which wasn't professional, by the way." I squinted at Fab and tried not to laugh. "Knowing Mother, she decided in an instant that coming here would be much more fun than shopping, so she set up the meeting."

"You're so dramatic," Mother admonished. "I'm more than happy to help Fab."

"Like you had another option," I interjected.

"Anyway…" Mother stared at me, my cue to be quiet so she could finish. "That sweet Gunzelman called, and I was trying to be supportive when he mentioned he had a family emergency and needed Fab's help. What would you have done?"

"Me?" I pointed to myself. "Hung up on him." I swear, the guys didn't know whether to roll their eyes or laugh.

"He's just a big ole sweetie," Mother said.

I did roll my eyes and kicked Fab's foot under the table as she struggled not to grin. "I, for one, can't wait to find out what his third cousin's granny wants."

"No wonder the man told me you try his patience," Mother said.

Now everyone was in agreement and laughed.

"I call Pot on that one," I said. "So you know, from this moment on, I'm keeping an eye on you." I winked at Mother. "Your husb would flip if he thought you were sharing a laugh with that felonious fellow, no matter how reformed, and I won't be blamed."

"I just won't tell him," Mother announced proudly.

"Take it from me, since I'm probably the sneakiest of the bunch," Fab said, "that doesn't always work, and then you have to suffer retribution." She leaned over and whispered in Mother's ear, and her cheeks burned bright red. "Oh look, Gunz just pulled in. Time to adjourn upstairs." Fab stood.

Brad covered Mother's hand with his. "You can keep me company."

Mother snorted and jerked her hand back. "I'm going."

"Hate to throw your words back at you, Mother…" I said, although clearly not. "Making noises like that will give you big nostrils."

Brad and I traded a smile.

"I'll catch up with you two," I said as they headed to the elevator. "Need to talk to Brad."

Chapter Thirty-Two

I stayed seated, and Creole and Didier went back to their office. "I don't have anything new on Cassie. She's dropped out of sight, which is probably not good news, based on the kind of people she's hung out with in the past. You were probably her first romp with a good guy."

Brad winced. "I read all the reports Xander sent me, and her background surprised me. She put on a good 'girl next door' act. Has Xander been able to trace her phone?"

"Turned off, and he thinks she removed the battery. Did Cassie leave anything behind that would give a clue where she might have gone?"

He shook his head. "She took all her personal belongings. I can't help wondering how she could walk off and leave her kid. But then, Logan's not hers. Still, he's family."

"Maybe whatever she was running from—" Or to, I left unsaid. "—she thought you were the better option for Logan. Considering the legal document she left behind, she gave it some thought, and it doesn't appear that she plans on coming back. At least, not anytime soon. And since I know you're going to ask—" I paused. "—

Xander hasn't been able to find anything on the other grandparents.

Brad's hand covered mine. "Do I say thank you enough? I talked to Tank and updated him on everything you'd found out, and he said that chances are next to nil that I'd be granted any kind of custody, since I'm not family. The POA she left is worthless."

"Did he have any good news?"

"He suggested that I apply to be a foster parent." Brad shook his head. "I should've been the one to make the trip to the Glades."

"Bad idea there. They were, to put it nicely, an odd family. They tolerated our visit since we weren't perceived as a threat, but you... not sure you would've received the same reception." I'd thought back to that trip a few times, and my neck hairs told me there was a lot going on out there in the wilds. "Have you asked Allegra to move out yet? I noticed her car in the parking lot, and when I find out who opened the gate for her, I'm kicking butt." I planned to invalidate her entry card after I talked to the Chief.

"I don't want you going off half-cocked and committing bodily harm. I have no desire to explain to my daughter about prison—the ugly uniforms and horrid food."

I sighed. "You want me to calm down—message received."

"Allegra thinks you're unstable."

"Let her think that."

"She and I had a long talk, and I told her she needed to move ASAP, that she owed me that much for the screwing she put my life through."

"Bet she was all broken up." I didn't even try to curtail my sarcasm. "Any explanation as to what the..." I was losing the battle to control my anger.

"Turns out she's still working for the FBI and says it's a big case, still ongoing. She befriended Cassie to get information about the head of the criminal ring she has ties to. She didn't think about us getting together, but when we did, it was convenient."

I gritted my teeth. "Does Allegra know where Cassie is?"

"She said that Cassie dropped off the radar right after she packed up and left. She didn't say it, but I gathered she didn't think there'd be a good outcome."

"There's something we agree on. I'm surprised, if Allegra is working this case, that she'd leave the area. Unless her involvement has ended?"

"I think she's more worried about what you're going to do." Brad laughed. "I didn't bother to tell her you probably wouldn't lose it and shoot her anytime soon."

I didn't care what the woman thought of me. But in light of what I just learned, I needed to not provoke her. "Is she going to continue to work for the Chief?" I nodded to the floor overhead.

"I wanted to ask what he knew or didn't know, but decided a little ignorance was a better option. I need to get along around here. Allegra did tell me that I needed to get with a lawyer and get the legalities of Logan's living situation worked out."

"At least she didn't send over Social Services, which she could have easily done. That would've been the last you'd have seen of Logan." That would've been a sad outcome all around. "So you know, I'm working on finding you a top-notch family law lawyer."

Brad nodded at something behind me.

I turned and saw Gunz holding the elevator door for Mother and Fab. I lowered my voice and said, "So sad that I missed hearing the latest about whatever relative's life has gone off the rails."

"How many does he have?" Brad eyed the man as he said his goodbyes.

"A wad-load. I think the blood relatives suck in every friend, acquaintance, and probably stranger to dump their problems on him. Gunz never says no. At least, not that I've heard."

Gunz winked at Lark, who giggled. He waved as he went out the door. That's when I noticed the bouquet on her desk.

"You better institute a 'no dating Fab's clients' policy, or yours for that matter," I told my brother, who shook his head, not willing to stick his nose into someone's personal business, unlike his sister. "I promise that it'll come back to bite you, and not in a pleasant way."

"Are you two discussing Logan?" Mother asked as she sat down. "You could've waited for my input."

Fab—about ready to burst, smug look and all—also sat down.

All eyes were on Mother, and nobody said a word.

"Keep him. There's always room for one more in the family. His bio family sounds..." Mother made a face.

"It's not that simple," Brad told her. "Once I've spoken to a lawyer, I'll let you know my options."

Mother's suggestion didn't surprise me; I didn't think there was anyone in the family that wouldn't support Brad's decision to do just that.

"Isn't anyone going to ask how the meeting went?" Fab bubbled with excitement.

"I'll bite," Brad said.

"You're going to be sorry," I murmured.

Fab whipped out her phone. "I have to set this up, since I wasn't able to capture everything on video."

"You give me that." Mother attempted to whisk the phone away, but Fab was quicker, and she came up with air.

"My best client comes in to avail himself of my services, and it's not a boast when I say I have an impeccable record for dealing with his issues."

Fab waved her phone.

Brad looked at me like I was the one who snorted. I pointed to Mother. He shook his head, not believing me.

"Gunz gets comfortable and starts to detail the job. He'd just gotten started, and that's where the video begins."

Mother glared at her.

She held up her phone, pressing play. It showed Mother jumping up from her chair and slapping the desk with her hand. "Now you listen to me, young man."

Young man. Both Brad and I smirked.

"That's not the kind of job Fab will agree to take," Mother told him in no uncertain terms. "For one thing, her husband will kill her. Well, probably not her, but you anyway."

The video showed Gunz grinning at Mother and enjoying every minute of his rebuke.

"It's in your best interest to find someone else." Mother shook her finger at the man.

"Don't you think we should hear what Fab has to say?" Gunz asked.

"You already have your answer." Mother turned a squint eye on Fab. "You better not think about sneaking around."

Brad and I laughed. We'd heard that speech before. Behave or else something you hated would befall you.

"The end," Fab said with a flourish, looking disappointed.

"The video doesn't enlighten us as to what kind of job it was," Brad said.

"Convenient, huh?" I exchanged a smirk with Brad. "So sad that neither Creole nor Didier got invited to this little show, not to mention Spoon. He's going to be irritated to be the last to know. Sauce it up with a private showing." I winked at Mother. "Be sure you forward a copy of that video to Mother," I said to Fab, then stood and yelled, "Hey guys, get out here."

Creole and Didier came out of their offices, both men shaking their heads.

Lark, who hadn't missed a word, sat back in her chair and grinned the whole time.

"I assume you're yelling at us," Didier said.

"Come have a seat. You're not going to want to miss this." I waved to the chairs. "As you know, Gunz was here, and Fab videotaped Mother laying down the law to him. A little spoiler: he took it better than if I'd done it."

"What's the job?" Creole asked as he sat next to me.

"Gunz wants me to recover his Mercedes," Fab answered. "A woman friend made off with it, and he doesn't want to be a dick but wants it back."

"This isn't the first time he's been relieved of a spendy auto by a lovely young woman he's doing it with," I informed everyone, happy that Lark was still paying attention. "Last time, we were shot at, or maybe the time before. Let's hustle this heartwarming story along."

Fab handed her phone to Creole and Didier, and the two leaned together and watched the video. Both laughed.

"Tell me that Gunz took your mother's no as the final answer," Didier said.

"I smoothed over the situation, telling him I'd hand the job over to Toady and not to worry — he has prowess with the ladies and can charm the keys out of the girlfriend's hands."

I grimaced, thinking about that leathered old guy with the skin of a reptile. Fab had stepped in and given him a makeover — gone were the wife-beaters and tattered shorts, and he claimed it made him more popular than ever. "Toady's got a new woman in his life — Fuchsia, who we've yet to meet. If she can keep up with that old goat, then she's no shrinking violet."

"Thank you, Madeline." Didier smiled at her, and she blushed. "I'm willing to bet that Fab wouldn't have turned down the job if you hadn't done it for her."

"Since we're talking about your client, what happened to the man who was screwing him on the property deals?" I asked.

"He relocated for health reasons," Fab said.

"That means what?" Creole demanded. "If he doesn't want to die, he better head out of town?"

"Gunz assured me he was unharmed," Fab said.

Chapter Thirty-Three

Fab called early and invited me to lunch, promising a surprise. I'll admit, that made me suspicious about what she was up to, but I managed to stop short of questioning her.

Rummaging through my closet, I chose a full black skirt and paired it with a sleeveless black top that dipped in the back, then strapped my Glock to my thigh, just to be safe. Fab announced her arrival by laying on the horn. I grabbed my purse, walked out, and slid into the passenger seat. "Where are we going?" So much for no questions. "You look hot, by the way." I admired her black short-sleeve dress, with its square neckline and flared skirt.

"The Crab Shack," Fab said as she drove out of the compound. "It's been too long since we've been there."

I refrained from licking my lips but thought about it. "You must be buttering me up for something." I tapped my cheek.

"You're so suspicious," Fab said with amusement. "I thought, who better to share great food and a drink with?"

I squinted at her, then turned and checked out

315

the back seat. "You definitely mentioned a surprise, and I don't see a huge box anywhere."

"It's not that kind of surprise," she said and shot me the *behave* stare. "You didn't get your shopping day, and I'm going to make it up to you. There's a store that just opened in Marathon, and I thought we'd check it out."

"Sounds fun."

Fab pulled into the parking lot of the restaurant, which overlooked the cool waters of the Atlantic. She parked, and we walked up the steps to the entrance. It was a favorite, with its low-key atmosphere, decorated with fake palm trees and fish, mounted on walls strung with ropes of lights. Fab had made a reservation for an outside table—we both loved a view of the water. The server took our drink order and was back in a flash.

"To more fun times," Fab toasted.

"Ladies." A dark-haired man of medium height with cropped brown hair and a scruff of stubble strolled up. His blue eyes were trained on Fab, holding nothing but icicles. He sat down without being invited.

"That seat's taken," Fab stopped short of snapping. "If you don't move, and now, I'll call the manager."

"No need to be unfriendly." He cracked a small, insincere smile. "Michael Ashton." He stuck his hand out, which she ignored. "I'm a reporter with a local news outlet. I've tried to get ahold of you several times, but my calls have been routed to voicemail and not returned. That's why I'm getting in touch with you directly."

"About what?" I asked.

"This isn't any of your business." He briefly turned towards me, and I struggled not to flinch under his frigid glare. "If you would sit somewhere else, the two of us could conclude our business a lot faster." He glanced at Fab.

"That's not going to happen," Fab snapped. "Whatever it is you want, you can say in front of her, and if that offends you, tough. Now, you've got two minutes." She tapped her watch.

"I thought you'd like a heads up that you're about to be inundated with requests from reporters wanting to interview you, since you're an eyewitness to the disposal of the bodies that were recently fished out of the Gulf. You could head that off by talking to me. Tell your story your way, and once it makes print, other writers won't want to waste their time."

"You've got the wrong woman," Fab told him as he continued to stare at her intently. It was clear he didn't believe a word she'd said.

"Police reports say otherwise," he said with a 'gotcha' smirk. "A woman fitting your description was the one to call the cops."

We both knew that was a lie.

"Are you done with your fishing expedition?" Fab returned his intense stare.

"The report is that the bodies washed up in front of your house."

"You heard wrong." Fab held her cool despite his insistence.

I picked up the menus and waved them at the server. "Sounds like that's the end of the story, so if you don't mind, we're hungry."

"No one asked you anything," Ashton snapped. "You weren't invited to this interview."

I doubted he got a lot of interviews with his abrupt, cold attitude. Ashton was definitely taken with Fab, and I was sure that wasn't a good thing. The server came over, and I ordered, adding, "He's not staying," then nodded at Fab, who also ordered.

"I'm sorry you wasted your time tracking me down," Fab said. "I truly don't have anything to contribute to your article."

Ashton stared at her, and to Fab's credit, she didn't flinch. "Maybe we'll run into each other again." He stood, crossed the deck, and went into the restaurant.

"That was totally creepy." I took my phone out of my pocket and texted Xander: *Run a check on Michael Ashton, news reporter, might be local.*

"If you weren't here, no telling what he would've done." Fab checked out the bar area, but Ashton had left. "I knew if he tried anything, you'd shoot him."

"Without hesitation."

"Wonder what he really wanted?" Fab mused. "He was too intense for just a story. Several times, I thought about snapping a picture, but there wasn't an opportunity... not one where he wouldn't notice."

Our food arrived, and as always, it smelled good.

"We need to keep an eye out and make sure Ashton's not following us," I said. "You more than me, since all his attention was focused on you. Judging by his demeanor, he's not used to being told no."

"I'm sure he's heard it plenty; he just doesn't like it."

"I'll feel better when Xander gets back to us and tells us who he's employed by."

Neither of us enjoyed having our lunch intruded upon, and we both picked at our food.

"You know we both enjoy leftovers," I reminded her as I waved the waiter over and asked him to box our food.

"Can I owe you one on the shopping? I'd really like to go home. We can kick off our shoes and go for a walk on the beach."

"Love that idea. I'm going to get you a bucket so you can pick up shells with me. Won't that be fun?"

Fab laughed. "You've lost your mind."

"You laughed, which made me laugh, so mission accomplished."

I picked up our bag of food, and as we left the

restaurant, we went out of our way to compliment the server, so he wouldn't think our lack of appetite had anything to do with him.

Fab cruised out of the parking lot and took the direct route towards home, one eye on the rearview mirror. "I'm pretty sure we're being followed. The Jeep."

I tightened my seatbelt and looked in my side mirror, watching wide-eyed as the Jeep swerved around us and came within a hair of clipping the front bumper. Fab jerked on the wheel to avoid contact and quickly recovered. The Jeep sped off, weaving back and forth in the lane.

"Appears to be drunk," I said. "If that was intentional, and the goal was for us to end up in the ditch, the driver didn't have the skills to manage it. Besides, your skills are superior to most, and it takes a lot to knock this ride off the road."

"You know what they say about coincidences?"

"There are none. But maybe this time." I wasn't totally convinced. "I only had a clear view of the Jeep for a second, and I couldn't make out if it was anyone we knew behind the wheel. A man is all I got."

"One of us needs to call the husbands about the overzealous reporter." Fab pointed wildly at me. "Maybe save the almost car accident for later."

Chapter Thirty-Four

As Fab cruised up to the signal and turned off the highway, her phone rang. She picked it up out of the cup holder, glanced at the screen, and handed it to me.

I knew it wouldn't be a fun call and took a quick glance—Toady, swell. "Bonjour, Mr. Toads," I answered and hit the speaker button. "Fab fluffed you off on me, so she must know this is going to be a doozy of a call."

Toady growled a laugh that would unsettle most, but I knew to be harmless. "I love the Frenchie stuff; reminds me of my girl."

Fab shook her head, knowing he was referring to her.

"You're on speaker," I felt compelled to tell him, to save me from having to listen to him go off on some romantic tangent.

"Took nothing to find Gunz's car, but there's a problem..." He hesitated. "You two think you could hustle to the Kroger's on the main highway?"

Fab nodded.

"We're not far. Give us five, and we'll be

there," I said, and he grunted, his way of ending the call.

"You didn't think to get details?" Fab demanded in a bossy tone.

"Clearly your fault. You should've trained me better." Her lips quirked. Good enough for me. "Besides, we're two blocks away, and by the time I was done with the questioning, we'd be cruising into the parking lot. It's not like you'd turn him down, even though you're not hot over heels for him like he is you."

"I missed my opportunity. There's a steady woman in the picture now."

"Sarcasm aside, we both know you're his true love—one tiny indication of interest from you, and the new babe would be history." I made a heart with my fingers and batted my eyelashes.

"I think I'm going to be sick."

"Not in my car. Had that happen once in college, and not me either. Robin was her name— you never forget barfers, especially when the smell reminds you every time there's a hot day." I made a gagging noise.

"Enough." Fab had morphed into Mother, using her *behave* voice. She pulled into the parking lot and, after a quick glance around, saw Toady leaning against the bumper of his beater truck. His hands shot in the air, and he waved wildly. She coasted over and parked next to him. We both got out.

"Hey girls." Toady winked as he closed the

space between us. "The Mercedes with the engine running..." He pointed to a shiny black model with tinted windows. "That's the coach Gunz wants recovered, except there's a slight problem. There's a little kid in the back in a car seat, sound asleep."

"What the heck is wrong with people?" I said.

"The woman left the air conditioning running, which is good. I followed her here, and she got out and bolted into the store. Figured, I only had a small window and hopped behind the wheel. Had it in reverse when I noticed the kid. I jumped the hell out, not wanting to get charged with kidnapping. Even if she'd taken the kid with her when she got out, I'm not such a turd as to leave a mother without a ride."

Fab stormed over to the car and peered in the window. "What the devil is going on? Gunz didn't say one word about her having a..." She stared again, taking a closer look. "A young child."

I backed up a couple of steps, thinking we should just leave and let Gunz handle his own personal issues for a change. I agreed with Toady; I wouldn't leave the woman stranded, and I was certain Fab wouldn't either.

"There's another thing you should know," Toady said, then stared over my shoulder. "But you're about to figure it out for yourself." He nodded to a woman barreling down on us, pushing a shopping cart.

The young blonde was so ginormously pregnant, I suspected she was due in the next minute or two.

Fab and I shared the same look of shock.

"What's going on?" The woman skidded to a stop, ditching her basket. Toady kept it from rolling away. "Is my son okay? I didn't want to wake him... I did hurry." She flew to the passenger door and hit the key fob.

Fab gently touched her arm. "No worries; your son is still asleep."

"I don't understand what you're all doing around my car."

"Your car?" Fab questioned. "Gunz claims to be the registered owner and sent us to retrieve it."

The woman burst into tears. She covered her face and stumbled backwards, but Fab caught her and kept her from falling.

What a messy situation. I stopped short of bolting back to the car. People constantly pointed a finger, calling me a do-gooder; time for Fab to step up and give me some competition. I could think of two reasons—it was an icky situation and her client.

Toady reached in the window of his beater and pulled out a napkin, handing it to the woman and awkwardly patting her shoulder.

"You can't." She sobbed and then blew her nose. "I know what I did wasn't right, but how will we get home?"

Fab appeared to be taking a deep breath. "Is Gunz the father?"

Nothing like direct and to the point.

The woman sniffled and rubbed her stomach. "This one is his baby."

"Toady, would you load her groceries in the trunk?" Fab asked.

Toady, who had a set of keys from Gunz, popped the trunk, pushed the cart over, and put all the cloth bags inside. While he did that, Fab stepped away, turned her back, and made a call.

The woman started to cry again. Toady finished, returned the cart, and came and stood next to the woman. "Don't you worry none; there's no chance that we're leaving you here." He patted her shoulder again.

Fab finished her call, stomped over, and pocketed her phone. "I don't want you to think I'm bugging you for details of your personal relationship with Gunz, because I'm not," she told the woman, then leaned forward and whispered something in her ear. The woman nodded in response. The two whispered back and forth.

Toady handed her another napkin.

"Gunz wants the Mercedes back," Fab told the woman. "I negotiated a deal for you. Toady is going to follow you home and then return the Mercedes to Gunz. He'll be back in an hour or two with a loaner for you to use. Just know that you can't keep the car indefinitely. In the meantime, you need to get with Gunz and work out your situation."

"Okay." The woman sniffed.

"My best advice is to deal with this quickly. Don't wait for Gunz to come to you—take the initiative." Fab walked the woman around to the driver's side and held the door while she got in, then closed it, motioned for her to roll down the window, and said something. "Call me, when…" She nodded to me, and I guessed at what she wanted. I'd know soon enough if I was wrong. I grabbed a business card from the SUV, walked back to the Mercedes, and handed it to the woman. She thanked Fab and backed out.

Toady saluted the two of us, then jumped in his truck and followed the Mercedes.

"You couldn't toss in your two cents? You had to stand back and do… what?" Fab demanded as she slid behind the wheel. "I watched you keep stepping back… surprised you didn't make a run for it. In case it slipped your mind, you're the one with the sensitivity skills."

"You're exaggerating. You were great with the sobbing woman, all calm, collected, and nurturing." I smiled at her. "I'm going to go against my better judgment and ask what's going on. Besides, it's no fun minding my own business."

"Tracy is her name, and she and Gunz dated." Fab made air quotes. "Anyway… her car was repoed for non-payment, she needed a ride, and the Mercedes was sitting in the garage, all neglected... her words. That's when she got the bright idea to borrow it."

"Tracy is lucky that Gunz didn't press grand theft auto charges. Although even when bodily harm is committed on his person, he doesn't call the cops." I shook my head. "Not to mention that she's the mother of his baby, about to be born any second?"

"Gunz claims he's not the father. I asked him how he could be so certain if they've been doing it. He mumbled something, and I let it go. Nosey and all, and there was nothing to stop me from poking around even more, so why not? I asked Tracy how Gunz could be so certain he wasn't the father." Fab blew out an aggravated sigh. "Gunz told her in all seriousness that it was impossible for him to be the father, as he'd had his dick twisted. She hadn't heard of that procedure and asked me about it. Me. Then went on to confide that she hadn't been with anyone else, and I believed her."

I covered my face and laughed. "How did you leave it?"

"Told her to get a paternity test when the baby's born; that way, there wouldn't be any doubt. Then assured her that if Gunz was the father, he'd take care of his kid. Any problems, call, hence the business card." Fab picked up her phone. "I'm going to tell Gunz..." She called the man in question. "Toady's following Tracy home, and he'll be by your office to pick up the other ride. You and Tracy need to work this out, and my advice to you is to get a paternity test, so you know for sure whether you're the father or not."

Since Fab never put him on speaker, no telling what he was selling.

"Don't ever involve me in this type of situation again. There are too many 'what ifs' about what could've gone wrong with a baby in the back of the car. Had I known all the facts, I'd have handled this completely differently." Fab ended the call abruptly.

"What would you have done differently?" I asked.

"Dumped it in your lap."

My phone dinged with a message from Xander: *Couldn't find anything on a reporter named Michael Ashton.*

Chapter Thirty-Five

Creole and Didier flipped when they learned a strange man crashed our lunch and went ballistic when they found out that Xander couldn't dig up any information on the man. They ordered us to keep a low profile and no more slacking off on checking in. Fab stomped off in a snit. I didn't miss the wink that Didier shot Creole before he took off in hot pursuit. In the days since, I hadn't gotten any emergency phone calls from Fab to come save her from boredom and assumed Didier had been keeping her quite busy.

Creole and I split our time between working and hanging out on the beach. I looked for sneaky ways to cheat at water bike racing, but he was pretty much onto me and wouldn't let me get close enough to knock him off course.

Eventually, Fab and Didier came out of seclusion. Didier and Creole got together to cook up a surprise, and I'd been sent to Fab's and admonished that neither of us better come sneaking around.

Didier arrived via the front door as I went out the back to hike down the beach. I was tempted to sit on the sand and watch the water lap the shore, but I knew Fab was waiting and would be impatient, wanting to brainstorm about what the husbands were up to.

I cut across her patio, slowing to dip my toe in the pool—warm and ready for a swim. We hadn't done that in a while. "Knock, knock," I yelled, not even slowing as I slipped through the open sliders and joined Fab at the kitchen island.

"Come in, make yourself at home." Fab pointed to a stool. She poured a glass of iced tea and set it in front of me, then lifted her glass. "Cheers. I think we've convinced the husbands we can behave. Not sure how, but starting tomorrow, we're on our own, since they have a meeting with the Zoning Department."

I clinked my glass against hers. "I've enjoyed being under Creole's watchful eye. I'm going to suggest that we do it more often."

"I told Didier that they were being overly worried and we have to get back to our life and not live in fear, just keep a watchful eye out. Then reminded him of our collective skills by shooting up the room. He wasn't amused. But I have my ways of changing the subject."

I groaned, "No details, please," and formed an X in front of my face. "I'm hoping our surprise includes food."

"I know it does. I spied on Didier, and he filled a tote bag with food from the refrigerator and left it by the front door. He wasn't happy that he had to hunt me down—I didn't make it easy for him to find me, knowing he wouldn't leave without kissing me."

"What you were really doing is covering up that you were spying. If one time he just left, you wouldn't do that again."

"He'd never." Fab made a shocked face.

I laughed.

Fab stared over my shoulder. Her eyes went wide, first with anger, then fear. She reached for her phone, pulling it closer.

I was afraid to turn around.

"Hello ladies."

I had my hand over my phone. Hearing the man's gruff voice, I pushed a button and pushed it again.

"Now, now. Too late to call anyone. Push it away, or I'll shoot it out of your hand."

I swiveled on my stool, unobtrusively pulling my phone closer, certain the man was talking to Fab but not wanting to take the chance of being wrong. I found myself staring down the barrel of Michael Ashton's gun, which he had aimed in our direction as he dripped water on the floor, his clothes completely soaked and sticking to his skin.

"That includes you," he barked, waving his gun in my direction.

Despite Xander's ongoing efforts, he'd found nothing on the man. One thing he'd been able to verify: he wasn't a reporter. Nothing in all of Florida carried his byline. Xander had located several Michael Ashtons, but none fit the description we'd given him.

"Listen up, girlies. Don't either of you move, or you'll be dead sooner rather than later." Ashton pointed his gun at my face. "You first."

"Who are you really?" Fab asked.

"Ted Roberts." He stuck out his hand and waved it up and down. The man barely resembled his booking photo.

"What do you want?" Fab asked.

She sounded calmer than I was feeling. If I'd had my gun, I would have shot him, hopefully before he could get a shot off.

"Let's see..." Roberts licked his lips as he leered at Fab. "You. I want you. And I'm going to enjoy every minute. You'll stay alive as long as you do everything you're told. Get my drift?" He was practically drooling. "As for her..." He trained his gun on me, making clicking noises. "She's a dead chick. Being the nice guy I am, you can have a minute to say your goodbyes."

"Not so fast." Fab shifted forward on her stool. "You want me compliant, biddable to your every command and servicing your every need, you need to rethink your plan. Kill her and I'll go to my death making sure I take you with me and you don't enjoy a single second of the rest of your life."

I side-eyed her in admiration, as her words matched the ferocity of his.

Roberts grinned, staring at Fab, and after a

minute, he laughed.

"Can you at least tell us why?" I asked, hoping my attempt to keep him talking didn't set him off. "Neither of us remember ever meeting you before the restaurant. Why would you want me dead? Either of us?"

Roberts gave up his post at the sliding doors, stalking through the living room and stopping at the edge of the kitchen. "Imagine my surprise when I found out there were witnesses to my dumping the bodies. Those two learned the hard way that no one puts one over on me. Greedy shits." He practically spit his disgust. "It wasn't bad enough that they testified against me and walked, but they stole a hundred thousand dollars. Probably figured why not, I was in jail, but they should've known that if there was a way to get out, I would. And here I am, and they're not. No way were they getting away without feeling my retribution. Once I knew my release was coming, they were at the top of my kill list. I might have changed my mind—I doubt it, but maybe—but the theft of the money sealed the deal. You know what it's like to get released from prison with five bucks in your pocket, then finding out there's no more?"

"You've done well for yourself," Fab said. "Boat. Nice car."

"I felt bad having to kill my old friend Hank. Unfortunately, he was the only one I knew that had cash on hand and lots of it. I also knew that he would never part with a cent." Roberts chuckled to himself and mumbled something under his breath. "Hank never gave his safety a thought, living out in the wilds of central Florida under the delusion he'd insulated himself from the crazies." He shrugged. "Never had a clue. After I drugged the dogs, it was easy to sneak up on him. I killed him fast. I knew if I didn't, I'd be at his mercy and there wouldn't be any from him. No way was I going to be the dead one after all I'd been through."

"You murdered your friend for his money and walked off?" Fab looked aghast.

"Gave him a nice send-off. It was hard work digging the hole for him. Lucky for me, I discovered some lime in the barn. That came in handy."

I shuddered, wishing Hank had gotten the better of this man.

"I haven't seen a news report about his body being found. So good work, I'd say," Roberts boasted.

"The men in the duplex?" Fab asked.

"A message for Paul and Bowe that I was coming for them. Ingenious, don't you think? I knew they'd be sweating every day—creeping around, looking over their shoulders. Oh, I made sure they knew what happened to their friends. But I wasn't about to hold off on taking my revenge until after someone stumbled over the bodies. Your discovering the bodies was just icing on the cake."

Roberts' eyes glittered with a glee that made him seem more deranged, if that was even possible. "I suppose you're going to ask about Pierce next. Stupid ass. Who signs onto a job while drinking at Custer's? After I snapped a couple of his fingers, he confessed to how ineptly he handled a simple request. Paid big time to get his body pitched over the wall; not happy where he landed." He sighed. "I told the man 'front doorstep,' but he whined about not being able to get in. I was short on time, so... What are you gonna do? Incompetent help. But a businessman can't do everything for himself."

Businessman? That was a stretch. I glanced over at Fab, who winked at me. I didn't know how to explain it, but one look at her face, no matter how impassive, and I knew she believed that she had the situation under control. I wasn't so sure. But I forced myself to do what she wanted — stay in the moment and not get freaked out and do something stupid.

"Why would you go to the trouble of tracking us down?" Fab asked. "Aren't you running the risk of being caught, and for what?"

"When you discovered each of my men dead? You showed up at one crime scene after another. You were a loose end that needed to be tied up." He winked. "You play your cards right... you never know."

I grimaced. Roberts was delusional.

"You say you want me willing, snap your fingers and I perform; does that cover it?" Fab stared at Roberts intently as he nodded. "I'll come with you and you'll get all those things, as long as she remains here and alive." She cast a side glance at me.

"How stupid do you think I am? I leave her here, and eventually, it will bring the cops hot on my trail."

It would be sooner than he thought.

"I hate to be the bearer of bad news," Fab said, though she wasn't. "But you're already on the cops' radar, and last I heard, they'd issued an APB. Your best bet is to get away while you can. I'll help you with that."

True or not—which I suspected it wasn't, since there'd been no word about the cops having a suspect—the last thing Fab should do was go anywhere with the man.

The house was eerily quiet in between the manic confessions of the man holding us at gunpoint. He was proud of his accomplishments, and his eyes glimmered as he bragged.

I gauged the distance between Roberts and myself, waiting for him to be momentarily distracted as he lusted after Fab. My plan was to hurl myself at him and hope to not get my head blown off.

"How do you plan to get me out of here without the neighbors noticing and either stopping you or calling the cops?" Fab asked.

Slim chance. But he didn't seem to know that, which told us he hadn't been able to access the compound before now for a look around.

"You're full of questions."

"The one I'm most interested in hearing the answer to is, do we have a deal?" Fab managed to stay calm and didn't show any sign of backing down from any of his stare-downs. He'd been the one to look away every time. "You and I hit the road for some adventure and leave her behind."

"Much as I want to make you happy." Roberts flashed her a smarmy smile. "I only brought one piece of rope." He pulled a length from his back pocket. "This here is to truss you up. Can't have my prize getting away."

"Lock her in the hall closet and barricade the door." Fab nodded toward the hallway.

Roberts shook his head. "Fetch me a frying pan. A few good whacks, and then we'll make our getaway."

I flinched. He was a decent-sized fellow and "whacks" could easily leave me dead. Except he'd have to get a heck of a lot closer to me than he was now to beat my brains in, and game on. I wouldn't go down without a fight. I sucked in a breath and adopted Fab's calm-and-cool act.

"Let me see what I've got." Fab opened a cupboard and dug around, banging items together. "I don't do the cooking," she said over her shoulder. "Not sure what's in here." She raised a pan over her head as several others tumbled to the floor. "Here you go." She stepped forward, the frying pan at her side.

"Not so fast." Roberts laughed and turned his gun on her. "You do the honors. Knock her unconscious. If you attempt a double-cross and force me to kill you before we have a leisurely tango, you'll watch while I slice her up a piece at a time." He ratcheted his already creepy laugh up a notch.

Chapter Thirty-Six

I caught a glimpse of movement from behind Roberts and saw Creole and Didier slink silently across the patio, guns in hand. I bit the inside of my cheek to keep from uttering a sound and kept my full attention on Roberts.

The men slid quietly through the sliders and into the living room, coming within a foot of Roberts, whose attention was focused on Fab.

Not sure who coughed, but it startled Roberts. He turned.

Shots rang out.

I hurled myself to the floor.

A thud on the floor. Another body down.

I lifted my head. Roberts was slumped on the floor, his lifeless eyes staring at me. He looked angry and surprised as a dark puddle spread beneath his head, which lay at an angle.

Fab had done the same as me and dropped to the floor.

Didier holstered his weapon and ran straight to his wife, pulling her into his arms.

Creole stepped forward and nudged Roberts with his foot, rolling him onto his side, then another nudge, leaving him face down. He turned and closed the space between us, scooping me into his arms, setting me on my feet, and wrapping me in a hard hug.

"Are you okay?" both men asked in unison.

I nodded into Creole's chest.

Didier roared in French.

"Our friend wants to know what the heck happened," Creole translated. "As do I." He tightened his hold and led me out to the patio. He sank down onto one of the chairs and pulled me on his lap, faced away from Roberts. He ran his hand over my arms and legs, then cupped my chin. "You sure you're okay?"

"Promise." I leaned forward and brushed his lips with mine.

Didier had picked Fab up, carried her outside, and sat down opposite us. The two murmured to one another.

Creole pulled his phone out of his pocket.

Before he could make a call, I pushed his hand down. "Can't we just throw him in the water and let the fish eat him? Use that rope he was going to use on Fab and drag him out of here?"

"That great idea has my vote," Fab said emphatically.

"Ladies, it makes the fish sick. Not positive about that, but I heard it somewhere," Creole told us.

"If only we had a few hungry sharks," Didier said. "But I haven't spotted any in the water, and no coverage on the news."

I wrapped my arms around Creole and hugged him hard, then pushed back. "Not to be snarky, but what took you so long?"

"We both left our phones on the outside bar while we were finishing up inside." Creole grimaced. "Good thing the alert Xander installed keeps ringing until answered."

"At the same time I heard the phone ring, I caught sight of a boat anchored down the beach," Didier said. "Was about to go check it out when Creole barked that he'd get us both guns."

"We raced down the beach and across the patio." Creole nodded to his friend and called 911. "No ambulance needed. Send the coroner." He opened an app that opened the front gate and locked it in place.

"The dead guy was…? And why our house?" Didier asked. "Tell me it wasn't a disgruntled client."

"Ted Roberts." I nodded to Fab and laid my head on Creole's shoulder. She was calm and collected. I felt like I was going to lose my lunch.

Fab launched into the story and didn't skimp on the details. It shocked the guys to learn of the man's murderous rampage, and they were both ready to explode when they heard what he'd had planned for the two of us.

"Good riddance." Didier tightened his hold on Fab.

"Six murders? And two more, if he'd had his way. No way he would've kept the two of you alive long." Creole shook his head. "If anything had happened to either of you, when I tracked him down, he wouldn't have been sent to hell as fast as he was today."

"Thankfully, you two arrived in time." I smiled at him.

"You okay?" Fab asked me.

"You're the best — staring down a gun and trying to talk him out of killing me. You slowed him from what I think was his original plan — to dispatch me as soon as he walked through the door."

"Trust me, I had a plan for that frying pan, and it wasn't beating you over the head. Too bad he's dead."

"I wanted to take aim from the patio," Didier said, "but Creole called for caution, not wanting a bullet to hit either of you. We agreed to get closer and then shoot him. I didn't breathe until I knew that the two of you had hit the floor of your own volition."

Fab laid a loud kiss on Didier. "We need to get Roberts out of the house before he begins to smell."

The grimace on Didier's face made me smile. "Crime scene cleaner dude hasn't heard from us in a while," I said. "By the time he's done, that spot will sparkle and there will be no sign of... anything."

"You make that call," Fab said.

I nodded.

The banging on the front door stopped all conversation. Creole stood, set me off his lap, and went to open the door, Didier at his side.

"Check the peephole first," I said to their backs.

Creole turned and grinned.

Fab crossed over and sat down next to me. "You really okay?"

"I did my best to suck up some of the calming energy you sent my way and not do anything that would provoke Roberts to shoot."

Fab put her arm around me and gave me a side hug. "His eyes were a vacant, icy wasteland. Not sure how I held out for so long in his game of stare-down."

"He's dead now, and I'm happy. It means he won't be terrorizing anyone again."

"Xander gets a bonus for coming up with the code alert," Fab said. "And forcing the caller to shut it off was a great idea."

"You should be the one to tell him. Also that you were the one to suggest the bonus."

Fab flicked her gaze over my shoulder and groaned. "Guess who's leading the cop parade?"

"Kevin's calm in intense situations. It's when he thinks we're gaming him that he gets all grouchy." I grabbed Fab's hand. "Don't leave me until we're separated."

"Creole intercepted Kev and has the situation under control. Didier's picked up a few tips for dealing with cops and can hold his own." Fab half-laughed. "I'm lucky he doesn't trade me in for someone not so high-maintenance."

"Boring."

"I asked him if he wished he'd chosen a more housewifey type, and he laughed. Then said, 'Hell no,' for which I rewarded him."

"You two doing okay?" Kevin asked as he walked up and sat down on one of the ottomans.

"Roberts was a psycho freak," I said.

Kevin questioned me, then Fab.

"You should tell Kevin what we knew about the man before today." I nudged Fab.

She gave him the rundown on Roberts and didn't skimp on details, telling him everything we'd learned about the man.

Kevin shook his head. "No need to worry about him getting out of prison this time." He stood. "Don't go anywhere, in case I have a few more questions."

We pushed our chairs closer to the edge of the patio and stared out at the water.

Chapter Thirty-Seven

When the police told us we were free to wander off—not in those words—Fab and I hotfooted it over to my house with no hesitation. Fab and Didier were our house guests for three days, and I barely made a dent in showing them the same hospitality they'd shown Creole and me when we stayed with them.

The husbands issued the edict that all talk of crime and criminals was banned and took over, orchestrating fun and cooking all the meals.

I put in a call to the crime scene cleaner dude, who said he'd sprint right over. He arrived with his crew, and they disinfected Fab's house in short order. One of the workmen remarked to Didier that, "This was an easy clean-up compared to some. You know, blood splattered everywhere." Didier told us, "I was happy when one of the other men whistled for his attention." Neither Fab nor Didier were creeped out about returning, and as soon as their house was spotless, they went back.

It had been fun to have them as guests, and they promised, when they were on their way out the door, that we'd do it more often.

Another week went by, and Fab and I kept a low profile, which pleased the husbands. It didn't escape our notice that they were keeping an eagle eye on us, making sure we didn't sneak off... at least not without one of them.

Finally, the day of the welcome party for Cruz's relatives arrived.

I'd decided I needed something new to wear and found the perfect dress in one of my favorite stores. I twirled in front of the mirror in a loose-fitting, knee-length, hot-pink, spaghetti-strap sundress. The crisscross opening in the back made the sell. I slid into a pair of pink wedge flip-flops and decided on several bamboo bracelets, then pulled my hair into a high ponytail.

My plan was to arrive at The Cottages early and leave early, putting in a brief appearance with a smile pasted on my face to make the guests happy. To say that life had been hectic would be an understatement. I hadn't stayed up on the party plans and hoped that it turned out to be a low-key day. If that was possible.

Creole had gotten up with the birds and disappeared; I suspected he didn't want me making him feel guilty for not being my date. I'd teased that I'd guard his body from the eager women, which didn't elicit a laugh; instead, he'd kissed me before changing the subject.

I grabbed my purse and headed to the kitchen to grab a cup of personality in a mug, maybe some whipped cream. It surprised me to see my favorite threesome sitting around the island. My neck hairs warned me that something was up, but before I could voice my concerns, Creole's and Didier's matching smirks distracted me. Fab slid off the stool and stepped back, showing off an oversized terry bathrobe. Who knew she owned something so un-sexy and would wear it out of the house? She probably wasn't sweltering, despite being all wrapped up like that, since the air was on.

"Not to be rude—" I eyed Fab up and down. "—but I didn't know you wore any intimate apparel that wasn't silky and sexy." I sidled up next to Creole and brushed his cheek with my lips. He looped an arm around me.

"I wore this special for you." Fab curtsied.

I laughed. "So sweet of you."

Didier worked some magic with the latte machine, added ingredients I couldn't see, then turned and set a steaming brew in front of me, which the mind reader topped off with a generous serving of whipped cream.

I licked my lips. "Hopefully this tastes as good as it looks... but know that if there's the slightest bit of ick going on, I'm pouring it out."

"Bonjour." Didier winked. "I promise—" He crossed his heart. "—not one healthy ingredient."

I took a drink and sighed. "Caramel latte, my favorite. You're the bestest."

"These two are slugs." Fab motioned between

Creole and Didier. "But me, I'm the best friend ever."

"Ever?" I laughed.

"Yes." She shook her finger at me, then stepped back, untied her bathrobe, and shucked it off, letting it fall to the floor and revealing a flared black v-neck, a-line swing dress. "Surprise. I'm going to be your date for today's festivities."

I rushed around the island, fighting the urge to get emotional, and wrapped her in a hug. Then I took a step back, lifted the hem of my dress, and flashed my Glock, strapped to my thigh.

"Me too," Fab squealed and flashed me.

Creole and Didier stood back, both sporting amused looks.

"You really are the best." I smiled.

"I got to thinking, and what if... I missed something really fun? You know how much that would bug me?" Fab slung her arm around me. "Don't worry about us, boys; we'll be back when we get here." She herded me toward the door.

I turned and said, "Don't you worry your pretty heads about what could go wrong." I winked at the two men.

Fab and I laughed and let the door close on their answer.

I gave her a shove toward the passenger side, then ran around and slid behind the wheel quick, in case she tried to stop me, which she didn't. That surprised me. "I want to show off a little." I backed out of the driveway and hit the gas, squealing toward the gate.

"Whatever you're up to, stop now. If I'm the one to barf, I won't be rolling down the window." Fab imitated the sound.

"The hot, sexy French woman barfing in the car." I laughed. "You can bet I'll get pictures. Try living that down. For now, hang onto the sissy bar and let me demonstrate what I've learned from you. You can decide for yourself if I've paid close enough attention."

"You're going to impress me with your driving skills?" She turned her head both ways as I cut across the highway.

I patted her arm. "I'll get us there in one piece."

"So you know, our husbands are up to something."

"Hopefully that means something fun for us." I curved into a residential area, turned into a driveway and, figuring out quickly it was the wrong one, had to U-turn. Backtracking, I found the shortcut, not missing Fab's smirk.

She slapped the dash. "I know what you're up to now. When you get lost, I get to drive."

"This shortcut business that you pull off so flawlessly isn't as easy as you make it seem." I made several more unnecessary turns, Fab laughing, but I got us to The Cottages in one piece.

I backed into Mac's driveway and parked.

We'd had permission since she moved in, and it had never been rescinded.

Fab clapped. "I had my doubts, but you got us here."

Chapter Thirty-Eight

Fab and I leaned forward and stared out the windshield. There were so many things to look at, it was hard to know where to turn our attention. Police tape blocked the entrance to the driveway. Tied from the palm tree to a pole on the other side, a string of inflatable mannequins flapped in the wind. A man I vaguely recognized had parked his butt in a chair, wearing a multi-colored umbrella hat that shaded his shoulders and holding a clipboard in his lap, a small ice chest at his feet. He opened the lid, removed a beer, twisted off the cap, and sucked it half down before shoving it between his legs.

"What the heck is going on?" Fab asked, a bit of awe in her tone. "So much for me thinking this was a 'free beer around the pool' get-together."

"I don't know why you didn't remind me to ask more questions." I tried to make out what was happening underneath the hundred balloons that floated overhead, hovering along the line of tables and umbrellas that ran the length of the driveway, where several women had claimed chairs. "I wonder if Cruz's relations have checked in?" I turned my attention to the barbecue area, where the two benches were crowded with more women. That was a first. One of them jumped up, waved, and ran over to the tables. She was directed down the row, where she took a seat.

Fab said, "For a big-time lawyer, it surprises me that Cruz lets his relations jerk him around. Is Granny included in this celebration?"

"If Ms. Bag of Trouble is in attendance, I'm going to make it your responsibility to keep her in line." I ignored her scrunched up nose. At one hundred, slight exaggeration, Cruz's Granny had the libido of a spring breaker. "You've got the inside track, since she likes you and finds me lacking in all areas."

Fab shook her head, clearly not in agreement.

The short bus pulled up wrapped in streamers, balloons hanging out of every window. Oversized gloved hands were attached along the side, waving wildly.

Fab laughed.

Mac came running out of the office dressed in a bright-red maid's outfit that barely covered her cheeks, her girls pushed up to her chin. She grabbed a whistle from her cleavage, stuck it in her mouth, and blew a blast loud enough to wake the dead. The bus doors opened, and people trooped down the steps. Casio's brood, Mila, and Logan, came running around the corner from the pool, Larry trailing behind, not letting them out of his sight.

"Kids?" Fab said, aghast.

"If I'd known they invited a dog, I'd have brought my cats."

Fab snorted, then laughed.

After instruction from Mac, the kids—except for Logan, who hung onto her hand—each darted to one of the guests, singing a welcoming 'Hello.' Alex raced to the office and was back quickly, wheeling an oversized wagon. He opened the back door of the bus and unloaded the suitcases, piling them haphazardly in the wagon. Crum hustled through the trees in a pair of baggy shorts six sizes too large, a rope tied around his waist, a pair of coconuts strapped to his chest, and a lei around his neck that even from a distance we could see sported fake flowers, a number of them in sad shape. He was wearing a straw hat, the ends sticking up in all directions. Bungee cords in his hand, he secured the luggage to the wagon.

The hearse pulled up, capturing everyone's attention, and all the talking over one another stopped. The guard kicked the beer box he had his feet resting on, and it landed in some nearby flowers. He jumped to his feet and removed one side of the tape to allow the car to enter. The driver slowed, and the two talked. Then the hearse continued down to the end and parked, clearly on display, not pulling all the way into the space. The tape was replaced.

"Joseph died, and no one told me." I covered

my faced with my hands.

"Don't think so." Fab knocked my shoulder. "Look." She nudged me again. "What the heck are they doing?"

I opened my eyes and saw that Dickie and Raul had opened the back door. I expected a stretcher — coffin? — but they unloaded two rolling makeup cases, each man grabbing one and rolling them toward the tables. Female squeals greeted their arrival.

"We might as well check this out." Fab got out.

I grabbed her arm. "I heard there'd be an open bar; I'd rather make that our first stop."

"No." She sounded too much like Mother. "You need to save saucing it up for later."

It turned out that the barbeque area was the waiting area to have your makeup and hair done. The handful of women, who I assumed were guests, were all excited.

A flashy blonde, half of her hair purple, pointed at one of the women and motioned her to follow. She and another woman with a neon do were styling hair.

"Those women have drinks. I want one," I whined, pointing to the women waiting to avail themselves of Dickie's makeup skills, which he usually used on dead people. This must be a nice change for him.

Fab turned me away from several sets of eyes that were closely scrutinizing the two of us. "You behave." She gave me a slight shake. "I'm going to talk to our digger friends."

"Are you getting your makeup done?"

"Have you lost your mind?"

"I'm thinking yes."

"You go find Mac and get an update; then we'll compare notes." Fab headed over to the line of tables, every chair filled, the laughter a good sign everyone was having a good time.

Mac was easy to find. She'd finished getting everyone checked into their cottages and stood in the middle of the driveway, surveying all she'd done. I crooked my finger, and she came stomping over in white platform shoes with red crosses on the tops.

"Before you start—"

"This is a lot," I interrupted.

"Oh no you don't, not in that tone." Mac crossed her arms, pushing her boobs up further. "I told you all about this special day. Now don't toot on it."

"I wasn't… uh… complaining or anything."

"Oh yes, you were. Now just suck in a breath and have a good time. Get liquored up." Mac pointed me toward the pool, as though I didn't know where the tiki bar was located.

Fab joined us. "It was very special of you to arrange for the ladies to be made over. They're enjoying every minute." Out of view of Mac, she smirked.

"They bury people," I said, as though they

didn't know. "I'm sure the two of them have… uhm… talents…" Dickie for sure.

"If you hustled your backside over there, I'm sure you could cut in line, get your makeover, and be able to calm your reservations." Mac smiled like she'd just had the best idea ever.

"I do not need a makeover," I grumbled. "Besides…" I twirled in my new dress. "I look good."

Fab nodded.

"I should've been more specific," Mac said. "The theme is Festival, and a costumey outfit would be more appropriate."

"I wouldn't want to spoil your festival." I'd wanted to leave early, and now Fab and I could go to lunch.

"Don't you dare even think about sneaking out of here." Mac shot me the stink eye. "Walk around, introduce yourself; that will make the guests happy. I've got to run and check on everyone, reiterate that there's fun to be had." She skipped off in her platforms.

"I had a couple of questions for her, and she thought I was going to go all 'tudey. I'm so misunderstood."

Fab laughed at me. "I'm thinking you were right when you suggested that we have a drink. Because it's kind of early, we'll sip slow." She grabbed my arm, and we headed to the pool. "Don't ask Crum about Nix," she said conspiratorially. "She met someone with the same IQ, and the two skipped down to Key West. Left the return date open."

"If he brings it up, I'll pretend it's the first I'm hearing about it."

We rounded the corner and halted at the gate to the pool, which stood open. Crum, clearly in charge, had the women up and dancing, not a one in a costume, all in bathing suits. Under the thatched umbrella, a group of men were playing cards. Brad and Casio supervised the kids, who were now done with their heavy labor and jumping around in the pool, Logan in a sailboat floatie, hat on his head.

Fab ordered two drinks from Joseph, who had Svetlana strapped to his back.

"Good to see you both." I waved to the man as we slipped onto bar stools. "Svet comfortable up there?"

"Got to keep an eye on her, since she's a man magnet. Don't want anyone pawing her."

I nodded, unsure what to say.

Fab nudged me and nodded toward the gate. I turned as Creole and Didier walked into the pool area, both men in shorts, their shirts unbuttoned, giving any woman who wanted to look an eyeful of abs. And they were all staring in appreciation.

The men walked up and greeted Joseph and Svet.

I pulled Creole down to face level. "You need to button up."

He laughed, as did Didier, who'd heard me.

"I thought you wanted man candy. Here we are." He hooked an arm around Didier's shoulders, and both men stuck their chests out.

"I never said one word about you being half-naked."

He laughed again and swung me around, laying a big kiss on me.

Didier swooped in and kissed Fab.

I looked over Creole's shoulder and saw a woman standing at the gate, waving. It took me a minute to recognize her, and then I slipped around Creole and went to meet her. "You came." I enveloped Emerson Grace in a hard hug. She was a friend of the family and an old love interest of Brad's.

She breezed into the pool area, her bright-blue sundress swirling around her legs, brown hair tucked up under a sun hat. "New York was a bore. You called with such a fun invitation, how could I not show up?"

I had an ulterior motive, which I'd fully disclosed. Emerson was one of the best family law attorneys to practice in Florida before she inherited a fortune from her grandmother and went north to get the family affairs in order.

Brad climbed out of the pool, wrapped a towel around his waist, walked over, and threw his arms around her, lifting her off her feet and swinging her around. "Good to see you." He laid a big kiss on her.

"I told you I'd find you a brilliant attorney,

bro-ski, and here she is." I smiled at the two of them, hoping for more than just Emerson figuring out Brad's legal issues.

"You'll be happy to know that I've researched your options and started mapping out a plan of attack." Emerson smiled up at Brad.

"My sister is, as you know, so nervy," Brad said. That made Emerson laugh. "We'll get you a drink and introduce you around. But later, we'll have a long talk." The two walked away, laughing and smiling at one another.

Creole appeared at my side, hooking his arm around me. "It was nice of you to get Emerson to come."

"I was honest with her about everything. If anyone can help him figure out Logan's custody, it's her, and she won't let anything bad happen to either of them."

Creole kissed the top of my head.

The kids called him and Didier over to the pool.

I made the rounds of the guests and talked to each one, noticing out of the corner of my eye that Fab was doing the same thing. She had the attention of both the men and the women. I'd be reminding her the next time she complained she couldn't do personable.

About to take a seat and enjoy a margarita, I caught sight of a string-bean blonde cutting through the palm trees from the front, stopping to look over her shoulder. She was headed to the pool area, and I'd be the one to stop her. A guest wouldn't be tromping through the bushes, so it was more likely an uninvited neighbor, though she wasn't familiar to me.

I caught Fab's eye and nodded in the woman's direction, silently indicating, *I'll take care of it.* I had the advantage and could cut her off before she made her way into the pool area. It worked out perfectly, the two of us meeting at the open gate.

"This is private property," I informed her as I stepped through and closed the gate behind me.

"You're a hard woman to catch up with." Her smile was hard and calculating. "You don't know how many times I had to tell myself to be patient, that we'd meet up. And here I am."

Something about her, more than just her skulking around, had me on alert. "Have we met?"

"Lime."

The same color as her cotton dress, which tied at the waist. It was a name I'd never heard before; if I had, I would never have forgotten it. I was better at faces than names, but I couldn't recall ever meeting her.

Lime made several attempts to move around me, but I stepped in front of her, forcing her to back up.

"Those your kids?" She peered around my shoulder, then focused her attention back on me. "It doesn't matter; everyone's going to die." She pulled a gun from her pocket and pointed it at me. I took a step back, and she jabbed me in the stomach. "I wouldn't move if I were you."

"I'm certain that we haven't met, so why don't you tell me what this is all about?" I said in the most patient tone I could muster. I sized up the way she held the gun and figured she'd had little practice. "Be unfortunate if you had the wrong person." I planned to take advantage of Lime's first moment of hesitation and kick her on her butt. I casually tapped the small of my back.

"You murdered the love of my life. The fact that you're not in jail disgusts me. I'm going to mete out justice. He'd want me to get even, and I want it for the both of us."

"Does your true love have a name?" So much for not wanting to sound snarky, but she hadn't noticed.

"Ted Roberts." She sighed with a big smile.

Definitely wasn't happy to hear that name again. I really hoped that the two of them hadn't mated and had kids. "I did not kill Roberts. The cops took him out." An ex-cop, anyway, but she didn't need to know that.

"He was obsessed with you."

With Fab. But I wasn't about to enlighten her.

"He spent a lot of time tracking you down, and the last time I saw him, it was his plan to permanently shut you up, since he couldn't be certain what you knew. I never saw him again. I had to hear about his death from the news." She swiped at her eyes with the back of her wrist.

I took half a step back.

Lime jammed her gun into my stomach. "I told you once already. Move again, and I'll drop you and everyone else."

Her gun didn't have that kind of firepower, and she'd never get the chance to reload, but I wouldn't take the chance. "I can identify the officer that killed Roberts and help you get your revenge."

"I don't believe you."

"Roberts wouldn't want you to kill a bunch of innocent people."

Lime's laugh was brittle. "You didn't know him very well."

Fab appeared at my side out of nowhere, catching her off guard. I planned to insist that she teach me that trick of hers once we'd dealt with the woman.

Lime pointed her gun at Fab and then back at me. "You should've minded your own business."

"I don't know what the problem is, but I'm certain we can come to a reasonable agreement. One that doesn't end with anyone hurt and you dead or in jail," Fab said in a deceptively patient tone, her eyes sparking fire.

"Lime here thinks I murdered her boyfriend, Roberts. I told her that the cops shot him."

"Sorry for your loss."

I almost laughed at Fab's insincerity. Lime, on the other hand, soaked it up. "She also threatened to kill the kids once she dispatched me."

"Did she now?"

For the first time, Lime appeared indecisive, not knowing which of us to turn her attention to. The gun wavered in her hand.

"Would you like to know why that's not going to happen?" Fab asked Lime, but didn't wait for a response, instead kicking the gun out of her hand. It went airborne, and a shot went off.

Lime yelped and grabbed her hand.

I planted my foot in her lower abdomen. She clutched herself and doubled over, and I shoved her to the ground, where she landed on her butt and screamed.

Fab drew her gun and pushed the barrel up against Lime's forehead. "You have gutter taste in boyfriends," she growled.

I turned and yelled, "Grab me a bungee cord."

Alex jumped to his feet, raced out of the pool area and over to the wagon he'd left parked in front of Crum's door, and grabbed several.

I pulled my Glock. "We need to trade here; you'll do a better of securing her." I smiled at Fab, who turned and took the cords from Alex.

The pool area had gone silent, the guests open-mouthed and wide-eyed.

Creole and Didier shot out of the gate. Creole hauled Lime to her feet, and the two men had her trussed up in a blink despite the fact that she fought them, the whole-time screeching that she was going to avenge Roberts' death and nothing would stop her.

"That's what you think," Creole growled at her and shoved her back to the ground, standing over her.

"Murderer," she hissed at me.

"She thinks you killed Roberts?" Didier asked. I nodded. "I killed him."

Creole took out his phone and called 911.

"You two are cops?" Lime sputtered.

Ignoring her, Fab said, "I knew the second you touched where you'd normally holster your Glock that something hinky was going on."

"I just wanted to know why she was on intent on mass murder before I kicked her teeth out." I leaned my head on Fab's shoulder.

"Let's hope Roberts doesn't have any more friends willing to crawl out of whatever hole they're in to cause more ugly surprises."

"I'm thinking whoever's left was happy to hear of his demise. They no longer have to wonder if they're next for a well-placed bullet."

Fab nudged my head.

Kevin ambled up in his day-off attire of bathing trunks, impressive abs on display and a beer in hand, and exchanged a few words with Creole. He toasted us. "You're getting another officer today."

"That gives you a pass on the paperwork, but the ladies are going to want to ride you like a wild pony." No smile, but his lips quirked, so good enough.

"I'll take the short version," he said.

That set off Lime, who ranted and bellowed filthy words.

Fab nudged me again and nodded towards the pool. The guests had lined up against the fence, trying to pretend they weren't hanging on every word. Brad and Casio had herded the kids back into the pool, and Emerson was sitting on the side, encouraging them by throwing wayward beach balls back into the water.

"Enough," Creole snapped at Lime and hauled the woman to her feet. He struggled to walk her towards the front, as she attempted to fight him off, and when that didn't work, she went limp, fell to the asphalt, and tried to roll away. "Roll in the dirt; I don't care." Creole let go of her arm and took a step back, not taking his eyes off her.

Two cop cars rolled into the driveway, and an officer got out of each car. They acknowledged Kevin and talked to him first, then split up. One of the cops hauled Lime to her feet, and she went without any trouble until he tried to put her in the back of his patrol car. She fought him like a wet cat, but he prevailed.

The guests gathered around the gate hooted, hollered, and clapped. "Great show," they yelled.

"What the...?" the cop asked.

Creole and Didier grinned.

"My guess is that they think this was a show

put on for their entertainment," I said. When his eyebrows went up, I added, "The answer is no, we haven't done it in the past and will not be doing it in the future."

He nodded, but didn't appear completely convinced.

"I can vouch for her," Kevin said, *you owe me* on his face.

The cop made the rounds and talked to the rest of us, finished up by talking to Kevin again, and left.

Creole and Didier came over and hooked their arms around us.

"By the time we're done testifying, that woman won't be getting out of jail," Creole said.

"Good place for her," Didier agreed.

They led us to chairs under one of the umbrellas by the pool.

"I'm tired of having guns pointed in my face," I told Fab.

"We lucked out with Lemon. She knew nothing about her firearm. I wouldn't be surprised if she stole it."

I snickered but didn't correct her on the woman's name. I didn't care.

"I'm just happy we were able to disarm her before she shot one of us or the kids." Fab winced.

Creole and Didier were back, handing us each a drink—a margarita for me and a martini for Fab. They both sat down. "We're here to guard you so you can get your drunk on in peace."

I side-hugged Fab. "Thanks for coming to my rescue."

"You didn't need it. You could've taken her on your own."

Madison and Fab had a sign made for the front gate of the compound.

> **PRIVATE PROPERTY**
>
> **NO TRESPASSING**
>
> **VIOLATORS WILL BE EATEN BY A PACK OF DOGS**
>
> **AND THEN PROSECUTED**

~*~

PARADISE SERIES NOVELS

Crazy in Paradise

Deception in Paradise

Trouble in Paradise

Murder in Paradise

Greed in Paradise

Revenge in Paradise

Kidnapped in Paradise

Swindled in Paradise

Executed in Paradise

Hurricane in Paradise

Lottery in Paradise

Ambushed in Paradise

Christmas in Paradise

Blownup in Paradise

Psycho in Paradise

Overdose in Paradise

Initiation in Paradise

Jealous in Paradise

Wronged in Paradise

Vanished in Paradise

Fraud in Paradise

Naïve in Paradise

Bodies in Paradise

Deborah's books are available on Amazon
amazon.com/Deborah-Brown/e/B0059MAIKQ

About the Author

Deborah Brown is an Amazon bestselling author of the Paradise series. She lives on the Gulf of Mexico, with her ungrateful animals, where Mother Nature takes out her bad attitude in the form of hurricanes.

For a free short story, sign up for my newsletter. It will also keep you up-to-date with new releases and special promotions:
www.deborahbrownbooks.com

Follow on FaceBook:
facebook.com/DeborahBrownAuthor

You can contact her at Wildcurls@hotmail.com

Deborah's books are available on Amazon
amazon.com/Deborah-Brown/e/B0059MAIKQ

Made in the USA
Las Vegas, NV
16 October 2024